The Book of
True Believer

A Novel by M. Funk

WILD ABANDON
BOOKS

Published in the United States by Wild Abandon Books
WildAbandonBooks.com
MFunkWrites.com

Library of Congress Cataloging-in-Publication data is available upon request.

ISBN 978-0-9983016-5-5
eBook ISBN 978-0-9983016-4-8

Printed in the United States of America

Text set in Centaur
Book design by M. Funk
Cover illustration by Naomi Hart

First Paperback Edition

*With gratitude
for all the love,
encouragement,
and inspiration.*

How did I get here?

Nine.

One.

One.

Send.

I remember that part clearly.

Nine-one-one dispatch. What's your emergency?

Lately, the question has been nagging me. I don't readily remember the details, you see. I don't want to. I wrote them down so I wouldn't have to.

Upended handbags, scattered possessions, keys, tissue packets, dollar bills crunching under my knees, searching for one thing—ah! Hands shaking, I dialed.

The details are coming back in scattered flashes, unwelcome and uninvited.

I touched my friend's arm, and sheer chaos hit me with the force of a tidal wave. I absorbed it nerve ending by nerve ending, layer by layer, with no defense against the surges of pain.

Sometimes they come to me in dreams.

Tripping, falling bodies crushed us from above. My friend's rigid fists were wedged between us like gargoyle claws, and they knocked the wind out of us both.

Relentless futility, that's the worst part. The battle to save him rages on and on, though it's much too late for that now.

My yell was but a whisper.

That, and the brief lapses.

Make way for the Man Himself!

Those moments when the particulars are lost to memory
and the feeling fades.

He towered above us—that silhouette of salvation, piercing the twilight with dread.
"Get back!" he cried.

The sweet split second of amnesia upon waking.

He will cast out the demon!

Standing at the sink, washing dishes while the mind drifts toward
peaceful things, and the conscience is almost quiet.

Praise Jesus, hallelujah!

And then.

BEFORE

How shall I begin?

Dear Diary?

To Whom It May Concern?

Scene One? Act One?

Wait! I know.

Once Upon a Time, there lived a blithe, bookish young lady with cork-screw curls and extra-wide eyes. She dwelt in a sunlit cottage at the edge of a deep, dark forest and spent the better part of each day alone. Of course, she was uncommonly good at entertaining herself.

The young lady was mostly content, but she realized in time that one facet of her happiness was wanting. Deep down, she desired that a kind and handsome prince would rescue her from the ennui of her somewhat sorrowful, but otherwise satisfactory life.

Years passed, and he did not come. Though the young lady made the best of things, her heart darkened a shade or two with despair.

Then one bright and sunny day, her prince appeared. He galloped into town on his trusty steed, Adventure. He was everything that she had hoped for and more—gifted, brilliant, worldly, and mysterious. He brought definition to her dreams, and each minute she spent with him unlocked decades of uncharted aspirations. Though his visit was brief, their connection was profound. The prince offered the young lady a seat astride his steed and Promised to carry her off into an infinity of happily-ever-afters. At last! She readily accepted.

The End.

No.

The Beginning!

Life is a marvelous concoction of endings and beginnings laced up in ribbons of fantasy and fairy tales. I take up my pen today to declare that I am happy! I am a balloon so overfull with joy that I may burst— and when I do, I hope to be standing near a crowd of people, so the confetti of my elation sprinkles over everyone.

My life has changed suddenly and forever. Forever, I tell you, and it all happened in under an hour. Can you imagine anything so spontaneous and profound?

Guess why. Go on, guess. I've given you a hint already, but I'll give it to you again: this day was full of Promise, and *that promise* has been fulfilled.

Anticipation is so delectable. Let us not ruin it by rushing ahead. I shall begin at the beginning and build up to the best part.

I woke with the dawn. My eyes fluttered open, following the sensation of soft wings stirring my hair. I thought I caught a glimpse of a dream flitting out the window. Though its details escape me, its auspices linger.

All was right in the world this morning. The velvet breeze contained a note of moldy leaves. Dozens of red, pink, yellow, and orange tulip tips peeked up at the sun like an untidy platoon of toco toucans.

I meandered through the garden on my way to the gate, delighted in my anticipation of the many tiny green shoots that would soon emerge from the freshly planted soil. As Mom used to say, "Brave is the seed that cracks open and issues forth without knowing what it will someday become." It takes an act of faith to stir from winter's sleep and undertake the formidable strain of growth and change. Yet this is what life must do every year during this season.

Spring! My favorite.

I retrieved my brother's old bike and walked it toward the road, tapping each fence post along the way as Dave used to do for luck. I saluted the Sentinel, my granddaddy's oak, as I passed through the gate. He nodded deeply upon the breeze. Once my tires hit the pavement, I pedaled sunward toward the meeting place.

Several cars were parked in front of the old town hall when I arrived. How promising! One of them undoubtedly belonged to the Man Himself. I wondered which one it was. At the same time, I didn't want to know. Let us preserve our image of the Man Himself as a rider of trusty steeds named Adventure.

Up the rickety steps, I skipped, careful to avoid the rotted stair third from the top. Inside I found the main room filled with rows of folding chairs. A few handfuls of people milled about, maybe enough to fill half the seats. There was a steady hum of conversation. Some faces turned to look toward the door when it clapped shut behind me. Some nodded to me, and I nodded back. There were several from town: Cameron and Sarah Halsberg, Moira and Finn Olson, Susan Marshall, Graham Tucker. I spoke with each of them as I made my way across the room.

I spotted Ms. Mary Cooper seated at the end of a row with her walker parked in front of her. Atop Mary's snowy white hair sat a most extraordinary nest of tulle with two little cardinals perched at its edge. Her arthritic hands lay folded neatly in her lap. As soon as she laid eyes on me, she launched into a discourse about her daughters. I listened politely as Mary told me the details of Amy's pregnancy complications, Jolie's work promotion, and Tabitha's move to Ohio. I took care to lean forward and express awe and sympathy at the proper moments, though these sorts of undertakings were all foreign to me.

Oh, precious Mary Cooper, proud mother of three (and grandmother of seven). She will talk for days about everyone else, but only spend a few moments on herself when pressed. I asked after her health. She tittered and made light of her arthritic aches and pains. With stars in her eyes, she declared that after today, *they* won't vex her anymore!

I glanced at the wall clock as it ticked past the quarter-hour. Everyone was seated by then. The hum of voices, which had temporarily hushed at the top of the hour, was surging again. I sent a smile around the room and sympathized with everyone's impatience. Most of them had never seen the Man Himself before and didn't know that he almost always arrived late.

Boom! Boom! Boom!

The people jumped in their seats. A hush fell. All heads turned to look toward the back of the room. Showtime! I reached into my purse and pressed the button on my mini recorder. I did not want to miss a sound or syllable of the marvels to come.

We all watched the heavy wooden doors shudder on their hinges. Eyes flashed as people exchanged looks. The urge to comment nearly broke the tension barrier, and then—

Boom! Boom! Boom!

A godly fist pounded three more times at the doors.

"Do you hear that, Lord?" A voice resounded from the front of the room. Heads whipped the other way. I patted Mary's trembling hands and smiled warmly. *Fear not, love, these are only theatrics!*

"I SAID, do You hear that, LORD? That's the sound of a thousand souls come seeking salvation!" There was more thunderous pummeling at the door, more rapidly this time.

"Do you hear that, God's Children? That's your *Lord* and Savior come to SAVE you!" The pounding at the door continued, multiplying, expanding, coalescing into chaos, before settling into a rhythm.

"He cannot save YOU unless you invite *him in*. Invite Lord Jesus into your life, into the deepest chambers of your heart, and He will endow YOU with riches beyond your wildest dreams. He will bless YOU with life *everlasting*. Can I hear an AMEN to that, brothers and sisters?"

A chorus of *amens* trundled forth.

"Brothers, sisters, now heed the MAN who does the Lord's work."

That man appeared at the front of the room. Even with his head bowed and hands clasped, he arrested our attention. He remained perfectly still and waited for silence before raising his gaze to the audience.

Three years it had been—nearly. Three years of clutching his memory to my heart like a faded photograph, ready at every moment to recognize him the instant he reappeared. His dark locks, chiseled features, and powerful frame were slightly changed, but the blaze of his fiery blue-green eyes was precisely the same. It was he. The Man Himself.

Someone in the back row blurted out the *bad name*, followed by a crude accusation of criminal misconduct. Concentric gasps rippled through the surrounding folks. The Man Himself turned with laser precision toward the Critic. "Is that why you have come?" he asked. "To *crucify* me?"

His accuser attempted a feeble comeback. He seemed to have already exhausted his vigor. I strained to get a good look at the opposition, but he stood cloaked in the shadow beside the sun-blasted window.

"You dare sully this sacred space with the name *Bartholomew Lambrecht?* That wicked man is not the problem here. No, the PROBLEM is my heavy heart." He clutched his chest. "So heavy has it become that I lack the strength to lift it anymore. I am grieved to look today upon the bleached bones of a once-mighty congregation. I am grieved to see the EVIL at work in this town. The Devil chips away at the souls of God's Children with the hammer of *indolence* and the chisel of *doubt.* You know

it to be true!"

Amen.

"VALUES!" he bellowed. "Christian values are the casualties of modern society. Who here can testify to the concerning lack of solid Christian values in their fellow men and women?" He leaned into the congregation as if he really wanted an answer.

Murmur.

"Who here can testify that the Devil's hand has never touched them, nor have they ever associated with anyone touched by the Devil's hand? Let me see a show of unblemished hands!"

No hands went up.

"'He that is without sin among you, let him cast the first stone!' Whose words are those? Is this not an utterance direct from Jesus Christ, our Lord and Savior?"

Amen!

"We are all SINNERS in the eyes of God. But don't tell me about it. I'm not here to hear your confessions or forgive your sins. I am a humble servant and prophet of God. Our Lord sent me to heal your bodies, but I do NOT have the power to heal your wayward souls."

His lips curled, and he turned again to the Critic. The Man Himself jabbed a finger into the air. "Your sins are between you and God," he exclaimed. "You are polluting our sacred space. Leave, and don't come back until you get straight with HIM." With that, he spun on his heels and strode offstage. Protests and exclamations erupted all around me.

My heart felt as if it plunged into my gut. Was this it? Had the moment come? It was unfolding much differently than I imagined, but it would have to do. A force like a magnet pulled me from my seat and launched me onto the stage.

I spoke to my fellow spectators. "Have faith!" I cried. "Wait here!

It's not over yet." Then I raced through the side door in pursuit of the Man Himself.

By the time I reached the back hall, he was out of sight. I scoured the parking lot and all the inner corridors and chambers before I found one closed door that seemed to press outward with self-righteous indignation. I touched the cool wood with my fingertips and knew this was the one. I called through the door and asked to speak with him. After a minute passed with no response, I turned the knob and peeked inside. There he was, slumped in a chair with his back to the door.

"Jeremiah Promise, sir." My voice wavered. My nerves nearly failed me. The muffled din in the next room seemed to intensify. I couldn't make out what the people were saying, but I could guess. The Critic was out there right now spreading misinformation about the infamous bad man and his sullied associate, Jeremiah Promise. The vapors of hope and despair mingled in the air like vinegar and baking soda.

I summoned the energy to go on by reverting to starchy formality. "It's an honor to be in your presence. On behalf of my friends and neighbors, I thank you for coming here. Please believe that, despite the criticism of one, most have come in full support of your mission and work."

"I don't believe you," he said.

"That's ironic," I responded.

"What is?" He turned slightly toward me and cut a stark profile against the sunlit window behind him. That image seared into my memory like a holy brand.

"You—saying you don't believe," I explained. Should not a man who dedicates his life to faith know how to better deal with skepticism? He must encounter the fears and stings of disillusionment daily.

Jeremiah Promise turned all the way around to look at me. The force of his gaze nearly pushed me over. I planted my heels to steady myself.

"Why have you come?" he asked me.

A few years back, an ominous shadow crossed the blithe, bookish young lady's path...

I did not expect the Man Himself to remember me, as I had been but one grain of sand in a high, rushing tide of miracle-seekers. So, I recounted the story of our first meeting: it was about three years ago at the Madison Revival. I had recently been diagnosed with stage four ovarian cancer, and my prognosis was grim. Pretty hopeless, in fact, when we reviewed all the treatment options. I did a lot of research and fretting at the time, but the one thing I didn't do was pray.

It was acutely uncomfortable to admit to this holiest of men that I had never been much interested in God. No, I never conversed with Him, not even at my lowest point. But when a kind doctor's best offer lands down around seventeen percent, a person's mind begins to open to ideas it has never conceived before. That's when I heard about the miraculous healing convention in Madison—just a few weeks and a few hundred miles away.

Grim and skeptical though I was, I found my way to that Revival and went up on stage to stand before the Man Himself. He lay his hands on me, and a week later, the scans confirmed that my cancer was absolutely, positively, undeniably gone. The miracle had worked as advertised.

Well, what then? I had just faced death and been given a second chance at life! I figured that meant something, but I wasn't sure what. I searched for answers. I learned a lot about health and human needs, nutrition, exercise, social connection, faith, the universe, and oh! So much more. But I was never quite satisfied because I had this unshakable feeling that I needed to find Jeremiah Promise again. He himself had something more valuable to me than any book or correspondence

course. He had the gift—the means—of making a difference in this world, and that's what I wanted to do, too.

Jeremiah Promise sat stone still as he listened to my story. His brow remained furrowed, his steepled fingers pressed to his lips. Only his eyes moved: they deepened and dilated.

"You were an unbeliever?" he asked. "Did you accept Jesus Christ as your Savior after that?"

I faltered. "I accepted *you* as my savior after that."

This seemed to trouble him at first, but the lines on his forehead gradually smoothed, and his demeanor softened.

"Praise be. I think you may have just redeemed me, sister," he said. "I've been through so much, you understand. I've grown weary. I spent this past year wandering the country without friends or followers. Persecution has damned me with doubt, and bitterness has placed me in peril. The Devil's whispers have polluted my gifts and turned me into poison for my people."

All he wanted, all he'd ever wanted, was to heal the sick, bring hope to the destitute, and help God lift every soul to grace. Years of preaching the Gospel of fiery damnation had left him jaded. He had always felt that it was somehow wrong to use fear to drive sinners to salvation. There must be another way, he thought. Now, the living proof stood before him!

"You're a True Believer!" he exclaimed. "You have been baptized in the Holy Spirit, and this is the name God has given you! May I call you by your rightful name, True Believer? More than that—may I ask you to join me in my sacred mission of salvation? With you by my side, we will take this world by storm. Think of all those we can heal! Think of all the souls we can save!"

He clasped my hands in his and talked of starting a new enterprise

called Wholesome Healing Ministries. His warm, broad, electrical palms zapped me to distraction, and I could barely follow his words. I instinctively withdrew, broke the circuit so that I could collect the fragments of my thoughts.

This seemed too easy. It *was* too easy! All was not settled yet—the hardest part was still ahead.

I cautioned that Jeremiah Promise's redemption was not in the room with him, but out there with all those other good people. They were his faithful followers—his true believers. They might not be a mighty congregation, but they had come here today despite every disparaging thing they'd heard about the great Jeremiah Promise because they loved and trusted him. Those people didn't deserve to be reproached or abandoned by their idol. He might be the closest thing to Christ that some of them would see all year. His duty was to inspire hope the way that only the Man Himself could and recognize that the appreciation of a dozen true believers was worth the approval of seventy-times-seven fickle followers.

Storm clouds hastened across Jeremiah Promise's brow. I braced for his backlash. After a time, he softened again. "I wondered why God sent me to this odd little town, but I trusted His wisdom. There must be a reason, I thought—and here it is."

He told me that he had reached the end of his rope this very morning. He had run out of hope. This was to be his last week of preaching.

"If I go out there and humble myself to those good folks, will you partner with me in this great new endeavor?" he asked me. He was, if not yet redeemed—then renewed! The error of his ways was now crystal clear. He knew what to do: start fresh with this new ministry and do everything differently.

"Come, my True Believer! Don't keep me in suspense. Promise you'll

come with me. We will save the world, you and I. With God on our side, we cannot fail."

His enthusiasm was irresistible. My whole being vibrated from head to toe. I clenched my teeth to keep them from chattering. This was it—the moment I'd been waiting for. I said the word. *Yes.*

Jeremiah lifted his face skyward and reveled in ecstasy. When his gaze returned to me, it flared with viridian fire.

"Tell me what you would have me do, True Believer."

The world whirled, and I grappled for the anchor of an idea. The puzzle pieces of a plan fell into place one by one. "Apologize for chastising them so harshly just now," I told him. "Heal this rift, and you will begin to heal the others." I assured him that his people were eager to forgive. By showing up today, they very nearly did. But they still deserved to hear him tell the truth and repent—for his behavior today, and for the scandals of his former ministry partner as well. The fact that Jeremiah walked free while Bartholomew Lambrecht sat in prison was evidence of his innocence, sure, but his followers still needed to hear the whole story. Maybe not today, but soon.

Jeremiah turned abruptly and strode back to the assembly room. He hopped up on the platform, reached up high, and snatched everyone's attention out of thin air.

"Children of God!" he exclaimed. "I am but a humble instrument of the Lord, gifted with the healing touch, but not with the grace of tongue. Please forgive my brashness. Just now, an angel came down to deliver a message direct from God. This angel relieved me of my wicked ego and told me to recommit my life to healing bodies and saving souls.

"Please, hear my sinful confession. I have done you wrong. I have accused you all of imperfect faith when I am the one that entertains doubt. I allowed my faith to be shaken by the Devil, and it was I who abandoned my flock in their hour of need. God saw the sin in my heart and chose to test me. He rescinded His Gifts and replaced them with sorrow. Does the Lord test us when we are strong? No! He tests us when we are at our weakest! Can I hear an Amen?"

Amen!

"I confess that I intended to give up today! I was at the Devil's door with my fist raised high, ready to knock. Then. Then *this* angel came to me." Jeremiah Promise pointed at me. "And her name is True Believer. Praise Jesus, hallelujah!"

Hallelujah!

"She told me to forget my troubles. Why? Because God's Children need me. Praise Jesus, hallelujah!"

Praise be!

Jeremiah Promise fell to his knees and clasped his hands before him. "You fine folks have hearts of pure righteousness. I kneel in awe of your perfect faith. I kneel as your servant and ask that you grant me the honor of proving my renewed faith by laying hands on the most deserving among you and healing your earthly pains. Can I hear an amen if you feel God's divine presence this morning?"

AMEN!

This time, no sour notes of dissent intruded on our consensus. Where was the Critic now? He must have melted into the shadows and vanished! United, our tidy group of true believers forged onward, toward our reward, with Jeremiah Promise in the lead.

His eyes rolled back in his head, and he shook with convulsions. Guttural, foreign-sounding syllables emitted from his throat. Then he called out, "Mother, is that you?"

He pointed toward a little cluster of onlookers.

"Mother! Is that you? Mary, mother of our Lord Jesus Christ! Mary

Cooper, mother of three beautiful daughters and seven glorious grandchildren? God whispered your name to me!"

Mary Cooper nodded vigorously. Her eyes were keen and bright.

"How long has your arthritis been troubling you, Mary Cooper?"

Mary fumbled with her words. Someone beside her bent down to hear the answer then called out on her behalf that it had been twenty years, at least.

"That walker, is it yours, Mary Cooper?"

Jeremiah bounded off the stage with the spring of inexhaustible youth. He jumped up onto the seat of a folding chair and hopped from one to the next until he reached Mary, who was still seated in the same spot I had left her half an hour ago.

He towered over her and quoted Hebrews 11:1, "Now faith is the assurance of things hoped for, the conviction of things not seen."

Jeremiah leaped catlike to the floor, knelt tenderly beside Mary Cooper, took her hands, and focused intensely on her.

"Mary Cooper, God has sent me to heal your arthritis today. He tells me that you can walk without that walker and without pain. Do you believe Him?"

Mary nodded timidly.

Jeremiah Promise laid his hands on Mary's shoulders. He looked around to address the others.

"Do you have faith today? Do you BELIEVE? I can't do anything if you don't believe—Amen!"

Amen!

"God believes in you, Mary. I believe in you. Let's see you take a step right here and now all by yourself, just to spite the Devil!"

Mary swayed like a chickadee in a March breeze. She placed her gnarled hands at the edges of her chair and lifted her delicate rump off the seat. She rose.

A few onlookers gasped while others held their breaths, and all were in suspense to see if Mary's hip would hold her. The woman straightened up, smoothed her skirt, and took a step forward. She took a second step. Then she performed a quaint little jig while standing in place.

"*Praise Jesus, hallelujah!*" Jeremiah Promise bellowed.

Everyone gathered around and implored Jeremiah to lay hands on them. I stood to the side and watched with bursting pride. Even in my wildest dreams, I couldn't have devised a better ending to this beginning.

Monday, April 12

I feel youthful. I feel enthusiastic. I feel fresh. The world amuses me. My internal machinery hums along in perfect working order and produces a never-ending river of loving warmth that sometimes ebbs and sometimes flows but never runs out.

I marvel at life: Is this for real? Did it really happen? What's next? I can't wait to find out. I'm so eager to begin this adventure that everywhere I look, there it is.

I decided to go out for breakfast this morning. One step beyond the garden gate, I plunged into the Yucatan Peninsula's dense and humid jungle. Crowded by oppressive vegetation, I scanned left and right, forward and back, ever watchful for marvels and dangers. Now and then, I caught a glimpse of the upper gable of some ancient temple peeking over soft, green plumes.

I tiptoed past the marble ruins of the cemetery where centurions of arborvitae slept standing up. Shhh, don't rouse them. Onward, around a broad bend of the Circus Maximus and across a sun-bleached expanse

of the sub-Saharan veld. Onward, past the moss-covered stairs to no-where, past the manicured English lawn. Onward, toward the lakeshore whose aspect switched from Mediterranean beach to Scottish moor depending on the strength of the sun.

I crouched down near the Moroccan medina (an educational institution in a distant dimension, I'm sure). Here, a cascade of ants erupted like lava from a weedy crack in the road. It was a sight to behold. At this level, the pavement seemed to stretch out like a sandless desert as far as the eye could see. *Move along*, said the cracked asphalt. *You're not done yet.*

A few paces further on, I reached the Dotted Line. Here I halted.

There come times in every child's (and child-like adult's) life when she must acknowledge the semi-permeable frontier between fantasy and reality, and this was one of them. Should I cross? Should I turn back? These are the sorts of questions with which I grapple daily.

Pancakes called to me from the diner up the street. My appetite had sprung teeth by this time and had begun to gnaw me up from the inside. Such is the peril of being a first-class dilly-dallier.

Propelled by hunger, I crossed the Dotted Line, tore through the tissue paper of fancy, and tumbled out onto a crosswalk in the middle of South 7th Street in Luck, Wisconsin, USA, Earth.

Sheldon's diner was but a dash away. I was pleased to find Sheldon himself behind the counter. Upright! Not smiling—though, that part was not surprising. There was a sparkle in his eyes that I hadn't seen in quite some time.

"Migraine-free since April three," he quipped.

I was thrilled. "Absolutely thrilled," I said as I clasped Sheldon's hand in both of mine.

Should I have told him that I had prayed for him? Probably not. He periodically reminds me that he's not a religious man. I'm sure he thinks me a quirk for broaching spiritual topics, especially since my beliefs are nebulous. I claim no denomination and draw no demarcations when it comes to good morals and good ideas.

Someday, I might take the time to explain to Sheldon that prayer is a ritual of gratitude. In scientific terms, it is a means of willing good things into the world by pressing one's semi-conductive hands together to close a natural electrical circuit. In abstract terms, it's the ever-expanding desire for connectivity that must be shared and should not be suppressed.

Someday, but not today. Today, I sat at my favorite little table by the front window and kept my musings to myself. While I waited for breakfast, I studied my favorite painting of a ship sailing through turbulent waters. Its moment of crisis was frozen in time forever. I often wonder what became of that ship's crew. Was their distress frozen in time, too? Or did they carry on after history stopped and grow bored from hanging so long at the precipice of danger? If so, I would gladly trade places with them. The crew and I might both do with a change of scenery.

Sheldon served me extra pancakes this morning with all of the toppings. I may be prone to hyperbole, but I swear to you that these pancakes were—if not the very best I've ever tasted—then in the top three of all time. I asked for a to-go box.

Macy Martin and her son Joyce had just taken seats at the counter when I went to the register to pay. Joyce is a darling boy. Wonderfully smart! Whenever the library receives new books on a scientific topic, I set them aside for Joyce. The boy's appetite for knowledge is a joy to behold. He reminds me of a young lady that I knew once upon a time.

Little Joyce looked over at me shyly, and yes, there it was: that conspiratorial spark. I nodded and gave him the hand signal. A book about space travel was waiting for him at the circulation desk that very moment. He wiggled with delight. We would see each other again soon.

I took a different way to work this morning. I believe that changing one's routine even a little bit every day can lead to all sorts of brilliant discoveries and adventures.

I sneaked through a crevice between two buildings and came out in the alley behind Main Street. Today felt like a good day to examine the flip side of everything.

When I entered the back alley, the first things I saw were two giant crows perched on the edge of a dumpster. They were busy fighting over half a fish sandwich and didn't notice me. The birds managed to rend their second-hand prize in two, but one got greedy. It dropped its portion and pursued the other's share.

There followed a needless flurry of feathers and snapping of beaks for which I had little patience. I hurled my to-go box into the fray and knocked both birds into the trash. Eventually, they emerged again, each toting its own prize (one had a pancake and the other the fish sandwich). Off they flew in separate directions.

I like to think that everything in life is connected to a higher purpose. The purpose of those leftover pancakes must have been to keep the peace this bright Monday morning.

A few doors further down, I came upon a glorious sight. On the brick wall behind the hardware store, I found a striking and beautiful specimen of graffiti. It was a portrait of Edgar Allen Poe, done in the style of Edvard Munch's *The Scream*. Words from the poem "A Dream Within a Dream" radiated outward around his head like lightning bolts.

I delighted in imagining some somber young virtuoso sneaking through the shadows to paint this illicit masterpiece. Could it have been someone I knew?——Gloria Foley, for instance. Minivan-driving mother of five with recalcitrance hidden in her heart. Romantic.

I came to the end of the alley and stood for a moment, blinded by the warm spring sunlight.

The final gift of this morning's adventure was the chorus of wind chimes on the porch behind the co-op. There were at least a dozen of them, all shapes and sizes, some metal, some glass, and each singing a different, breathy tune. Together they orchestrated chaos. Yet the longer I stood on that spot and listened, the more those random sounds seemed to converge into a sophisticated sort of harmony.

Tuesday, April 13

It's been two days. That's 3,031 minutes since serenity flew the coop. I know it's essential to live for the moment and such, but dangit! I'm anxious for my new life to begin.

The call could come any day, so I have wasted no time packing, cleaning, and preparing the garden for an absence of uncertain duration.

Delivering my resignation to Candice wasn't the hardest part, though I feared at first that it would be. She expressed her displeasure with heavy sighs and numerous rounds of paper shuffling. How was she supposed to find another storytime host on such short notice—one that will do *all* the voices for the children? By abandoning my post now, I would surely incite a munchkin revolt and imperil the whole institution.

Ha! she was kidding. I was relieved. We parted on good terms.

The hardest part of my preparations was spending the afternoon next door, attempting to convince Missy of my sanity over a single pot of coffee. She drank hers in short, skeptical sips and asked a lot of trifling questions about "this so-called holy man." I cannot blame her for this. I'm quite certain Mom had made her promise to look out for me. Missy was only doing her due diligence.

I answered her question to the best of my ability, laughed merrily, and swore to her that I knew what I was doing. This decision was not as impulsive as it might seem. Jeremiah Promise had been a significant figure in my life for a long time. Years. And I always had this... feeling... that I'd see him again. It was almost as if I manifested his coming ... (but I didn't say that part out loud).

I assured Missy that I *knew* I was on the right path now. It might look strange and new underfoot, and when I look forward, it might be foggy up ahead. I don't know what's to come, I admitted, but I believe with all my heart that I'm headed somewhere I want to go. I'm ready.

Missy shook her head at my words but agreed to look after the house and garden. I insisted that she take the whole lot of fruit and vegetables if I wasn't back by harvest time. Will it come to that? We shall see.

WEDNESDAY, APRIL 14

The call has come at last! Plans are underway, and things are about to unfold quickly.

Jeremiah Promise has found a place for us to go. His good friend, Pastor Ormand Kenneth, oversees a small church in Texas, and he has offered an assistant pastorship to Jeremiah. He's invited us both to stay with him and his family while we get situated.

Miraculously, Pastor Ormand called Jeremiah out of the blue just yesterday. It had taken him several months to track Jeremiah down, as Jeremiah had been living off the grid since last September. The pastor knew about the ministry scandals, the police investigation, the trial, and Jeremiah's many months of subsequent hardship. He never doubted Jeremiah's innocence for an instant and couldn't stand to see a good man tarnished by the deeds of another. Pastor Ormand decided to hire a private detective to track down the renowned faith healer. He was determined to help his friend in any way possible. Jeremiah Promise needed to be absolved and restored to prominence. The people needed him back.

During their three-hour phone conversation, Pastor Ormand begged Jeremiah to ask any favor. Jeremiah refused several times but reluctantly admitted that the ministry's assets had been frozen months ago. He had been running on the financial fumes of God's grace ever since. Despite this, he would not accept charity—only honest work that would ultimately benefit all involved.

For this, we must go to Texas. My flight to Dallas leaves the day after next.

Jeremiah deeply regretted asking me to buy my own plane ticket to Dallas. He promised that it would be the only money he'll ever ask me to spend. Once we're in Texas, I won't have to pay another penny.

"This is God's plan," he said. "God will provide."

I don't mind. I have some savings to fall back on in case his God takes a while to come through.

I'm enormously relieved that it won't just be Jeremiah Promise and me alone together, twiddling our thumbs in some seedy, cracked-plaster motel room.

The Kenneth Family! What will they be like? All I know so far is that there's a mother, father, and ten children ages five to twenty-five (half are already independent). I'm excited to know them all. There will likely be a constant hustle and bustle around us all the time.

I look forward to sometimes plunging into the noise and vigor of

youthful activity, and at other times, escaping to some inconspicuous corner with my sketchpad on one knee. I can't wait to absorb every detail and moment of this strange new journey.

FRIDAY, APRIL 16

I spent the entirety of last evening saying tearful goodbyes. *Goodbye, leaky faucet. Goodbye, creaky stair. Goodbye, stained-glass window.* My home, my dear friend, deserved a proper farewell. I went around touching doorknobs and windowpanes and explaining how our lives were about to change, and why. To ease the pangs of parting, I promised to return before too long.

As I drifted into the twilight of sleep last night, I vowed that, now and forever, I will *always* feel happy, joyful, and fulfilled. No matter what comes next, I shall let nothing take these away from me. By morning, grief was gone, and my whole being had clicked into focus. My mind was clear as glass. The moons, planets, stars, and galaxies were all in sharp alignment, and I was ready for anything.

Thank goodness for this bold start to the day, because in practice, my journey began haltingly. At several points, the frustration was great, and I was tempted to turn back. But I did not.

The first stumble of the day came at three o'clock in the morning when I knocked at Missy's door and received no response. This prompted some panic. I depended on her for a ride to the airport. Fortunately, Missy was able to get out of bed, get dressed, and start the car in five minutes flat. We arrived at the airport before dawn.

My quiet, peaceful existence burst like a soap bubble as soon as I stepped through those sliding glass doors. I tumbled into a torrent of rushing and scurrying, interrupted by intervals of waiting and worrying. I stood in this line, that line, the wrong line, the right line, always immersed in roiling whirlpools of impatient strangers. Hurry up, slow down, step to the side. *Excuse me, miss—you can't bring this through security.* In the blink of an eye, Teddy's Swiss army knife thunked into the trashcan. It felt as if someone had just yanked a thread that was connected to one of my vital organs. I felt sick about it but had no chance to protest. *Keep the line moving!*

At the end of all this hustle and bustle, I expected to be swept up directly into the air and have my first-time-flying anxiety dispatched before I knew what hit me. Not so! I spent the next seven hours staring down a long tunnel of flight delays.

First, a problem with one of the engines rendered our plane useless. We lost our pilot while we waited for a new aircraft to be brought up. By the time we had both plane and pilot, our flight crew had been reassigned, and a new one had to be rustled up. To pass the time, I reviewed everything I knew about extraordinary heights in an effort to minimize the unknown.

I made a list of up-high things that I love: mountains, clouds, trees. Though I have not sat atop any mountains or clouds, I have climbed many trees. Sitting high up in their branches, I've imagined what it would be like to ascend a thousand times higher.

Good news! I love to fly.

I was fortunate enough to be assigned a window seat so that I could enjoy every line, ridge, and shadow of this new point of view before the sun set on it. It is a curious experience to watch while the landscape flattens out, and every horizon is stripped of its mystery. I overcontemplated the crisp details of a foil peanut packet in my hand compared with the distant haze of a hundred thousand lives beneath my

feet. (Sometimes I get lost in trifling analysis and must take a moment to step back from it and laugh.)

When I reached the other side, Jeremiah was there to soften my landing. He had driven all day and all night to arrive in Dallas ahead of me. He whisked me off the curb out baggage claim.

The drive to Redbird was full of whispers and shadows. Jeremiah told me tales from the road, and I told him my tale from the sky. He commended me for bravely flying alone for the first time. It was a flattering overstatement, but I soaked up my idol's praise in silence, rested my head against the car window, and watched streetlights gleam past. The sound of gravel crunching under the tires roused me from a momentary half-slumber. We had reached the house. It was dark. We slipped silently through the front door, and Jeremiah directed me to a couch where I could collapse for one night.

The moment my head touched the pillow, my heart began to pound. My senses quickly convened and recalled me from the brink of sleep. It's all too strange and new, and I have far too much to think about. We have lives to save, a reputation to restore, an empire to build. No rest for me tonight.

Here I sit on a stranger's couch a thousand miles from home, writing by flashlight and awaiting the dawn. It is not far off now. Soon, I'll meet the pastor and his family. Soon, our real work will begin.

SATURDAY, APRIL 17

This evening after a big family dinner, Jeremiah Promise and Pastor Ormand Kenneth stood up from the table, went directly to the study, and closed the door. They seemed to have established this understanding beforehand. Margaret, the pastor's wife, and five of her children had a different understanding. They all retired to the family room to watch Bible study videos.

Nobody hinted that I was welcome to join them, so I floated in the hallway between, alert and attentive. The low rumble of voices droned behind one door while the violet glow of an electric Aurora Borealis emanated from another. I did not seem to fit in either world. Eventually, I retreated to the dining room with my sketchpad and pencils and settled in for an evening of creative reflection.

After a while, Jennie (the second youngest child) found me there. She passed through on her way to refill the snack bowl, and her trajectory bent and slowed as she drew near, like a small celestial body pulled off track by the gravity of a larger one. I felt her presence at my elbow. Her big blue eyes peered at the half-rendered scene on my paper.

"Where is that?" she wanted to know.

I told her that it was from my home. She wanted to know how I drew it "without looking." I explained to her that it was a blend of memory and imagination, and she began to say that she wanted to try it—but a chorus of protests from the other room reminded her of her errand. Jennie retrieved the snacks and delivered them to her brothers and sisters. Then she came back and pulled out the chair beside me. I provided her with a pencil and paper. Soon she was wholly absorbed in an artistic endeavor of her own. The girl took to drawing like a sponge to water, and I didn't want to squelch her independence. I offered a few words of encouragement now and then but otherwise left her alone with her vision.

When Margaret came searching for her second-smallest duckling, Jennie ran to her mama with her drawing in hand, eager to show it off. Margaret met her with indifference. She accepted the paper only so that

she could return it to its presumed owner (me). It was late, and Margaret instructed her daughter to brush her teeth and go to bed.

Alone in the dining room once again, I felt strangely sad and restless. A void seemed to have been created where there wasn't one before. Where were Jeremiah and the pastor? The murmur of voices had ceased. They must have slipped past me without pausing to say goodnight.

Tuesday, April 20

I miss home.

The elegant balance of my whole existence was obliterated on my first day in Texas. None of my habits nor carefully cultivated efficiencies fit in this cramped household of nine. I feel like a puzzle splayed out on a table. I am anxious to be put back together again and see the new picture of my life with Jeremiah Promise in it.

My chief occupation for these last few days has been to study this new world and find my place in it. So far, I have discovered:

1. It's best to keep my toothpaste under lock and key.
2. It is unwise to end up last in line for dinner.
3. To avoid being trampled underfoot in the morning, I should rise early and sneak outside.

My morning walks are helping to acquaint me with the neighborhood. Each day, I venture a little further in a new direction.

Today, I headed west along the main road. A city bus roared a few inches past my elbow and tossed my hair in my face. I leaped back with fright and hurried off on the first side street I came to. This road led to a quiet, slightly forlorn neighborhood. Not a creature stirred here, though I had the eerie sense that I was being watched.

Texas is not what I expected. I envisioned high desert: rolling tumbleweeds, gunslingers, and bleached bones swamped with sand. Here on the south side of Dallas, I'm finding a land reminiscent of my own. There are trees and bushes aplenty, roads, ditches, driveways, gardens, and gnomes, much like the ones at home. The ways in which our two lands differ seem to manifest in its subtle textures.

It appears that the south was forged from harder metal and filed down to a sharper point. Its fences stand taller, and its slats cluster more tightly. Coils of barbed wire glitter in the sun and signs with curt tidings abound. *Private Property. Keep Out! Beware of Dog! Never Mind the Dog—Beware of the Owner! CAUTION. Community Watch. STOP. No Trespassing. No Parking. No U-Turns. No Outlet.*

A broken sippy-cup here, a discarded scratch-off ticket there. Peeling paint, barred windows, flickering neon—an auto-body shop slouching on the corner. Plastic bags swaying in the bushes like ragged angels.

An empty cardboard six-pack cartwheeled past me down the sidewalk. There was my Texas tumbleweed. *Corona, Coors, Budweiser, Miller Highlife, Modelo.* Empty glass bottles lay half-buried in the dirt like old bones. There were my sand-swamped skeletons.

Birds roosted on wires, and a lopsided basketball hoop gawked at me over a picket fence. *Cheetos, Starburst, Milk Duds, Blow Pop.* Dusty snack food labels peeped at me from cracks and crevices like leering townsfolk. They all seemed to be holding their breath—for what? For whom? For the gunslinger. I rounded the next corner and saw her long shadow stretch out in front of me.

By then, I must have been a mile or two from the house, so I skipped on back with a heart full of awe and wonder. Oh, what a marvelous dance life can be, with its elegant intersections and subtle meanings. Sometimes the most profound delights are waiting to be discovered in

the most ordinary of places.

Friday, April 23

This evening, as every evening, I helped clear the dinner table and waited for everyone to disperse so that I could settle back into my chair to read and draw. I expected to have the evening to myself, so I had to suppress a little bounce of anticipation when I heard footsteps in the hall. I instantly recognize the gait. Not wanting to appear too eager, I held my breath until Jeremiah touched me on the shoulder and invited me to join him for an evening walk. I tossed aside my book, and away we went.

Jeremiah began with thanks for my patience. The waiting must not be easy for me, he empathized, and it was never his intention to neglect me. He was pleased to finally have good news and progress to share with me.

"Our mission is a delicate and potentially dangerous one," he reminded me. Thanks to his former partner's dirty dealings, Jeremiah Promise had accrued several powerful enemies by association. These enemies would take advantage of any opportunity to complete his ruin. Some of them were too close for comfort.

Here, I couldn't help but glance around us nervously. Under these circumstances, should we be standing so near a busy street? Jeremiah seemed to be unaware of this risk and went on talking. He explained that when he launches his official comeback, it has to be robust enough to provide him the protection of notoriety. His enemies will not want to attack him out in the open.

Jeremiah Promise and Pastor Ormand had been holding secret meetings, tirelessly strategizing, and securing alliances. How to blaze the

trail safely and effectively to a new era of healing? That's the question they've been hammering away at. The rampant corruption within faith-healing circles has left a bitter taste in many mouths. Reforms are long overdue, and he knows that rebuilding trust is tricky. Every detail of the new ministry must be taken into account.

Jeremiah feels that we are getting very close to the unveiling.

I nodded with relief and asked what I could do to help. Jeremiah mused over my question at considerable length as we strolled toward the chapel. He invited me to sit on the chapel steps while he leaned against the railing with a doctor's air. The authority of his stance put me at ease.

A peculiar half-smile played at his lips as he nodded slowly. Yes, there were things I could do. Once the ministry is active, I will play a critical role in its success; but in the meantime, if I wished to work, he would find tasks for me.

What are my skills? This question caught me by surprise. Doesn't he know? No, of course, he doesn't. I feel as if I've always known him, yet we've only just begun. I recited a list for him: organizing, researching, writing, drawing—

Jeremiah stopped me there to marvel at the fact that I could *actually* draw. He complimented me for being multi-talented and suggested that I help create the promotional fliers that we will use to spread the word of our first Crusade. Ah, yes, this would be the ideal job for me; he just wished that it had occurred to him sooner!

By the end of the hour, he had given me so much praise that I had begun to sweat. When the Man Himself approves, he leaves little room for self-doubt.

Darkness had fallen by the time we returned to the house. I felt chilled and listless like the sea after a storm. I thought I would sleep

well tonight, but here I lie, sharply aware of the wee hours of morning. My mind is alive with ideas, ideas, ideas! Now that I have something to do, I shall do it with all my might.

TUESDAY, APRIL 27

Jeremiah was grave and quiet this evening. I asked him questions and made cheery remarks, hoping to provoke his usual loquaciousness, but he would not stir. Jeremiah did not speak to me until we reached the farthest corner of the lawn. He then revealed that he had been doing a lot of soul-searching over the past few days and determined that he needed guidance. His ego had grown unchecked for too long. His arrogant outburst at my hometown revival was a symptom of this, and he was ashamed. Could I ever forgive him? Would I help him root out the evils of his disposition and correct them? I must teach him all that I know about humility.

I laughed aloud. In truth, I was embarrassed. That word is an abstraction and an enigma to me. I know little about humility, aside from the general rule that one who touts her humility cannot be genuinely humble. Jeremiah would be better off seeking guidance from books or wise elders of the church and community.

He insisted that I teach him whatever I *do* know. And I should promise to hold him to the high standards of integrity and humility modeled by Jesus Christ himself. If I should see him falter, then I must confront him. He doesn't know why, exactly, but he finds himself compelled to heed whatever I say. He trusts my senses, he said.

I was terribly embarrassed—but flattered and aflutter too, I'll admit. To appease Jeremiah, I agreed and hoped that he didn't really mean it.

Such an awesome responsibility ought to be divided between better, wiser people.

THURSDAY, APRIL 29

The tasks that Jeremiah appointed me are proving to be more ambitious than I anticipated. For one, he expects me to design a flier for our first Crusade by next Monday. I don't know much about creating extraordinary marketing materials. What magical phrases should I use? What entrancing images and color schemes should be employed to entice our true believers hither?

Brainstorm: I could cut out letters from magazines and spell our message with colorful, mismatched characters. Nothing grabs attention quite like a ransom letter. Glitter? Everyone likes shiny things. Perhaps I should design a pop-up card—the unsuspecting recipient opens it and out leaps the Devil waving a pitchfork!

Next idea, please.

I have not used graphic design software before, but Margaret has. This task initially belonged to her, but Jeremiah reassigned it to me. Not wanting to step on any toes, I tried to talk to Margaret about this (awkwardly), but she shrugged me off. Without ever expressing her displeasure directly, Margaret disappeared to her bedroom complaining of a migraine and has been there ever since.

Jeremiah and Pastor Ormand invited me to join them in their study to discuss strategy. It was my first trip to the secret room. As you might expect, the walls of the study were adorned with leather-bound volumes, and a Tiffany lamp roosted on the corner of a massive mahogany desk. The scent of stale cigar spurted from the stuffing of the easy chair when I sat down. The meeting began with golf chat. I glazed over. After about ten minutes, the conversation turned to business. The men discussed flier designs while I sketched out their ideas. They agreed that Margaret would be persuaded to teach me the software. The pastor seemed apprehensive, but he promised to speak with Margaret privately and make sure that she complied.

What's with the reluctance, I wondered? Lately, I've felt an odd sort of discord in the house, like the vibration of an overtightened string. But up to that point, its tune was still too faint to make out.

During our evening walk, it came out that a certain mother might have become jealous of a certain child's admiration of and devotion to her drawing mentor.

This surprised me! I had no idea that Margaret disapproved of my spending time with Jennie. She always seemed indifferent, and I assumed that I was doing her a service by keeping one child occupied for a few hours a week.

Thank goodness Jeremiah clued me in. The last thing I want to do is give offense. I may have to curtail the drawing lessons for now.

MONDAY, MAY 3

Today we hit the streets. The time has come to introduce Wholesome Healing Ministries to the world.

Jeremiah was quick to correct my use of the word *campaign* to describe today's mission. We are neither politicians nor troops, he explained. The purpose of our errand is divine, so we call it *discipling*. Whatever the name, I was eager to begin. Jeremiah's words rang in my ears and filled me with single-minded determination. *We have to get the message out by what-*

ever means possible. Lives depend upon it!

The children were granted a free day from school so that they could accompany us. Each adult was assigned one or two little ones. This was strategic. Jeremiah and the Kenneths agreed that strangers on the street tend to be more willing to accept religious pamphlets from cherubic five-year-olds than from insistent adults.

The adults disbursed to different quadrants of the city with their wards in tow. Susan, the eldest, and Tyler, the youngest, were mine for the day. We wove our way up the street against rush hour's current and planted ourselves near the transportation hub at Ervay and Elm.

Our thick stacks of fliers thinned by the hour. As noon approached, exhaustion manifested in the form of numb lips and toes. I was impressed that the children did not seem to find this work fatiguing. Perhaps their efforts were more efficient than mine. My appeals to strangers were earnest and emotional. The children's strategy proved more straightforward: hand over the paper and say thanks.

Sometime after one o'clock, I turned around just in time to spot Jeremiah Promise and little Joe coming up the sidewalk. They had cheeky expressions on their faces as if they were attempting to sneak up on us. Was the Man Himself being playful? With a chuckle, Jeremiah admitted that his ninja skills were wanting. In honor of my team's shrewdness, he'd like to cordially invite us to join him at the 7-Eleven across the street and select a few treats at his expense. The five of us then commandeered a bench in the shade to rest and eat.

Even in the shadows, it was a hot afternoon. I marveled that Jeremiah's blazer was still buttoned up, his tie cinched tight. He looked excessively respectable. I teased him about rolling up his sleeves and flexing his biceps to attract additional attention from passers-by. Until then, I'd been careful to tip-toe around the topic that could not be ignored

forever: Jeremiah's exceptional appearance.

It's something that one really can't help but notice—especially when one shares common living spaces with him and must tolerate his presence at the dinner table dressed in jeans and a T-shirt. His limbs are—how can I put this—sculpted like a Greek statue, and his jawline could cut glass. I swear I do not care about such things! But at some point, they must be acknowledged.

I playfully pestered Jeremiah, but he did not see the humor in my suggestion. What a puzzler he is! One blessed with attractive features but too principled to show them off.

Jeremiah lamented the state of the world. It wasn't modest enough for his taste; he found the ways of modern women very disappointing. These days, many young ladies wear shorts that don't cover their derriere and skimpy tops designed to distract men from the deficiencies of their hearts, minds, and souls. He simply could not enjoy exterior beauty—not when he knew that it was hollow inside.

I chuckled. What could I say? He's a prude! His assertions were too broad, but still oddly flattering. I was tempted to feel smug that he chose me as his confidant. Not so fast, Miss Puffed-up! Let's not forget that a haughty spirit comes before a fall.

Still, I cannot fault him for valuing the interiors of people more than their exteriors. In mythology, the hero of the story is always pure of heart. His sound moral character guides his deeds, and because of this, he achieves great success.

Friday, May 7

I discipled alone for the first time today. The undertaking proved more challenging than I expected. Folks seemed to be less patient and receptive. Perhaps because it was Friday? Or because the presence of children did not temper their responses.

At least a third of the people crossed the street when they saw me. Another third averted their eyes or held up their hands to stop me when I spoke to them. I endeavored to take none of these things personally. A few people called me names, told me I was stupid, narrow-minded, blind, that I should get a life, get a real job, etc. One man pulled my hair (which was oddly childish), and a couple of teenagers distracted me while a third tried to steal my backpack. These unkindnesses were more difficult to bear.

By noon I felt thoroughly knocked about and worn out. I gathered up my things and sought shelter in the gentle shade of the Thanks-Giving Square garden. There I sat and read my book until it was time to head home.

I shall dwarf the difficulties of the day by focusing on the positives. I met several exceptional strangers today, one of whom lingered to talk to me for over a quarter of an hour. Her name was Katya Novak, and she looked young enough to be in high school, yet she had wisdom beyond her years when it came to the differences between self-confidence and self-esteem.

I saw something in her, and perhaps she saw something in me, too—that special little spark. A spark of what? Recognition! Though we were strangers, we seemed to instinctively know that we could skip the small talk and dive straight to the heart of any topic in a matter of seconds.

As Katya spoke with me, her manner was polite but firm. Her feet remained planted on the ground, and her whole body tilted forward with a determination to be understood.

Here's a person who exemplifies the self-confidence we are discussing! I thought. It was a pleasure to discover an admirable trait in a passing stranger and have the opportunity to draw it out. What other delights may hide in plain sight?

TUESDAY, MAY 11

A lady walked right up to me on the street, shook my hand, and said that she hoped I would die in a fiery car crash. Her words landed like a hard slap with reverberations that stung me to the core. They hurt all the more because I didn't see them coming.

The woman was nice looking, well dressed, and approached with a smile. I supposed her to be an employee of some nearby law firm or financial institution. She accepted the flier that I offered her and contemplated it for a few moments. I stood by quietly and waited for my chance to engage her in conversation. When the woman looked up, the smile was still there—only in retrospect did her expression seem asymmetrical. Without batting an eye, she grabbed my hand, seared my skin with her fingers like a hot brand, wished an excruciating death upon me, tossed the flier on the ground, and walked off.

I was stunned. How can a person so casually curse someone she doesn't even know? Why? The woman disagreed with the ideas that I represented. That's the only reason I could imagine. She didn't even take the time to speak *with* me. If she had, we might have discovered that we were similar people, even if our ideas differed.

The parade of polite, well-meaning people that came along after her could not un-shake me. All afternoon, I was adrift on some faraway tide, my senses swamped with seawater. At dinner this evening, I could not focus on anyone or anything, so I did not hear Margaret's request to pass the green beans. Jennie elbowed me to get my attention. The bowl was at the corner of the table closest to me. When I reached for it, my elbow knocked it to the floor. The bowl shattered, and beans flopped everywhere.

Margaret shouted and leaped to her feet. I suddenly found myself at the center of eight piercing stares. It was more than I could bear. I burst into tears and sprinted for the girls' bedroom. Though I share that room with three of the children, it seemed like my best chance of privacy at the moment. I collapsed on my bunk, sobbing.

No *one* thing was the matter. Everything was the matter.

It troubles me that anger and unkindness leaps out of strangers so readily, though we live in a world in which compassion and acceptance are the supposed ideals. Within the last week, I have been spit at, yelled at, cursed out, and had a cigarette flicked at me out of a car window. One man tried to kick me. Stacks of fliers periodically go missing, and sometimes I later discover them crammed halfway into a gutter or trash can down the street.

It doesn't help that I haven't slept more than three hours in a row since I first arrived here. I'm exhausted!

Eventually, my self-pitying tears subsided. When Jeremiah came to find me, I scrubbed my face on my sleeve and went to open the door with a smile. We went for a walk. Jeremiah patiently waited for me to speak my mind. I was reluctant, but once I began, the whole story tumbled out. I described every instance of rudeness and inhumanity

that had plagued me this last week.

Jeremiah sighed and shook his head. He apologized for the petty and sometimes profound cruelty of man. God Himself endorses our mission, but that doesn't ensure our safe passage.

"When we stand up for our beliefs," he said, "others will always seek to test us and tear us down." Jeremiah knows that I am unused to the ways of the world. It takes great vision to see the world the way that he does. Unfortunately, people don't always see the good in new and novel things. Their fear drives them to shun the unconventional. When people lash out, they know not what they do. Jeremiah urged me to see these negative encounters as opportunities to identify my weak spots and strengthen them.

We arrived at the edge of the property near the street and stopped there. Jeremiah drew my attention up to the freestanding marquee beside us. *Sunday Services at 9:30 and 11:00.* He told me to look past the plain message that was presently there and envision what soon would be: his name in big, block letters.

"There's power in a name," he said. Jeremiah Promise's name is his pledge to the people to do everything in his power to save them. He will put his name on this sign when, and only when, he is ready to make good on that *promise.* Thanks to me, that time is close at hand.

Jeremiah reminded me of my name. I am True Believer. My powers of faith and conviction are some of the most potent in the universe, for they are the building blocks of manifestation. "Take heart," he said. "Your faith is essential to our success."

We slowly walked back toward the house, and I marveled at the heroic confidence of the thoughtful figure beside me. When I was with Jeremiah, I felt protected by the umbrella of his wisdom. He seemed to have an answer and a plan for everything. He melted my worries away.

At the door, Jeremiah paused. "Let's shake on it," he said. He clasped my hand, and his long fingers brushed my wrist. I averted my gaze, not because I didn't want to look him in the eye, but because I was suddenly gripped with fear that he'd see straight into me. He wouldn't have had to look too deep to see traces of something more than gratitude there.

THURSDAY, MAY 13

I was nervous about going out on my own again today, but as luck would have it, I was not alone. Around ten o'clock, a small group assembled at the end of my block. They held up signs and cheered whenever a car honked at them in passing. I enjoyed their spirit but was uncertain of their cause.

Debt = Slavery!

The Power of the People > The People in Power!

End Austerity!

Where's the Humanity?

After a while, I got up the courage to walk over to the knot of demonstrators. Most of them ignored me at first. One woman shot me a wary side-glance, so I approached her with a bright smile and wished her good morning. I apologized for my ignorance and asked if she would please tell me what they were doing.

"Protesting corporate corruption and greed," she said. She pointed at the two skyscrapers on either side of us and informed me that they housed two of the biggest, most corrupt banks in America.

The woman's name was Miriam Coffy, and I learned from her about the home foreclosure epidemic that's been sweeping the country.

Of the group of protesters, Ellen, Francisco, and Victor had all been

bum-rushed (her word) to financial ruin within the last six months. Floyd and Markus lost their homes while they were on active duty overseas. Mateo lost his ranch because he couldn't afford to pay both the mortgage and his wife's medical bills. Sylvana, Doris, Frank, and Samson were all victims of subprime loans.

"It's criminal, and it must stop!" Miriam proclaimed, and the others cheered. I looked from one to the next and felt for their loss and displacement. I felt compelled to do something. How could I help? Could I join their protest for the busiest part of the day? Miriam chuckled and said sure, why not?

The experience was invigorating. I merged easily with the current of like-minded anger that surged just below the faction's diverse exteriors. Their cause drew more fire than mine ever has. Perhaps that's because they were more raucous. They were not there to politely get along with people, no! They were there to evoke emotion, attract attention, and stir things up. Any kind of noise was better than no noise.

For the first time ever, I was called a "c-word" to my face. Fortunately, Miriam was close by and overheard. Before the insult had a chance to sink in, she snorted and said, "He's just jealous." I laughed. Miriam was right—it wasn't personal. That man probably would have said the same thing to me if I'd been standing on the opposite corner promoting a different cause. He was trolling for any opportunity to be rude.

After the lunch rush, I returned to my corner and resumed ministry discipling. Before parting ways with Miriam, I handed her a thin stack of Crusade fliers. She looked at me skeptically. "I don't go for this sort of thing," she said, handing the fliers back to me.

I quickly agreed that it's not for everyone. But it might be for *someone* she knows. I asked her to do me the honor of telling her people about us. Let them decide for themselves. In the end, Miriam agreed. That goes to show that a little discipling outside the box can benefit everyone.

SATURDAY, MAY 15

It's the eve of our first Crusade, and my heart is full of everything. Of love, of people, of drawing, of summertime and dresses and sandals and flowers, of adventures and discoveries, and of having my senses pulled in so many directions that I hardly know where to focus. Of heat-shimmering pavement, feet up on the dash and windows rolled down as we sit in traffic. Of sprawling in the grass reading books. Of soulful music and swaying. Of dripping sweat and refreshing gusts of relief. There seems to be no obstacle in the world, great or small, that Jeremiah Promise cannot eventually overcome.

All is well—much too well! It's as if a garden hose has un-kinked inside me, and all the love in the world gushes freely through my anatomy. It is painful at times, but never mind that. I'd rather burst from joy than let drought hollow me out.

SUNDAY, MAY 16

When I opened the front door this morning, it was with a gust of exultation. Cars were parked on the front lawn, and the churchyard bustled with activity.

Jeremiah was fussy and fretful. He complained that it looked as if half the seats would remain empty. I laughed, knowing that his nit-picky pessimism was just an expression of nervous excitement. As Jeremiah's confidence briefly abated, mine surged to make up the difference.

I told him not to worry! The turnout would be exactly what it ought to be for his first step back into the public eye.

Pastor Ormand served as Worship Leader of the Crusade. With tact and well-timed humor, he built a bridge of amity between Jeremiah and the audience. It was wondrous to behold the soft glow that spread through the room as trust took hold. Bodies began to loosen, arms began to rise. Exclamations of praise and agreement cropped up like popcorn.

Jeremiah opened with a dynamic sermon about the need to lovingly detach oneself from life's drama to seek divine clarity. We all grapple with our desire to control our lives, he said, but God, in His infinite wisdom, encourages us to release control so that we may know true freedom.

Cue my entrance.

I was dressed in a lacy white gown and wore a wreath of fresh flowers on my head. We had found the dress at a thrift store, and it was a little too big. Margaret pinned me into it. I was nervous about the various calamities that might befall me—tripping, stumbling, pin popping—but I was careful, and all went well.

Thank goodness I did not have to speak. My job was to stand there and smile and allow Jeremiah to introduce me as the pure, white lily that had once grown in the wild. His God told him to pluck me from an un-Christian field and bring me here so that his people could behold God's grace.

He told my story of miraculous healing and related it to similar Biblical miracles—the faithless lepers that Jesus healed in Luke 17, the Jewish man Jesus saved in John 5, and the boy possessed by the demon of epilepsy that was cured by prayer in Mark 9.

"Heal the sick, raise the dead, cleanse the lepers, and cast out the devils!" Jeremiah bellowed. He asserted that his God exhibits His real power and mercy by healing the *unfaithful*. People like me. When God empowered Jeremiah to defeat the cancer demon that ravaged my body, he also saved my soul by inspiring perfect faith. I became True Believer!

Hallelujah!

"If everyone here today already lives in TRUE faith, then the lion's share of God's work is done!" Jeremiah exclaimed. "Come, children, come to the front and let God's instrument lay hands. Let Him use me to unburden you of your earthly suffering!"

Surges of heartfelt adulation swelled and strained against the confines of the small chapel. The congregants swayed and sang, hugged each other, clasp their hands together, or reached toward the heavens with open palms. A small fleet of ushers was deployed into their midst with donation baskets. People dug into wallets, pockets, and purses, impatient to proceed to the ceremonious climax of the day: the healing procession. Most people stumbled over each other in their haste to approach the pulpit. Some held back, but their resistance was no match for Jeremiah's mighty allure. In the end, all but the most stubborn succumbed. Those few holdouts remained watchful but quiet.

During this next part of the Crusade, my assignment was to help catch the anointed as they fell.

The job of "catcher" is more critical than one might think, as most people fall down after Jeremiah Promise raps them on the forehead and declares them cured. Some get right back up again, some of them lie still, some convulse, and some go limp and must be assisted back to their seats. Anyone with a free pair of hands is encouraged to serve as a catcher.

What conviction from Jeremiah! More than fifty people passed under his hands today, and he was as patient and sincere with the very last

of them as he was with the first. His face gleamed with sweat, and at some point, he tossed aside his blazer, loosened his tie, and rolled up his sleeves.

"God is touching your thyroid condition right now," he proclaimed.

Healed!

"The tumors are gone in Jesus's name, and a surgeon's knife will never cut your flesh again. Hallelujah!"

Healed!

"I sense a darkness of the pancreas here beneath my hand. I revoke that darkness in Jesus's name!"

Healed!

"Lord, help me deliver this man from drugs!"

Healed!

"God has a miracle with your name on it!" Jeremiah raved, and everyone cheered.

Knees bent, and bodies collapsed one by one as if they were scored to fold just-so. With each wave of the hand, Jeremiah closed out years, perhaps even lifetimes, of illness and suffering. I marveled at the ease with which he defeated grief, disbelief, and the laws of physics. I wouldn't, I couldn't conceive of such a thing if I didn't watch with my own eyes as people discarded their crutches and freely flexed their gnarled, arthritic fingers. How did he do it? Not without the element of total surrender, I suspect. God or no God, belief or no belief, when the moment comes, each of his subjects must be—above all—willing.

Worship music played throughout. People sang, danced, and prayed aloud in garbled tongues. Some slid to the floor and writhed in ecstasy and adulation. Others tilted their heads back and held their arms high in the air. Some wandered around, hugging everyone they encountered. Others cried. Sensitivities heightened and converged into a perceptible pulse. Intangible connections wove here and there, in and out, back and forth across the room like a spider's web. It became impossible to move in any direction without triggering a collective vibration. Heads turned to look across the room and nod as if I'd tapped them on the shoulder.

Jeremiah tossed a curveball into the mix today that even I wasn't expecting. After he had healed those that approached and taken a ten-minute break to straighten his tie and splash water on his face, he returned to the stage. The Crusade wasn't over yet: one important ritual remained.

He explained that it's customary for the church and the faith healer to split the donation money collected from the congregation. It usually goes straight into their pockets.

Not today.

No, Jeremiah Promise understood that times were tough, and people needed more than miracles. They needed something to live on, too. Today, Wholesome Healing Ministries collected $966.16 from his faithful flock, and today he intended to give it right back.

"The amount is auspicious!" he exclaimed. "For it is on page 966 of the Bible that I find book 3 John, chapter 1, verse 2—'Beloved, I pray that all may go well with you and that you may be in health; I know that it is well with your soul.' So, shall one of our congregation prosper today in both health AND wealth!"

Jeremiah said that his God had whispered a name in his ear. It was the name of one of the most faithful and deserving among his flock. He described the woman: she wore a wig of long dark braids that covered her bare head. Until today, she had battled breast cancer. Though her body was healed and her soul saved today, she still had three young children to care for and a pile of bills to pay.

"Ebony Clark of 4978 Harmony Place, where are you?" Jeremiah

called out. "God beseeches you to step forward!"

Someone from the middle of the audience cried out. Ebony stood up and made her way to the front. Jeremiah presented her with a thick envelope. He proclaimed that this was but one small gesture to help her "slay the giant of debt" in her life. The woman cried and hugged him.

My heart sang. At that moment, I reached a new tier of admiration for Jeremiah Promise.

After the service, I couldn't wait to extol his altruism. He shrugged off my praise. "It's easy to give away other people's money," he said.

"It's still a sacrifice to give away the donation money when you don't have a penny to your name," I reminded him. Jeremiah didn't respond, but the faint hint of a smile played at his lips.

It took a while to clean up after the Crusade. There was a marked element of entropy entangled in the whole experience. Bibles were tossed about, and a few were torn. Entire boxes of tissues had been emptied and scattered all over the floor. Miscellaneous items—keys, jewelry, sanitary napkins, makeup, photographs, and bus passes—everywhere.

Jeremiah pitched in to help the rest of us put the chapel back together. Good man. He spent the most time with me at the lost-and-found table, helping sort through mounds of personal items. At one point, I opened a wallet to look for an ID. Inside I saw pictures of a happy, smiling family. I showed the picture to Jeremiah.

"This is what we're trying to preserve," he said thoughtfully. He reached over to take the wallet from me, and his fingers enveloped mine. It was just a touch, which may signify very little to some. To me, it was a jolt of tingles that took a long, long time to fade away. I wonder if he felt that, too.

WEDNESDAY, MAY 19

Today was a *strange* day. One stranger accosted me, and another stranger came to my rescue!

I was out discipling downtown this afternoon when a stout, pasty-faced man glommed on to me and loudly declared that I was a cult recruiter. *Here we go,* I thought. Something like this was bound to happen eventually.

I tried reasoning with the man, and then I tried ignoring him. He would neither be appeased nor leave me alone. I hoped that he would grow tired and go away, but the man only seemed to build steam, and his brute-force attacks gradually wore me down. My patience grew thin as the spectacle continued to drive people away.

The short man called me a brain-dead zombie and accused me of drinking the Kool-Aid. I consider myself an independent thinker that relies on fact and intuition to form careful opinions. *Remember, True, this man doesn't know you at all,* I thought to myself. I tried not to let his words sting my pride, though it was challenging to disregard false accusations when they were shouted in my face. Finally, I turned to confront him and asked him if that's what he *really* thought. If so, then I was sad for him! I was sorry his heart and mind were closed, and I doubted that he could enjoy much of the beauty in this world. I wished I could help him see it.

The man shook, and his face turned a deeper shade of red. For an instant, I feared that he would strike me. That's when the tall man intervened. Out of nowhere, he lunged at the short man while furiously flapping the wings of his jacket. The short man stumbled over a planter,

crawled, fumbled, and scurried backward until he rounded the corner and vanished from sight.

The tall man stopped, smoothed his coat, adjusted his hat, and came back to me. His eyes crinkled when he smiled. He bent down to pick up a flier from the top of the stack, folded it, and tucked it in his pocket. He tipped his hat to me and strode off without a word.

Eventually, I saw the humor in it and couldn't stop laughing. What might have been a cautionary tale about bullying turned out to be a lighthearted pointer: when reason fails, sometimes it is best to chase off one's foe like an angry goose and call it a day.

SUNDAY, MAY 23

I made a million friends today!

Crusade number two was twice the size of the first. We filled nearly every seat in the chapel. We saw many familiar faces, and they all clamored to introduce us to their friends, second cousins, family dentists, and other guests.

Irma Feldman showed me pictures of her new grandbaby. Rodney Thomson introduced me to his mother and told me all about her heart condition. I received hugs and handshakes from every angle and heard stories of numerous miracles. Crystal Williams swore that her husband's eczema had completely cleared up since Jeremiah laid hands on him last Sunday. Blythe Grange was totally free from knee pain. *Praise Jesus!* There wasn't a single complaint in the bunch. Jeremiah's healing success was mind-boggling.Don't think I let all this hustle and bustle distract me from the duty of filling out "prayer cards" for each person I met. Jeremiah stressed the vital importance of these cards: they will keep us streamlined, standardized, and professional. We must write down full names so that we can address people respectfully. We must write down specific medical conditions so that we can pray for them thoroughly. And we must record their complete mailing addresses so we can send them newsletters (whenever we get around to creating them).

Jeremiah is militant when it comes to Crusade conduct, but I respect his standard of excellence. When he is entirely in his element, it is a joy to behold.

Over the past weeks, I've been fascinated by the minor details of Jeremiah's interactions with strangers. I have studied the absorptive and unwavering intensity of his gaze. Again and again, I've watched him enthrall his subjects with both his words and the spaces between them. He seems to have no difficulty understanding anyone, regardless of language or accent. When I observe him from a distance, I cannot hear what he says to them or what they say back. I can only see the mystical shimmer of amity that ensues. His social instincts are truly remarkable. They border on the supernatural. I wish I had a tenth of his charisma. If I did, I imagine that nothing outside the present moment would ever matter again.

Alas, I am not a gifted speaker, so I endeavor to be a good listener.

The stories. Oh, the stories.

I'm astounded by the tales of hardship and perseverance that I've heard from real, honest, well-meaning people. I haven't yet met a single person that I didn't respect more after speaking with them.

Rose Sylva had suffered from fibromyalgia for her entire adult life. Her world was one of considerable highs and lows—sometimes peaking in periods of extraordinary productivity and sometimes plummeting into pits of such physical pain that she had to shut herself up in a dark bedroom and sleep for days at a time. She prayed Jeremiah Prom-

ise would take away the darkness today and leave her with nothing but light. *Praise Jesus!*

All of Isaiah Brash's fingers had become gnarled by arthritis. He could no longer hold the hammer and chisel that he used to make a living for seventy-one years of his life. He prayed that Jeremiah Promise would straighten his fingers so that he could make toys for his grand-children. *Praise Jesus!*

Andre and India Tillman's oldest child was narcoleptic. They brought their boy (Bobby) to the Crusade in a wheelchair flanked by their younger children. Now that he was getting bigger, the whole fam-ily had become captives of his condition. They could not make social plans outside of the home for any length of time for fear that Bobby might pass out at any moment, fall, and injure himself. They prayed that Jeremiah Promise would free them all from the "demon that makes him sleep." *Praise Jesus!*

Today, Jeremiah preached about Baptism in the Holy Spirit. He viv-idly described each of the nine Gifts of the Holy Spirit that were likely to manifest after baptism, emphasizing the Gifts of Miracles, Healing, and Tongues. Then he hastily dispatched the fleet of ushers to collect monetary "seeds of love" from the congregation before diving into the healing process. Time was short, and he had many miracles to perform before the day was done.

How does Jeremiah Promise heal abstract maladies like these, I won-der? How does he know where in the body they reside? I have been watching him closely for clues as to the science of his healing touch, but I have noticed little variation in his technique. No matter what ails them, he almost always anoints people on the head. Why the head? Per-haps to commission the brain to deliver his God's medicine wherever it is meant to go?

As a catcher, I fortuitously found myself paired up with a pleasant, good-looking man named Kevin McVae. He and I had exchanged half a dozen meaningful smiles throughout the day. We chatted during brief lulls here and there, and he had a lot of questions for me. He said he hoped to see more of me as the ministry took root, and I agreed.

We collected $1,762.24 today! That's almost twice as many "seeds" as last time. The money went to a man named Jamar Wilson, whose cancerous vertebrae were repaired by Jeremiah's powerful touch. An hour earlier, the man had cast off his brace and run from one end of the room to the other. Evidently, God saw fit to reward him twice in one day!

As the men shook hands, Jeremiah suddenly seized theatrically and announced that a spiritual baptism was happening right before our eyes. Could it be?—Was it possible?—Had Jamar Wilson just accepted his Lord and Savior Jesus Christ into the deepest chambers of his heart? Had he been anointed with one of God's Spiritual Gifts?

"Dedicate your life to God, and be elevated by His love," Jeremiah proclaimed. He exhorted the man to speak. If his first utterance was the language of the Holy One, we would know that he had been endowed with the Gift of Tongues as evidence of his transformation. Cheers and exclamations subsided as people strained to listen. Jeremiah held the man's hand in both of his and mouthed quiet words of encouragement to him. Slowly, the man began to utter a string of strange syllables. Jeremiah grinned and clapped him on the back triumphantly.

Monday, May 24

These Crusades are really knocking me for a loop. They treat me to a strange concoction of excitement and exhaustion beyond anything I've experienced before. It takes days to quiet the echoes of sights, sounds, and conversations, and to still the buzzy jitters that keep me up at night. I have started drinking coffee in the morning to help me cut through the fog. Coffee with lots of cream and sugar, of course.

Wednesday, May 26

Jeremiah has appointed me another ministry role. I am Miracle of God, Graphic Designer, Street Discipler, Backup Catcher, and now Congregation Liaison.

The Man Himself has more faith in my abilities than I do at this point. I was reluctant to accept. But this might have been due in part to my bleary-eyed, brain-dead state after having just spent all night tossing and turning in bed and all day crafting the first draft of our ministry handbook.

Jeremiah did not appreciate my lack of enthusiasm. He clarified that this was a prestigious role. Our following was growing, and so too was the demand for his attention. The last Crusade reminded him how draining it was to perform over a hundred miracles a week. The time before and after the Crusades was precious, and he needed space to mentally prepare and recover. While he did this, he needed someone he trusted to guard the gate, so to speak.

The way that he leveled that viridian gaze at me and smiled—what could I do but say yes? Congratulations to me! I'm now the designated people-person.

It took me a while to understand why Jeremiah would ask me to do this. Doesn't he know by now that I'm better suited to non-speaking roles? My words are like handfuls of marbles that might scatter if I squeezed too tightly. Last Sunday, I was sick with worry about saying the wrong things.

I've spent hours lying in bed with a head full of concerns. Tired though I am, there is no room for sleep. It bothers me that Jeremiah seems to have an unrealistic amount of confidence in me. What happens if I cannot live up to his expectations?

I must conclude that Jeremiah knows what he's doing. He *trusts* me, he said, and I must trust him. He means to challenge me. Teach me. He wouldn't do this if he didn't see the potential in me to learn, grown, and adapt.

Jeremiah is an ambitious man, and he seeks a worthy partner, no doubt—one who can hold her own in this world and is not held back by fear or corruption. I want to be her.

Deep breath.

Thursday, May 27

I had nowhere in particular to be today, but I couldn't stay in the house. Margaret scheduled a team of professionals to scrub the carpets and polish the hardwood. So, I claimed the bench outside the church offices for an afternoon of reading and drawing.

It was not a quiet spot. A steady stream of visitors came and went

all day. Most had healing consultations with Jeremiah or counseling appointments with Pastor Ormand. A few were walk-ins, and they waited in the hallway with me. Sometimes I'd move to the floor to make room on the bench when more than two people were waiting.

Kevin McVae showed up around three o'clock. He grinned, and I smiled, and we chatted while he waited to see Jeremiah. I learned that he was born in Iowa, and his family had moved to Dallas when he was twelve. A Midwesterner! That explained his lack of Texas twang.

His reason for meeting with Jeremiah on a Thursday afternoon was a mystery to him. I suggested that his good ushering work must have earned him a raise. This was a joke, of course—as a volunteer, he received no pay.

The Man Himself emerged from his office and beckoned Kevin. The expression on Jeremiah's face zapped my cheery mood. Kevin must be in trouble. I couldn't imagine why.

The meeting lasted about ten minutes. When the two reemerged, Kevin's countenance had completely changed. Jeremiah gripped his slumped shoulder and said loudly and clearly, "Remember what we discussed, Kevin. If this happens again, you won't be welcome back."

Kevin nodded, grim and gray-faced. He didn't look at me on his way out. A moment later, Pastor Ormand came to speak to Jeremiah. Their tones were too low to hear, but it looked like a disagreement. The pastor sighed and shook his head several times. He made a slashing gesture with his hand and then went away.

It struck me as odd the way this whole drama played out right in front of me. Did they mean for me to witness it? Jeremiah grinned and winked as he walked past me to the water cooler. He told me I was welcome to use his office, as he had no more appointments this afternoon. He just wanted to grab a quick nap before he headed out.

Did I dare disturb his rest with questions about Kevin?

I went into the office and took a seat in the swivel chair behind the desk. Jeremiah came in, kicked off his shoes, and stretched out on the couch. He set his phone on his chest and closed his eyes. I opened my book and attempted to read, but my attention kept slipping over and around the printed page to poke at the still figure beyond.

What's this—the Man Himself *sleeping* in my presence? Had we reached a new level of intimacy? Friends do not always need to be alert and talkative in each other's presence. It's a special thing to be comfortable enough with another person to be quiet and unguarded around her.

This idea called to mind last night's dream. Jeremiah, Pastor Ormand, and I were lounging on couches like old friends. We had just successfully opened our first church in Dallas and were discussing plans for expansion. We talked and laughed, and all seemed right with the world. Jeremiah leaned over to show me the notes he'd been jotting down. He moved so close that I could feel the stubble of his chin on my cheek. The sensation startled and thrilled me, and I tried to hold onto it for as long as I could.

After twenty minutes, Jeremiah's phone buzzed. He silenced it without opening his eyes.

"She isn't much to look at, but she sure is comfortable," he said. It took me a moment to realize that he was talking about the couch. I laughed and said that I would take his word for it.

He asked me what I thought of Pastor Ormand. Not sure what he wanted to know, I cautiously answered that the pastor seems like a serious man that cares about his people.

"You think?" Jeremiah asked and paused to reflect.

Here I saw my chance to ask what had happened with Kevin McVae. Jeremiah shook his head and waved away my question. I shouldn't

trouble myself with matters of misconduct, he said. It was already taken care of.

He asked how I've been handling the Crusade life. I told him all the good things before mentioning that I might maybe possibly perhaps be struggling with anxiety. Anxiety is a common ailment, Jeremiah pointed out. He's observed its many manifestations in other people, though he's never suffered from it personally.

He credits God for holding him to a high standard of authenticity and providing righteous outlets for his passion. By living life without restraint or regret, he has no fear of death. Jeremiah hypothesized that the feelings most people identify as fear or anxiety may really be excitement in disguise. Think about it! All these emotions are attended by similar physical symptoms: increased heart rate, blood pressure, respiration, muscle tension, brain activity.

Is anxiety by any other name quite so daunting?

A chime interrupted our conversation. Jeremiah glanced at his phone, thumbed a few things on the screen, and then lay it face down on his chest again. I struggled to suppress a smile, glad that he did not let a distraction pull him away.

He mentioned that he was supposed to go to a "thing" tonight, but he didn't want to. It was more important to rest. He would make an excuse. I agreed that he shouldn't go if he didn't care to. Energy is precious.

Jeremiah posed the question: if energy is precious, how does one effectively conserve it? This was his ongoing quandary.

I leaped at the opportunity to share one of my post-cancer epiphanies. One day, a couple years back, I stumbled into this sort of...energy river. I perceived an invisible current of elation rushing through the center of all things and was struck by the notion that joy is not a finite emotion but a force that flows *through* a person. It was an infinite power source from which I could draw boundless energy and enthusiasm. If ever my joy waned, it was because my connection to its source had kinked, I had inadvertently drifted out of the flow, or I had become hung up on some troubling obstruction. Outside the energy current, I would quickly wither with illness or exhaustion.

These are the dynamics that underpin energy-related matters, I concluded. Energy is fluid. It doesn't seem to keep, so I doubt it can be *conserved*. Better to focus on methods of unblocking energy's flow. Do things that inspire and expand—writing, drawing, and walking in nature. Avoid things that deflate and constrict, like attending tedious social events.

I was surprised that Jeremiah allowed me to go on this long without interruption. I expected him to object to my views on sacrilegious grounds, but he did not. A smile played at his lips, and he squinted with interest as though trying to perceive the common threads that joined our ideas together. When I was finished, he remarked that the experience I described sounded like Baptism in the Holy Spirit.

Friday, May 28

I have become adept at counting to twenty-three.

Twenty-three hours a day, I wait and eagerly anticipate the golden hour when Jeremiah seeks me out. On sunny days, we walk around the churchyard and talk. On rainy days, we sit in the chapel and chat. The topics are always engaging and give me food for thought. When the hour is done, the clock starts over again.

For weeks, I have basked in the sunshine of Jeremiah's regular atten-

tion. I believe that he looks forward to our time together as much as I do and takes pains to secure it. This has made me complacent, the folly of which has become apparent.

Tears of disappointment sprang to my eyes around ten o'clock this evening when I finally accepted that Jeremiah wasn't coming to talk to me. The third day in a row. I dashed the drops away with the back of my hand before they could fall.

Jeremiah Promise is a very busy man. He has important work to do. I really have no right to be surprised when his schedule gets in the way of our daily appointments. Sometimes these twenty-three hours of anticipation must double or triple without warning, and this is the inevitable consequence of involving oneself in so great an undertaking.

I shall take this as a lesson to be more careful about how and when I develop dependencies.

Sunday, May 30

The congregation was smaller than expected today. Ushers seemed to be lacking, too. Jeremiah approached the stage with stoic determination, but I know he was disappointed.

After the service, I overheard Pastor Ormand chastise Jeremiah. Kevin McVae was one of the church's most active and committed members, and Jeremiah shouldn't have taken it upon himself to reprimand Kevin without consulting the pastor first. Kevin had called the pastor and threatened to withdraw financial support if he didn't "do something" about Jeremiah Promise. Undoubtedly, Kevin had complained to other members of the congregation as well. Dissension can spread like wildfire when trust comes into question.

Jeremiah did not appreciate the scolding—certainly not right after so intense an afternoon of healing that his brow still glistened with sweat. I sprang to the front of the stage to field questions and comments from the audience while Jeremiah slipped out the back door. It wasn't difficult to assume my role as Congregation Liaison when I felt it was a direct service to Jeremiah. He looked drawn and dismayed, but at least he could escape to peace and quiet.

I spoke with every individual that stayed after the service. I wrote down names and contact information and took detailed notes about our conversations. Most people had personal questions about the Man Himself. Some wanted to arrange for private healing sessions. A few wanted to address the rumors they had heard about Jeremiah from Kevin McVae. Without knowledge of the details, I didn't know what to tell these people, so I met their misgivings with warm smiles and said that I was sure Jeremiah's conduct was based on God's wise counsel. We cannot always comprehend His reasons, but we can have faith that they're for the best. Most folks accepted this explanation, a few grumbled, but eventually, the room quieted and cleared out.

One man remained seated midway back in the pews after the last of the other congregants left. He stood, removed his hat, and ambled toward me. It took a moment to recognize him. His friendly eyes gave him away—it was Angry Goose Man!

I was thrilled to have the chance to thank him properly for his help defeating the heckler the other day. The man placed his hand over his heart, and his face crinkled with delight. An awkward silence ensued. I apologized for not being able to personally introduce my Samaritan to the Man Himself. He ought to have that honor.

I offered to go look for Jeremiah and bring him back. The tall man smiled and shook his head. By then, the stiltedness of our interaction

had become apparent, and I was running out of tact. The man had not spoken a single word, and the reason for this hadn't yet dawned on me. I attempted to draw him out by initiating a handshake and introducing myself. The man looked distressed. He took a deep breath and scrunched up his face.

"Forgive me!" I exclaimed. Too late, it occurred to me that he had a speech impediment. I instinctively gave his hand a sympathetic squeeze. Our palms suddenly became very hot. I looked down with surprise.

The man took a deep breath, opened his eyes and mouth wide, and recited the poem, "Do Not Go Gentle Into That Good Night," by Dylan Thomas. It was a good choice! Thomas's epic lines about living life to its fullest and striving fiercely until the very end have long been near and dear to my heart. When the man was finished, I commended him for his selection and execution. He revealed that he'd never recited that poem in its entirety before. His tongue would always get tangled. He'd had an awful stutter all his life, but I cured him of it when I touched him. A miracle!

Cured? Ha! Not possible.

Embarrassed, I explained that Jeremiah Promise was the faith healer, not me. But the man wouldn't hear it. He was convinced that I had special powers—not only as a healer but also as an "empath."

A what?

The man was going to believe what he wanted to believe. There was no point in trying to change his mind. Also, I had a lot of cleaning up yet to do, so I walked him to the door and said I hoped to see him again. He said yes, of course, he was confident we'd meet again soon. Before he left, he had just one more thing to tell me: that I had a fine speaking voice, and when I was up on stage, I ought to tell my own story.

The man's name was Alfred Childress, by the way. He told me to call him Freddie. *Sounds like Teddy,* I thought. A brief flash of nostalgia intervened, but I shooed it away.

Freddie was certainly an odd goose, but he seemed harmless enough.

Jeremiah and I crossed paths in the kitchen around midnight tonight. His hair was tousled, and he was still wearing his starched white shirt and suit pants. He must have crashed as soon as he returned to the house. Glad to have an entertaining story handy, I told Jeremiah about Freddie, describing the peculiar way he rescued me a few weeks ago, but leaving out the alleged healing part.

I thought Jeremiah would be amused. He was not. He solemnly warned me to be careful—there are a lot of oddballs around, and their intentions are not always good.

I suppose it's true that people are not always what they seem. Jeremiah is worldlier than I. He knows more about the hearts and minds of men than I do, and I ought to defer to his judgment. I shall endeavor to be more cautious.

Monday, May 31

It's days like these that I don't even mind the isolation. I have everything I need under one roof, and my impatience to break free and see *more* of this new world, do *more* for our cause, briefly subsides. I do so love these quiet afternoons with Jeremiah when no disciples demand our attention and no networking opportunities require our time. Jeremiah sits at his desk and drafts sermons, and I tuck into a quiet corner and draw. Though he and I inhabit the same space, we generally preserve the peace. I am happy to leave him to his work—which is more than I can say for Margaret.

She came in several times this morning and pulled him away to consult on some household matter or other. I guess Margaret assumed that being a man automatically made Jeremiah handy around the house, though he had already confided in me that he wasn't. After he was called away and returned for the third time, Jeremiah collapsed beside me on the couch with a sigh. He hoped that he had finally made it clear to the lady of the house that he knew squat about kitchen disposals. We shook our heads and laughed.

Gazing thoughtfully into the distance and rubbing his sturdy, stubbly chin, Jeremiah said that he wished he had the means to abscond to Duluth for a week and hide away in some remote cabin on the shore of Lake Superior. How odd that he should mention Duluth! Just two nights before, I'd had a dream about walking across the Aerial Lift Bridge. The image must have been summoned up from the deep archives of my early childhood.

Jeremiah dug into his pocket and produced a small, reddish stone. He handed it to me. Close examination revealed it to be an agate with delicate white ribbons. He had found it on the lakeshore when he was last in Duluth a few years ago, and he carried it around with him for good luck.

"It must have worked," he said. Back in April, he had meant to stop in Duluth during his last tour through the Midwest, but the plan fell through at the last minute. An act of God bumped him off course and pushed him toward northwest Wisconsin instead.

Toward me.

Jeremiah's viridian gaze seemed to intensify until it hurt to look at him. I invented a reason to excuse myself from the room. I ran away. Now, I feel silly.

It's strange. Sometimes when our eyes meet, I see not a face or a body,

but a vast expanse. I feel like I am reaching into something rather than looking at someone. Impressions form in my mind that aren't native to its terrain, and I become sure of things that I am prone to doubt. I begin to feel . . . reckless. My cautious nature may be the only thing that prevents me from plunging headlong into the abyss. Whether it is a leap I ought to take or not, I don't know. My fear of falling precludes it, for now.

Wednesday, June 2

First thing this morning, Jeremiah bit into a bagel and broke his tooth. I witnessed the incident and was horrified until he explained through his cupped hand that it was not a real tooth. He broke a dental bridge that he's had for over a dozen years. Both of his incisors were fake, but the reason was not shocking or cringe-worthy. They had simply never grown in after his baby teeth fell out.

Jeremiah refused to uncover his mouth so that I could assess the damage. He disappeared to another room to make a few phone calls and schedule an emergency dental appointment. I begged him to let me ride along. Many weeks of cloistering at the Kenneth house has made me eager to break free any chance I get.

Jeremiah took me to the appointment, but his lips remained sealed for the entire drive.

He had found a dentist that practiced out of the front two rooms of a bungalow at the edge of a tidy residential neighborhood. I was prepared to sit in the waiting room with a book, but the light there was dim, and the air smelled of bananas, bubble gum, and mildew. Jeremiah agreed that I should go for a walk around the neighborhood, though he seemed reluctant to let me leave. He crowded the doorway so that I had to squeeze past him to get outside.

I took a left and wandered until I reached a dead end. I backtracked, took a turn, and meandered some more, minding none of the street signs. My sense of direction is top-notch, and I can depend on it to get back from whatever wilderness I stumble into—most of the time.

I absorbed the culture of the neighborhood. The houses were a curious mix of mansions and shacks. Cacti grew amid poppies, and yard decor varied from twelve-foot high birdhouses to human gyroscopes.

The street ended at a cemetery. Its gate was open, so I strolled on in. I paused to read several headstones. Most dated back to the 1800s. Some were so mossy and weatherworn that I couldn't make out the inscriptions.

I stopped beside a family plot and examined the stones closely. Two markers stood side by side in the center: William and Elizabeth Houston, husband and wife. Around these two were buried three daughters: Katherine, Dorothy, and Rose.

Baby Kathrine lived and died on the same day in September 1902. Baby Dorothy's stone showed only one date, and that was in May of 1903. I counted out the months on my fingers; the math didn't make sense. It would seem that poor little Dorothy never lived at all.

Daughter Rose came along in 1904. Her parents must have rejoiced to have a healthy child at last. Unfortunately, Rose lived only eighteen years, and her mother lived only one year longer. Perhaps she died of a broken heart.

Life sure was hard back then. I can see why one's faith would be of the highest importance during eras rife with hardships and tragedy. It's easier to make peace with loss when there's reason to believe that it's part of some God's plan. There's comfort in the notion that suffering is justified and that good deeds are rewarded.

I have never had a church or God to make sense of senseless tragedy, and sometimes I wish I did. I have struggled to understand why it is my lot in life to lose. Others have done worse deeds than I and paid very different prices.

Teddy. Dad. Dave. Mom. I know they are more than mere prices. Their fates were not in my hands. Still, I am the one left behind to remember and miss them every day, and sometimes that feels punitive.

I look to nature for solace. The natural world provides endless examples of the life-death cycle. It reminds me daily that I am a tiny speck among countless specks and that the machinations of creation neither heed my wishes nor punish my choices.

I've heard faith healers preach to their followers that illness is the consequence of sin and poverty a disease of the soul. They tell sufferers that their difficulties are their faults because they're not clean enough, straight enough, or don't pray hard enough.

Jeremiah Promise is different. He will overthrow this blaming, shaming culture with his relentless and indiscriminate mercy. My heart swells with gratitude when I think of all the lives he has saved and will save.

It's funny to think that the man back at the dentist's office—the one too mortified to uncover his mouth with a tooth missing—is the same man that embodies these pure and noble ideals. He is simultaneously human and superhuman.

A thought like a voice cut through my reverie: *The time is now, True Believer.* I checked my watch and realized it was late. I said a hasty farewell to the ancient family that had inspired so much reflection. Then I ran out of the cemetery and far down the road before I had to stop to catch my breath.

Jeremiah was on his way down the front steps of the dentist's office when I returned. He grinned to reveal two tidy rows of teeth. They seemed whiter and straighter than before, but perhaps that's because it was the first time I looked closely at them. He was in a good mood during the drive home, so it seemed like the optimal time to ask him if I could testify at the next Crusade. This seemed like a mere formality, and I expected an easy yes. Jeremiah did not answer right away. He promised to think it over.

FRIDAY, JUNE 4

It took Jeremiah two days to consider and approve my request.

Yes, I could tell my story in my own words but with the stipulation that I don't attempt to use the floor to teach or preach. Our congregation is very traditional, first-wave Pentecostal, and would not take kindly to a woman's interpretation of the Word of God. This stung a tiny bit, but no matter. I am not qualified to teach or preach anything from the Bible, anyway.

Jeremiah graced me with a clever, boyish smile and offered to edit my speech when it was done. Eager to make use of his time, I commenced writing straightaway. I shall include a copy of the rough draft here for posterity.

I was born on a balmy spring day and died on a frosty fall day.

At least, that's how my story was supposed to go.

Three years ago, my doctor delivered the news that I had inoperable stage four cancer. Cancer? How could that be? It was a shocking betrayal of the peace treaty my body and I had established at birth.

Cancer. The news was unreal.

But the back pain was real.

The cramps were real.

The exhaustion.

The abnormal pap test.

The biopsy results.

Real.

In the days that followed my diagnosis, my whole life was reduced to small, quantifiable units—months, dollars, probabilities, percentages—none of which offered any hope.

Even as I dangled at the end of a fraying rope, I would not invoke God's mercy or make promises to him that I didn't intend to keep. By then, the loss of precious life after precious life had already shown me the tragic futility of attempting to haggle with fate. But I wasn't beyond challenging whoever might be out there listening to my prayers to relieve me of pessimism and despair. Whatever is meant to be, make it clean and quick! Either finish me off or patch me up and point me in a meaningful direction. No more mediocre holding patterns, no more passive accumulation of woe, no more waiting and wondering what my existence will amount to.

As I roamed the streets on a bleak Thursday following a particularly depressing appointment with my doctor, the providential wind blew a newspaper against my shin. I looked straight down into the fiery eyes of Jeremiah Promise. His printed hand reached out to me. The headline read: Miracle Man Himself Is Coming to Save a City Near YOU!

I found my way to that city with doubt leading me like a blind man's cane. I stood on stage before Jeremiah Promise and his God and let him lay hands on me.

What happened when he touched me, I'll never forget. Something deep inside me rent and fell open like the hasp of a padlocked door. All that had lain trapped behind it burst forth in a flurry of feathers and shrieks while I fell back into a stranger's arms.

Two ushers brought me back to my chair, where I lay limp for a quarter of an hour and saw nothing but sparkling silver confetti. I tingled all over as if my entire body had fallen asleep and was slowly awakening. The truth was that I had fallen asleep—in

life, in ambition, and in love. Only Jeremiah Promise's touch could awaken me.

During the week following my first encounter with the Man Himself, I continued to feel strange and tingly. My mind swam with questions that all began with: what if . . . what if . . . what if?

I met with new doctors, underwent new tests, tolerated exhaustive pokes and prods, and patiently withstood the general air of perplexity. I could afford to bide my time because time was on my side once again. The cancer was gone. Absolutely gone.

The Man Himself profoundly changed my life.

He will do the same for you.

SUNDAY, JUNE 6

I'm working diligently to rewrite the narrative of my feelings. As Congregation Liaison, *I am excited and not afraid*—got it?

Just as I was getting comfortable with the dynamic of our little chapel in the woods, Jeremiah decided to mix things up. He accepted a last-minute invitation to perform at the Indian Pentecostal Church on the other side of the city, and we left the Kenneths behind. This change and the subsequent lack of explanation struck me as odd, but I figured Jeremiah and the pastor must know what they're doing. Every move they make seems to be part of some elaborate thousand-step plan. So, we plunged into a sea of unfamiliar faces and started all over with introductions. I was overwhelmed before I even walked in the door. It was all I could do to greet hundreds of new people today—I didn't have the guts to stand up and tell my own story on stage. Maybe next time.

The people were all polite and friendly, of course. A few spoke in a manner that I struggled to understand, but they were patient while I acclimated to their accents. We all learned to laugh at me today, and this was probably my saving grace. One woman took me under her wing and introduced me to people until I found the confidence to introduce myself.

Her name was Faiza Dubashi. I learned a lot about her and her dream of becoming a helicopter pilot. She told me that she had already completed most of her flight training by the age of twenty-two. She wanted to be a volunteer Air Care pilot, on-call to transport accident victims to hospitals. She said she couldn't finish her training or take on flying shifts because she became pregnant and soon had her hands full with kids and a husband. Then her mother was diagnosed with brain cancer and needed full-time care. There were always family matters that had to come first.

Years passed, and Faiza's dream of flying was always pushed off to some future date—when her mother was well again (or gone), when her kids were in college, when her husband was settled in his new job, and so on. I asked Faiza if she would resume her training now if she could, and without hesitation, she said yes. Unfortunately, that hasn't been possible because she's in the late stages of kidney failure.

My heart ached for her. It must have been unbearable to spend her whole life putting everyone else's needs before her own dream. She had to look up at the sky every day and feel that it was just out of reach. I cannot imagine a life of such sacrifice. I could not do it myself. Then again, it's not my place to pity Faiza. Having one unfulfilled dream does not necessarily make for an unsatisfying life.

Thursday, June 10

Switching churches was like changing channels, and the small ripples of dissension that were spreading in Kevin McVae's wake ceased to be any concern of ours. A month in, and we're grappling with growing pains. It's a good problem to have, but one that requires scrambling and strategizing. We are very near the tipping point at which we will have to find larger church spaces to accommodate Jeremiah's followers. We're also running into time constraints. Jeremiah can only heal so many people in one afternoon, and the ushers can only deal with so much cash.

During our strategy meeting today, Jeremiah proposed that we begin rolling donation money forward one week. That way, the ushers won't be tied up for hours trying to count all the cash just so it can be bundled neatly and re-donated before the end of the service.

Jeremiah and Pastor Ormand agreed to open a joint ministry checking account and deposit all the funds there on the Monday following the Crusade. Jeremiah could then add a little flourish to his presentation by pulling a check out of his pocket payable to God's chosen, and— *praise Jesus, Hallelujah!*

This seems like a reasonable plan. There's no rule dictating otherwise—in fact, there are no rules about this practice at all.

I am not as keen on Jeremiah and the pastor's solution to the healing time limit, however. They think that Jeremiah ought to divine the names of the two or three dozen most worthy of God's disciples and call them to the front to be healed one by one. This sounds to me like a holy lottery. The men insist that it's the only realistic way to grow. A Crusade should last no more than four hours. Once we push past the six-hour mark, everyone's energy begins to wane. Thirst, hunger, muscle strain, and medical limitations start to vie with spiritual aspirations. Jeremiah can't be expected to perform quality miracles late into the night. Crusades must always end with a bang, *not* a whimper.

SATURDAY, JUNE 12

Jeremiah's instincts are spot-on, as usual. The new technique of handing out a holy check is going over well. Today's Crusade ended on a short, sweet, and high note when Raveena Koshy kicked aside her walker and danced down the aisle to claim her reward.

Only a fraction of the congregation was called up on stage for divine healing today. This left a lot of people wanting. A huge crowd gathered to talk to us (to me, that is) after the Crusade. It took me three hours to write down names and notes about each person. I was inside-out with exhaustion by the end of it. Fortunately, Reverend Krish was still there at the end and lent me his cell phone to call Jeremiah for a ride home.

Jeremiah took one look at me and shook his head. He said I didn't have to go to such lengths. I said I know. I just couldn't pick and choose who to talk to and who to turn away. Their stories all matter—every last one of them.

SUNDAY, JUNE 13

I did it! I stood up and testified today. I told my story in my own words. It wasn't a perfect speech, but I did my best. As an added bonus, the one

who first encouraged me to speak was there to see me do it—though I didn't know he had sneaked in until afterward.

I was just beginning to wonder what had become of Freddie Childress. Would I see him again? Did he really lose his stutter? Then lo and behold, there he was. He waited until everyone else had cleared out, then approached me with a bundle under his arm—a gift. I tried to turn it down, but he insisted.

I unwrapped many layers of newspaper to find a small, ceramic birdhouse at their core. Freddie had made it himself and decorated it with an intricate, hand-painted pattern of leafy vines and purple flowers. It was beautiful. I thanked him. Freddie scrunched up his face with pleasure and said (with only a few brief catches in his speech) that he hoped we could be friends. He was sure we had met for a reason and were meant to know each other. I could not argue with this line of reasoning.

With hat in hand, the tall man expressed a wish to get to know me better. He'd love to take me to dinner or invite me to his home for tea sometime. Reluctantly, I agreed. Jeremiah's warning about oddballs echoed in my mind. At that moment, the Man Himself appeared in the doorway behind Freddie. An unsettling, half-smile spread across his lips, and all the heat in my body rushed to my face. I hastened my conversation with Freddie to an end and gathered up my things.

Jeremiah was quiet during the whole car ride home. It wasn't until we stood in the dark hallway, moments from parting, that he explained to me in low tones why it was unethical for me to accept gifts from congregants. I was mortified by the implication. If only I had had the sense to say "no" to the gift more firmly. Had I successfully refused, I would not now be burdened with the unhappy task of swaddling the evidence of Freddie's kindness in a scarf and tucking it in the corner of the garage like some shameful thing.

MONDAY, JUNE 14

Despite the dull, throbbing headache that dogged me through another sleepless night, I felt fine today. A morning walk in nature was all it took to refresh me. Who needs sleep when there are so many ideas to explore and so much life to live?

During my walk, my mind backstroked through rivers of inspiration. Possibilities trickled in from all over like tributaries of a spring thaw. As if on cue, a political lawn sign with an amusing slogan came into view. This was the spark that marked the merging of several prongs of thought into one, and voila! Suddenly I was struck with a great idea for our next street discipling. I scrambled to find my pen and notebook and scribbled down as many details as I could pluck from the creative current as it rushed past me.

Back to the house, I hurried, my head throbbing with impetus. Jeremiah was nowhere to be found. I sat down at the computer and typed up a more formal proposal for him.

When at last Jeremiah returned in the late afternoon, I eagerly requested an audience with him. But he was not in the mood to hear new ideas today.

"What's up?" he asked as he stared at his phone and thumbed through messages. I couldn't seem to explain my idea fast enough to capture his interest. I took care to build up to the thesis of my pitch, but it completely escaped him. A moment later, he excused himself to take an important phone call and didn't come back.

I was crestfallen, and it was my fault. My expectations were too high. I should have known better than to pounce on Jeremiah when he was unprepared. He's always extra sensitive and irritable for a few days following the Crusade, and I'm sure he can't afford to consider my feelings at every moment.

It's just that…he's the only one to whom I can divulge all my plots and schemes. His ideas are grand and revolutionary, and I want to prove to him that I can keep up. He has everything mapped out, you know—how many hours and minutes will be required to take each step toward world domination. I know he will accomplish everything he sets his mind to. I just hope he doesn't leave me in the dust.

THURSDAY, JUNE 17

Another migraine.

I'm not sure of the biomechanics behind them, but these migraines seem to correlate with the intensity of my feelings. One strong surge of emotion is all it takes to ignite the Bunsen burner in the center of my brain. The heat of that flame causes some sort of balloon-like structure to steadily inflate inside my cranium until it feels like one of my eyeballs is about to pop out. Eventually, the pressure subsides with a pop, and I'm left with a soupy mess of pain for the rest of the day.

It isn't all bad, though! The sentiments that trigger these migraines are usually exceedingly positive, such as admiration, love, gratitude, and appreciation. Today's trigger was a shining example of altruism: two young boys left their mother's side to help an elderly man collect his scattered groceries in the supermarket parking lot. One chased after canned goods that rolled under parked cars, and the other gathered up stray apples like they were baby chicks. The mother and the man stood by and watched the boys while I observed them from across the street.

It makes my heart sing to see such things—though, I hope my head doesn't have to hurt this much every time my heart fills with exultation.

Friday, June 18

I've been thinking more and more lately about the word that Freddie Childress used to describe me: Empath. He placed such emphasis upon it that I suspect its meaning goes beyond that which can be found in a standard dictionary.

My curiosity came to a head this afternoon. I finished designing next month's trifold pamphlet for the ministry and decided to reward myself with a research project. Since I was already on the computer, I tried searching the Internet first. Unfortunately, all the websites that I wanted to access were blocked on the pastor's computer. He had stringent rules about what the family was allowed to read, watch on television, and browse online.

I seized the opportunity to go for a walk. The sun was blisteringly hot and the air as dense as a swimming pool, but I was determined to break free of my constraints for a few hours. The library was three easy miles away, and I was due for a visit. The moment I stepped through the front door, the scents of musty paper and wood welcomed me home. I took my time perusing the stacks and caressing book spines. No need to check the catalog. Muscle memory guided me to the materials that I sought. I browsed volumes, skimmed tables of contents, and pecked at pages until my elbow crook was filled with the substantial weight of knowledge. Then I fled to a quiet crevice by the window to read.

What I learned about Empathy surprised me. There's more to it than the "psychological identification with the feelings, thoughts, or attitudes of another." An Empath is a person that's highly attuned to the stresses and emotions of others. They "read," absorb, and respond to the unseen energies around them far more than the average person. It's a *preternatural,* rather than supernatural, ability—and for some, Empathy is not so much a choice or skill as it is a natural imperative.

Does one absorb or take on other people's moods and symptoms?

Check.

Does one take a long time to recuperate after social gatherings and dealings with difficult people?

Check.

Has one ever been labeled shy, thin-skinned, or overly sensitive?

Checkity-check!

Empaths tend to favor harmony and shun conflict. They tend to adore animals and nature and abhor scratchy clothes, harsh sounds, and bright lights.

It's a compelling concept. How did Freddie identify this trait in me so quickly, I wonder? Is he an Empath? Does it take one to know one?

This disposition surely describes Jeremiah, too. He is sensitive, caring, and brilliantly in tune with people. Come to think of it; Mom must have been an Empath as well. And Dave. And Teddy. They all had a depth of feeling, an uncanny quickness of comprehension, that seemed to border on clairvoyance. I'll never forget the time that I was out in the woods alone, tripped over a fallen tree branch, and cut up my knee pretty badly. Nobody knew I was there, and I was too far out to call for help, yet Teddy came and found me. Somehow he just *knew.*

The pale light of understanding dawned over the succession of friends, family, teachers, and neighbors that have filled up my life. I think about all the inklings. The niggling notions. The unfounded impressions. The peculiar gleams and astute smiles exchanged with a few strangers over the years. I've always had this feeling that some of us had a secret we didn't even know about. Could this be it?

A few more of life's puzzle pieces just fell into place, but the puzzle is expanding at the same time. Questions are forming faster than I can find answers. Who is Empathic, and who is not? How many of us are there? Are we defined by absolutes or by degrees? Where does Empathy come from? What is it for? Is it a strength or a weakness? Can it be used for evil as well as good?

As I left the library and walked home today, I studied every person that I passed through this brand new lens. Is he an Empath? Is she? How could I be sure? Can people hide Empathy? Can they gain or lose it? Is there a switch somewhere that turns it on and off?

TUESDAY, JUNE 22

We are going to Chicago!

Jeremiah's alliance with the IPC has attracted the interest of its sister churches in other cities. Last week, he received the invitation from a church in Chicago—and today, he alerted me that we leave tomorrow.

I want to be excited about this next leg of our adventure, I really do. But my stomach is queasy. I have begun to refer to the Kenneth house as "home," and though it's an imperfect nest with prickles of awkwardness and tension, I now feel uneasy about leaving it. Will we be gone for only a few days? I'm not so sure.

Once again, we're stuck with last-minute travel arrangements. Jeremiah had to book our flights separately. He'll go in the morning, and I will go in the afternoon. The thought of navigating a crowded airport alone again invokes a specific strain of dread, but I'll do what I must.

Wednesday, June 23

Margaret drove me to the airport. Though she and I have not quite succeeded at becoming friends, I felt closer to her than ever during that final hour. Despite all my determination to embrace the exciting unknown, I still had an involuntary impulse to cling to the imperfect familiar. Silly, I know. Margaret was kind to me at the curbside drop-off. She helped me with my bags and hugged me goodbye. I imagine she and her family will be glad to have their house to themselves for a little while.

When I passed through the sliding glass doors of the airport, my world transformed. Once again, I underwent a challenging ordeal. It took nearly two hours to get through the ticketing line and check my bag. Security took forever, too. My flight was on time this time, and I had to make a run for it.

In retrospect, I see that the hours I spent waiting today served a greater purpose: they brought to my attention the group dynamics of Empathy. As I stood in a roiling sea of people and gasped for air with my head tipped back, it occurred to me that *I* should not feel so stressed and anxious. In general, I try not to worry about situations with predestined outcomes. By the time I'm standing in a busy airport line, for example, the question of whether or not I'll catch my flight is already decided. My fate was likely sealed hours in advance.

With this in mind, I noticed that the people *around* me were cooking in a stew of consternation. A sweaty man in a suit kept checking his watch. A woman tapped her cowboy boots nonstop. An older couple behind me anxiously discussed their approaching flight time until I of-

fered to let them go ahead of me.

When packed into so tight a space, everyone's emotional bubbles press together until they pop, and the contents spill onto others nearby. As soon as I broke free of the body jam, I felt well again. My spirit surged like an escaped balloon.

We're in the air now. We'll be in Chicago before long. My stomach has settled a bit, and I look forward to the n—

—Oops, fligt turblc—

Friday, June 25

Northern green, we meet again. Perhaps we needed some time apart to cultivate this excruciating sense of longing. At the sight of you upon my return, I knew what my life was missing: all your shades and shapes, soft edges, sharp points, and reminders of home that you bring.

This weekend we are staying with Reverend Shaji Thomas and his family. They own a lovely three-story house on a tree-lined street in Edgewater Glen. The sidewalks here invite shady strolls through the neighborhood. I was glad to have a few free hours this afternoon to venture out and explore.

A strange thing happened during my walk. While crossing Clark Street at the light, I glanced over and noticed a person on the corner. He stood out to me like the crisp focal point of a photograph while everything around him seemed to soften and blur. He was a large man in sweatpants and a blue jacket, seated on the concrete foot of a streetlight. I couldn't see his face because he was looking away over his shoulder, yet something about him arrested my attention. My breath caught in my throat, and I blinked back tears. A profound sense of sadness pooled inside me, dampening every other thought and sensation, and there it remained for the rest of the day.

It took me a while to realize that this pervasive sadness didn't belong to me. I thought about all the mysterious moods that have passed through me over the years, like clouds crossing in front of the sun. I sought justification for them in the obvious places—life choices, existential dilemmas, minor disagreements with friends, changes in the weather—no matter how insignificant or ill-fitting. Now I wonder if all or any of those moods were mine in the first place. Where do I end and others begin?

SUNDAY, JUNE 27

The danger passed hours ago, but its reverberations continue—whether from fear, rage, or fatigue, I hardly know. There was a shooting! At the church! Right in the middle of Jeremiah's sermon, we all heard the pop, pop, pop-pop-pop. Several people at the back shrieked and leaped from their seats, but from my place on the stage, I could only wonder why they were so stirred up over distant firecrackers. There was a delay between seeing the glass fall from the window above the doors and understanding why. A shooting—actual bullets—from a gun—in human hands—was the last thing I expected. Later, came the horror, when it occurred to me how easy it was for a deadly threat to slip into our lives.

Jeremiah Promise stood his ground. In fact, he seemed to grow taller when he stood up to adversity. He seamlessly switched the topic of his sermon from God's mercy to Christ's courage. He exhorted us to remain steadfast in our conviction. *Remember! A good Christian submits to the chaos and maintains serene confidence in the divine order.*

He gestured for the AV person at the back to crank up the music higher and higher. With the help of song, he recaptured everyone's attention and made them focus. The air grew dense with a syrupy sort of excitement that tasted of pennies and sweat. Bodies writhed with feverish elation.

Jeremiah walked through the aisles and performed several slayings in the spirit (this is where he raises his arms and—whoosh!—a whole row of worshippers collapses like dominoes). He concluded with John 17:15-16. "I do not pray that thou shouldst take them out of the world, but that thou shouldst keep them from the evil one. They are not of the world, even as I am not of the world." That passage seemed to perfectly sum up Jeremiah Promise himself.

Based on the full donations buckets that I saw go by, I think it's safe to assume we broke our collections record today. At the end of the day, Jeremiah presented a check for $5,889.03 to Siddharth Achri. His Lyme's Disease had advanced to the point of kidney failure before Jeremiah cured him. *Praise Jesus, hallelujah!*

Nobody got around to calling the police until after the Crusade was over. By then, witnesses of the shooting had scattered to the wind. Jeremiah and I stayed late to make statements, but that was about all we could do. There were no outside cameras or bystanders and no urgency to apprehend the shooters so many hours after the fact. I thought this would leave Jeremiah dejected, but on the contrary—he was fired up about it over dinner. He seemed excited by the idea that he had inspired so much ire.

"The shooting is a sign!" he declared. A sign that the ministry was taking root, his influence was spreading, and powerful forces were beginning to stir. He was ninety percent sure that he knew who had done it. He would only tell me that this enemy was a powerful one, too pow-

erful to do his own dirty work.

"We cannot afford to venture much further without protection," Jeremiah continued. He has been thinking about recruiting a security advisor for quite some time, and this incident was a call to action.

Tuesday, June 29

We are back in Dallas. I woke up in a room of my own this morning. What a luxury! After so many weeks of sharing a bedroom, bathroom, living space, eating place, and Jeremiah's attention with others, I'm relieved to have something to myself. My plan for the day was to move from one sunny nook to another while consuming copious amounts of the written word.

But I had scarcely turned the page of *Don Quixote* when I heard a knock at the door. The inner door, that is—the one connecting my room to Jeremiah's. I found him washed and dressed and ready to go. He cheerfully invited me to join him for breakfast at the diner down the street. I let him go on ahead to get a table for us while I pulled myself together.

The little jump of joy I feel when I spot Jeremiah in a crowded room has not failed me yet. I recognized his loose black curls over the top of the far back booth by the window and found him drinking coffee. A glass of water with no ice sat at my place at the table. He remembered what I liked!

We talked. Boy, did we talk—over coffee and water, over eggs and toast, over the red-checkered tablecloth after the dishes were cleared. I followed the shape of Jeremiah's lips as he spoke, admired the perfect harmony of all his features, watched the patterns that his fingers lightly

drummed on the tabletop, and marveled that his every movement was precisely what it ought to be. Sun-dappled time seemed to slow to the cadence of our conversation. Words interspersed with dimpled smiles, crinkled eyes, and thoughtful lulls.

I have never seen Jeremiah in such a supple and springy mood. He was alert, curious, clever, thoughtful. His gestures were loose and re-laxed, and his mood was effortlessly superb. Everyone around us seemed to notice. Without even trying to make a scene, he drew attention like a magnet. The waitress came by often and chimed with laughter every time Jeremiah spoke. The women at the neighboring table wheedled their way into our conversation more than once.

Despite all that was going on around us, Jeremiah's attention re-mained fixed on me. We might as well have been the only two people in the diner. I listened with utter fascination as he described what it felt like to heal people. The way his palms would become hot and begin to pulsate with an overwhelming abundance of energy that demanded to be unleashed. When he touched someone receptive to God's healing power, it was like completing an electrical circuit.

"I know just what you mean!" I exclaimed. I told him that I used this same analogy to describe the effect of pressing one's own hands together. We discussed the science behind the posture of prayer, and I admired Jeremiah more than ever for his willingness to mix religion and pragmatism.

Our thoughts soon hit a stride at which they began to merge. Each time we started to say the same thing at the same time, Jeremiah's grin widened, and his teeth sparkled in the sun. I wished that we could stay in this joyous bubble forever.

Noon arrived. The conversation slowed, and Jeremiah lapsed into a silent, steady gaze that continued three, four, five beats longer than it

ought. Then he reached for the check and suggested we head back to the motel.

My stomach flip-flopped. Did he mean?

No, of course not! We had simply lost track of time. It was time to get on with the day.

When we returned to the motel, I bid him a hasty farewell and retired to my room. I tried to read but was too restless to sit still, so I tidied up my space. I washed a few articles of clothing in the sink and hung them to dry. At last, there came a superb, startling knock at the inner door. Jeremiah asked if he could come in.

I thought we would sit at my little table by the window and talk, so I moved my suitcase out of the way. Instead, Jeremiah helped himself to my bed. He stretched out at the end of it like a big cat. I almost couldn't look at him. I'm used to seeing him upright, sharply angled, and locked in the chokehold of some buttoned-up number. It was shocking to behold him in a position of repose, all soft and curvy. Maintaining a respectable distance, I pulled up a chair and perched on its edge like a ruffled screech owl.

"I want to talk about Bartholomew Lambrecht," Jeremiah began.

Unexpected! What triggered this impulse to open up after so many tight-lipped months? Perhaps it was the appeal. At the airport last night, I glimpsed a news headline announcing that BL's appeal was successful, and his case was going to be retried. I didn't think Jeremiah noticed, so I didn't want to point it out, but I've been curious about the impact this might have on him.

He did not want to talk about court proceedings, however. Instead, he wanted to share with me the particulars of his personal history with his former ministry partner and mentor. I shall attempt to write down the details as faithfully as I can remember them now.

BL began his illustrious (infamous) career as a tent revivalist in the late 1970s. He spent his first few years working his way through the Bible Belt preaching hellfire and damnation. In the mid-70s, he added faith healing to his resume and began "saving" his followers by laying on hands—a practice that BL defined loosely and soon began to abuse. He developed a reputation for violence. He became known for slapping, punching, and kicking the demons out of people. At least once, BL used pliers to pull teeth out of a woman's mouth. The woman had Tourette's syndrome, and he claimed this was the only way to quiet the "Devil's tongue."

That someone would willingly submit to such barbaric treatment, I can hardly believe—but supposedly she did, and without reservation. Others did, too. People flocked to BL in droves because they had genuine faith that he could cure them of illness and deliver them from sin.

Jeremiah and BL first met at a revival near Houston five summers ago. Jeremiah had just completed his second year of seminary at the time. He was highly skeptical of the healer's shady practices but also curious to see if any of BL's purported miracles were legitimate. The reports were mixed. Most people swore up and down that BL's antics cured them, but a few vocal dissidents denounced him as a fraud.

Jeremiah plotted a ruse. He went to the revival with his arm wrapped in bandages under the pretense that it had been badly burned in a house fire. If BL was indeed one of God's prophets, then he should immediately recognize Jeremiah's deception.

It was easier than Jeremiah expected to peg BL as a charlatan. The man's technique was sloppy, and his execution was lazy. He didn't even "lay hands" on most people—he just held his blazer by the collar and flailed it at them.

As Jeremiah waited in line for his chance to stand before the famous

fraud, he conversed with the blind man behind him. The man's name was Montague, and he had been blind since the age of five. Jeremiah discovered that this would be Montague's sixth time standing before BL, hoping for a miracle. He hadn't regained his sight yet. The man lamented that this was his own fault because his faith was imperfect. He had spent the whole last year praying and repenting for hours every day, and he hoped that today would be the day God saw fit to restore his sight.

Jeremiah declared this Pelagian Heresy. He explained to Montague that no man has the power to earn his salvation through prayer or deed. God is sovereign, and men cannot control His will. Anyone who says otherwise must be a false prophet!

Jeremiah then took the full force of righteousness in his hands, turned to Montague, and placed his palms over the blind man's eyes. He summoned up the power of the Holy Spirit, and when he took his hands away, *the man could see.*

Chaos ensued. Jeremiah was hauled off to the so-called healer's private trailer and held captive until BL could deal with Jeremiah himself. Jeremiah was prepared for threats and violence. The last thing he expected was for an amiable BL to stroll in an hour later and offer him a job.

BL openly admitted that he was not a bona fide healer. His gifts were more along the lines of entertaining and storytelling. He employed psychological tricks and sleight of hand on stage to create miraculous illusions. People wanted to believe the outlandish tales of journeying through hell and raising people from the dead. He really didn't have to convince them.

The preacher had no formal religious education and—as far as Jeremiah could tell—hadn't even read the Good Book all the way through.

He blasphemously claimed that God spoke directly through him, so he didn't need to know Scripture.

A "crisis of conscience" had recently come upon BL. He had truly enjoyed captivating audiences, lifting spirits, and inspiring hope in people, but he didn't enjoy living a lie. He had prayed to God for deliverance from this mighty dilemma, and then out of the sky fell Jeremiah, right into his lap.

Here, Jeremiah paused and shook his head and sighed. If only he had known then that BL was not a man with a conscience.

The preacher certainly was the most charming and charismatic person that Jeremiah had ever met. No doubt about that. BL talked him into quitting seminary and signing on to tour the country with him. That's when he adopted the stage name Jeremiah Promise. It rolled off the tongue more easily than his real name did (though Jeremiah wouldn't tell me what it was).

Things were glamorous at first. Private jets, fancy hotel rooms, menus without price lists, limousines. Jeremiah tried not to think too hard about where the money came from. He remained ignorant of all aspects of ministry finance (in the end, this was his saving grace). Though he was uneasy about BL's "relaxed" morals, he decided that this was his best means to build a platform for his future endeavors. He focused every minute of every day on his burning desire to heal people through faith and convinced himself that the end would justify the means.

Unfortunately, BL's insanity was worse than Jeremiah imagined. Jeremiah was the proverbial frog in the pot of boiling water. For the first year, he was relatively insulated from BL's antics because he kept his apartment in Houston and stayed there during the week. But when BL abruptly moved the ministry headquarters to Malibu, Jeremiah found it impossible to travel back and forth all the time. BL offered him a suite

of rooms in his Malibu mansion, and Jeremiah thought: why not let BL foot the bill for a while?

As his housemate, Jeremiah was privy to a lot more of his ministry partner's personal business than he ever wanted to know. The preacher threw crazy parties. One whole room of the mansion was coated in plastic for his body-painting extravaganzas. Jeremiah attempted to steer clear, but he still had to pass by the open doorway on his trips to the laundry room. He couldn't help but glimpse disturbing streaks of red splattered all over everything. It looked like the scene of a gruesome mass murder. Sometimes he questioned whether it was only paint.

Other rooms of the house were reserved for other bizarre hobbies. The drawing room contained a scale model and detailed blueprints for his future City of Salvation, which included a hospital, university, and holy theme park. BL intended to purchase the state of Nebraska from the federal government and convert it to a sacred city-state called New Lambrecht.

In the library, there were no books. Instead, the shelves were filled with rows and rows of jars of lizards, snakes, and beetles preserved in formaldehyde. BL claimed that these were all the demons he'd cast out of his disciples.

While he lived under BL's roof, Jeremiah was the full-time, captive audience of BL's fits of mania and rage. One morning, Jeremiah opened his eyes to find BL dressed in a suit of armor, standing over him with an antique sword pointed at his throat. Another morning, Jeremiah came out of his room to find every dish in the house lying in pieces on the foyer floor. One day, BL had fifty-dozen bouquets of roses sent to himself but refused to accept the delivery when it came. Another evening, Jeremiah returned to the house to find that the electricity had been cut off, and the house was filled with burning, dripping candles. There was

no telling what version of BL he would wake up to on any given day.

I wondered aloud if he was on drugs.

"Oh yes, of course!" Jeremiah cried. "Coke, heroin, meth. What wasn't he on?" BL pressured Jeremiah to partake many, many times, but Jeremiah always refused. He was a little afraid that BL might lace his food or drink with something anyway.

"Bartholomew was a smooth talker," Jeremiah added. He seemed to carefully consider his next words. "Yes, very smooth," he said quietly. "I stayed off the drugs, but he talked me into some other things that I'd rather not say." For a while, Jeremiah looked dismal. The pause drew out so long that I was tempted to do or say something reckless. At last, he resumed.

"So, why didn't I just leave when things got bizarre?" he asked. Because at first, it came on slowly. When it did hit, it hit hard. He had never experienced anything like it before—not at home in Pernam, not at boarding school—and he was shell-shocked. Sometimes BL threatened to prosecute for a breach of contract if Jeremiah left. He wasn't sure if this was a valid threat or not. He also didn't know what he would do next if he left. His ambitions and livelihood were all wrapped up in the ministry, and it was unlikely that he could take any part of them with him.

On his bad days, BL could be very abusive, but he tended to run out of steam within a day or two. Jeremiah reasoned that BL's tantrums were not directed at him most of the time, and when they were, the abuse was short-lived. He could manage well enough from day to day by walking on eggshells and avoiding the man as much as possible. This went on for three years. It went on until one day, the bubble burst, the story broke, and the scandals came to light.

Jeremiah was astounded by the flurry of letters and donations that

flowed in after BL was arrested. No matter how many sordid details of his life came out, his most faithful followers continued to defend BL's actions and campaign for his release. But he's in prison now, and with any luck, he will stay there for a very long time.

Jeremiah concluded this story with a sigh and collapsed on the coverlet. I hardly knew what to say besides, "I'm sorry! How awful that must have been!"

My curiosity was piqued by a particular detail of his story, and eventually, I had to ask how he healed the blind man at the Houston Revival? Did the Gift of Healing spontaneously come to him that day? Or did he have it before then?

Jeremiah was pleased with this question. He propped himself back up on one elbow and prepared to tell the next tale. This one went much farther back—to India, to his youth.

Jeremiah's father was one of three Christian missionaries that established the First Pentecostal Church of Goa in his mother's village of Pernam. They met and fell in love instantly, but they never married because they could not. Jeremiah's father was already married to a woman back in England. Though it was a loveless union, there were children and a strong sense of duty.

When his father's missionary work concluded, so too did his affair with Jeremiah's mother. She discovered that she was pregnant just a few weeks after his father returned to England. Despite the difficulties that she faced, she chose to keep the child and raise him with the help of friends. Could I believe that Jeremiah's unusual green-blue eyes came not from his British father, but instead from his Indian mother? Well, it was true. It was evidence of the lasting scars left on his people by the centuries-long occupation of the Portuguese.

For nearly three hundred years, Jeremiah's home state was the seat of

the Goa Inquisition. It was a ruthless tribunal that forcibly converted native Hindus and Muslims to Roman Catholicism on pain of oppression, imprisonment, or death. Many Goan women (whether married or unmarried) were made to share foreign soldiers' beds during this period. Jeremiah's great-great-great-great grandmother was one of them. She was raped and eventually impregnated by a Portuguese officer.

At the time, she was married and would likely have had to terminate the pregnancy had her husband not been arrested shortly thereafter. He was charged with heresy and burned at the stake, leaving Jeremiah's last living ancestor to fend for herself. She yielded to the pressure to convert and eventually gave birth to a baby girl with dusky skin and striking emerald eyes. This feature passed down from one generation to the next, all the way to Jeremiah Promise.

His mother told him this story when he was very young, and it had haunted him every day since. He could never stray far from the awful truth of his lineage. It came to him each time he saw his reflection in a mirror or a stranger's double-take.

Jeremiah was a sensitive boy who abhorred the evils of men. A passion for justice burned within him, but for many years it had no outlet. He struggled with fits of rage, sometimes putting his fists through walls.

Then one day, God came to him.

He was ten. He and his mother were riding a ferry across the Terekhol River. He had been defying his mother by running around on deck. He slipped on a puddle and fell overboard into the water. The current was strong, and he could not swim. He nearly drowned.

He remembered bobbing up to the surface, opening his eyes, and being blinded by a light brighter than the sun. It was the light of his God.

God told Jeremiah to stop wasting his gifts on meaningless pursuits. He must learn to focus his passion and channel it into service. This was the only way he could balance the scales of good and evil and atone for the sins of his forefather. God would not send Jeremiah out into the world unarmed, so He anointed him with four Gifts of the Holy Spirit: He touched Jeremiah's forehead and instilled in him the Gift of Prophecy. He touched his heart and gave him the Gift of Faith. He touched his hands and gave him the Gift of Healing. Finally, He touched Jeremiah's chin and gave him the word of the Lord, thus making him a prophet. Then He instructed Jeremiah to go forth into the world and speak his God's truth.

A ferryman fished Jeremiah out of the water. When Jeremiah told his mother about the vision, she punished him for lying and forbade him from speaking of it ever again. He had to practice his gifts in secret by laying hands on small creatures. He healed a baby bird that had fallen out of its nest, a cat that had been run over by a bicycle, and his best friend's pet snake.

One day Jeremiah picked a bouquet of wildflowers and brought them to his mother. She placed them in a vase in the middle of the dinner table. Each time they began to droop, Jeremiah secretly laid hands on the flowers and restored them to perfect health. Months passed, and his mother began to wonder why the flowers would not die. Jeremiah smiled slyly and shrugged. At the end of a year, his mother sat him down and demanded to know if the flowers were demonic. This time, he touched the wilted flowers and renewed them before her very eyes. He reminded her of the day on the ferry. This time, she believed him.

Jeremiah's mother wrote a letter to his father, the missionary. She begged his father to arrange for a proper education in England. Wanting to honor the only request that his one true love ever made of him, Jeremiah's father set him up in a private English boarding school. He received an excellent education there and completed two years of under-

graduate work by the age of eighteen.

Jeremiah had no complaints about the school or about his father, a decent, if distant man. His only lament was the loneliness of his life. He was always engrossed in schoolwork and had difficulty making friends. The boys nicknamed him the Bombay Bookworm. While the others went out to play sports and pursue girls, Jeremiah stayed behind in the dormitory to study.

He was ready to return to Pernam as soon as his schooling was over. He missed home. But his God had other plans. A couple of months before graduation, he received word of his mother's death. He was shattered. Had he been there, he might have saved her.

He received a scholarship to attend seminary in the United States. He had no one else that wanted him and nowhere else to go, so he went to Houston, Texas. Jeremiah theorized that perhaps he stayed with BL as long as he did because (crazy as the man was) he served as a parental figure of sorts. Jeremiah craved the connection, the sense of belonging. He tumbled headlong into a madman's trap. He was no dummy, though—from the beginning, he sensed a corrupt soul crouching behind that high-gloss façade.

He should have heeded the signs. Now, Jeremiah is responsible for helping to wreak ten times more destruction on earth than he could ever repair in its wake. His debt belongs to God and the people. He will be saving souls until the day he dies.

"We must try, right?" he asked reluctantly. I wanted so badly to reach out to him. I nearly did, but at the last moment, I froze and let the impulse pass.

Jeremiah went to get a glass of water. He returned with a stack of takeout menus. It was already dinnertime!

We ordered food and dealt with all the details of payment, delivery,

and cleaning up. It felt odd but pleasantly domestic to do these things with Jeremiah Promise. This was not the end of our day together—not even close. We talked late into the evening about everything from business to travel and psychology to pizza toppings. We talked about books and about our mutual fondness for the ideals of classic literature.

We both admire old-fashioned sensibilities. I think we are both painfully aware of all the ways that the real world falls short of our ideals. Life is far from perfect. We struggle to reconcile the differences between what is and what could be. If only we had the power to change the world...

A favorite quote comes to mind here: *Everyone thinks of changing the world, but no one thinks of changing himself.* That's Tolstoy, if I recall. Mrs. Maple used to recite it each time one of her art students asked to adjust the still-life arrangement.

We discussed our mutual preference for meaningful conversation and our distaste for small talk. In school, Jeremiah dealt with this issue by joining the chess club. It was the one extracurricular activity that suited his analytical mind and social reserve—a partner sport structured around silent contemplation. It was a way to forge gradual friendships on a foundation of common interests.

With a gleam in his eye, he asked if I played chess. I was sorry to have to say no—but added that I've always wanted to learn. Jeremiah shrugged and remarked that there were plenty of books available on the topic if I wished to educate myself. His problem is that most chess players are intermediate level, at best, and he has grown weary of winning every game. He wants a worthy adversary.

To balance this boast, Jeremiah claimed to be bad at math. I immediately objected. There's no way that's true. He's methodical, organized, and precise, and that makes him a mathematician at heart.

 The day ended on an awkward note. I don't even recall what started it now—something simple that made us both laugh. Whatever it was, it prompted Jeremiah to lean forward and raise his hand in the air. What was this? A high-five? I reached out and tentatively clapped my palm to his. Our fingers intertwined, and I received a jolt that went straight to my head. Flustered, I giggled and said something silly.

In retrospect, I can't roll my eyes hard enough. I am a dufus! Despite this final flub, I feel that the day was ideal from beginning to end. It was a masterpiece of human connection, and I would happily frame it and hang it on the wall.

As I prepared for bed this evening, I thought about my last Christmas with Mom.

It was mid-morning. We had already opened our presents, eaten our holiday breakfast, and cleaned up the wrapping paper shreds. There was nothing left to do but sit by the fireplace and bask in its glow.

Suddenly, Mom became busy. She got up and scuttled around the house, initiating projects. This year, she was going to start her New Year's resolutions early.

She brought out her violin from its dusty home under her bed and began restringing and tuning it. I watched her handle the instrument with the ease of a seasoned musician. She had a passion for it when she was young. Grandma used to talk proudly about Mom's tenure in the Saint Paul Chamber Orchestra. Mom would just brush away the praise like a stubborn piece of lint. She gave all that up before my oldest brother was born. Being a mother meant more to her than anything.

Mom adjusted the violin strings with the help of a mechanical tuner. Once the tones were close to what they ought to be, she abandoned the device and continued tuning by ear. Finding the precise pitch of each string is more a matter of feeling than sound, she explained. Only a liv-

ing, breathing body can perceive that exact *right* moment when a note achieves absolute, perfect resonance.I think Mom's philosophy about musical instruments applies to people, too. When two individuals discover ways that they are alike that they didn't even know were possible, they begin to harmonize. An effect emerges that is not so much a sound as it is a feeling, a sort of boundless resonance that fills every space that contains it. Others can feel it, too. They may not know precisely what it is, like those folks at the diner this morning, but they can sense its significance.

Wednesday, June 30

I am high on a cloud with no plans to come down.

Jeremiah came for me in the late morning, and we spent all day running errands together. He bought me a cell phone. I tried to talk him down to the most basic model, but Jeremiah would not hear of it. I needed a quality business tool, he insisted.

After that, we went dress shopping, and he embarrassed me some more with his generosity. It wasn't entirely unwarranted—I do need better clothes for the Crusades. That pinned-up, second-hand dress is starting to look shabby. I was far too bashful to model any of the dresses for Jeremiah. Samantha, the shop assistant, brought me different sizes and styles while Jeremiah waited outside.

Despite the awkward moments, we were more relaxed and open with each other than ever today. Another layer of self-consciousness must have slipped away in the night. We dipped our toes in the stream of friendly teasing and laughed openly without fear of causing offense.

SATURDAY, JULY 3

He called me into his room this afternoon to look over the first edition of his ministry newsletter. Rather than hand the letter to me, he made me lean over his shoulder to read it. I stood close enough to Jeremiah to smell the freshness of his soap and the spice of his aftershave. From that position, I could examine him with impunity. His arms. His neck. His dark curls. As I stood there, I contemplated the pros and cons of casually placing my hand on his shoulder. Part of me feared that if I touched him, the next step would be to bend down and kiss him.

It seems ignoble to steal a touch. I mustn't forget my place—Jeremiah Promise is my mentor, my idol, and I am his devotee. The pristine communion of this type of relationship discourages other forms of intimacy.

Does Jeremiah even *think* of women at all, I wonder? He doesn't seem to take any special notice of them. At Crusades, I watch him dedicate the lion's share of his attention to the older disciples and toss nothing but crumbs to the pretty young females that follow him with their eyes and smiles.

At all times, the ministry is Jeremiah's sole focus and passion. It's my unique privilege to be an integral part of his mission (and thus, within the scope of his interests). But it occurs to me that I must be more careful going forward. My admiration for him has been growing unchecked, and I should not let down my guard around a man that too perfectly aligns with my ideals. I might be tempted to overstep the ethical boundaries of our mentor/mentee relationship.

There's no going partway down this path, no space for exploration—

it's too dangerous a game. I may resist, but eventually, I will succumb. Neither antibodies nor antidotes exist to protect my heart from total adoration—or annihilation, should anything go awry.

SUNDAY, JULY 4

Jeremiah was already gone when I woke up this morning, so I went out in search of my own adventure. A couple of miles down the road, I found a Unitarian Universalist church. The second service was due to begin in half an hour. I crept inside and took a seat.

The energy of this church was more gentle and bubbly than the intense Pentecostal services to which I've grown accustomed. It was all soft pinks and golds, and its opening song was a heartfelt rendition of *Morning Has Broken* by Cat Stevens.

Pastor Francesca Costello's sermon centered on the concept of *velad*, a Spanish word meaning *to keep vigil* or *to stay awake*. She spoke about spiritual vigilance and the exercise of peacefully centering one's attention on something worthy and weighty, such as love. Love is the greatest power in the world, she declared. But there is a critical difference between the emotion of love and the will of love.

As a noun, the emotion of love ebbs and flows naturally. The sea-changes of our feeling states are as sovereign as the tides. As a verb, love must be mindfully (vigilantly) cultivated. It takes effort to develop the will to love—to act with kindness, be respectful, forgive, and commit, even when it feels impossible.

After the service, I stopped to sit on a bench outside a coffee shop. An hour in that spot was a rich experience. I watched strangers, acquaintances, and couples interact and observed numerous small gestures of love and generosity.

I overheard a conversation between a private investigator and the parents of a young boy. They were discussing details of the couple's adopted son's Colombian heritage. As the investigator gave his report, the parents excitedly interrupted him with anecdotes about their child. They were proud parents, and their enthusiasm was a joy to behold. I was happy for the boy—glad that he could have so many homes and parents, pleased that his adoptive family was so dedicated to learning about his roots and sharing them with him.

Outside of this spirited microcosm, the world was restful. The sun shone, but not hotly. The breeze blew, but gently. I sketched the people sitting at tables out on the sidewalk. They were all wrapped up in their lives, their discussions, their digital devices. No one seemed to mind that I was watching.

Monday, July 5

Ironically, we sat together while we discussed our views on solitude.

I told him that I prefer to go on long walks by myself because that's the way to fully immerse myself in my environment. I enjoy the company of others, too, but being with someone else changes the experience. When I walk alongside another, I inevitably become preoccupied with their feelings, needs, and desires.

Jeremiah said that he prefers to be alone when he writes sermons, reads, exercises, and meditates. Only in solitude can he establish a pure connection to his God. Others introduce a sort of static interference that disrupts his link with the divine. Re-establishing communication with God is a tedious process. He'd prefer that people wait patiently for

him to finish communion before approaching him.

Noted.

Jeremiah is magnetic, and people want to bask in the sunshine of his attention. But he and I are both sensitive individuals that find the world challenging and overwhelming. I understand the need to sometimes steal away and hide from the frenzy of life for the sake of self-preservation.

Tuesday, July 6

We keep the doors between our rooms open most of the time. I figure this privilege is mostly due to my strict adherence to boundaries, so I am careful not to abuse this liberty. We only venture across each other's threshold if we have something vital to share.

This afternoon, I overheard faint sounds of frustration coming from Jeremiah's room. A protracted crescendo of paper shuffling seemed to summon me, so I bookmarked the page I was on and got up to see what was the matter. Jeremiah's bed was overlain with a thick carpet of documents, and he stood at the foot of it fussing with a handful of envelopes.

"This week is going to be fun," he remarked without looking up.

"In an ironic way?" I teased.

Jeremiah feigned misunderstanding. I've noticed that when he is supremely annoyed, he pretends not to hear or comprehend what others say. Unwilling to be so easily dismissed, I explained the meaning of irony to him. He glanced at me and chuckled. *Touché.*

When pressed, he would only comment that Ormand Kenneth was a terrible record keeper, and now he had a disaster to deal with. I offered to help, but Jeremiah wouldn't hear of it. He would figure it out himself. He wasn't at liberty to say anything more at present, but he'd know more within a day or two.

That certainly sounded ominous. Did Pastor Ormand do something wrong? That would explain a lot. Within the last few days, it's become acutely apparent that something is amiss. Camping out in a motel. No Sunday Crusade. That faint souring of Jeremiah's mood without discernable origin or explanation. The mention of Pastor Ormand finally gave a name to my misgivings.

Now that I think about it, there were signs of discord before we left for Chicago. Jeremiah's vexation on more than one occasion when he and the pastor returned from sponsor meetings. His grumblings about his partner's lack of conscientious preparation. The abrupt switch to a different church.

Perhaps Jeremiah and Pastor Ormand are not suitable partners. I'm sure the pastor is a good man, but he has a plodding and phlegmatic nature. He prefers his comfy chairs, his two o'clock tea, and to solve the world's problems with quiet chides and pats on the shoulder. It's hard to imagine the fiery, ambitious, and ironically unorthodox Jeremiah Promise combining well with him in the long run. Perhaps their differences are coming to a head. Better it happens now than further down the road.

WEDNESDAY, JULY 7

I dreamed that my cottage went up in flames while I was still inside. Missy was at the door, beckoning me to follow her to safety, but I was paralyzed with indecision. I could only take with me the things I could fit in one backpack, but I couldn't decide what to grab. The photo al-

bums? The sketchpads? Clothes? Toiletries? I kept putting things in the bag and then taking them out. Where was Jeremiah? He would have known what to do.

When I awoke, it was still dark outside. The anxiety was slow to dissipate. I waited until a reasonable hour in the late morning to borrow Jeremiah's cell phone and call home.

All is well. Missy gave me a weather report and a garden report and shared a few funny stories about her grandchildren. The cottage is fine. She checks on it daily.

Thursday, July 8

Jeremiah was away all day, and when he returned to the motel this evening, he had quite a tale to tell. He had recently discovered some irregularities in the ministry's financial records, so he went to confront the pastor. The pastor denied everything at first. They spent hours going around and around in conversation, but eventually, Ormand Kenneth confessed to skimming funds from their joint account. He agreed to peacefully relinquish all financial and intellectual claims on Wholesome Healing Ministries in the past, present, and future. They dissolved the partnership in one sitting, and now we're free and clear to preach where we want and manage the ministry as we see fit.

I was stunned. Pastor Ormand—a thief? How was that even possible?

It was his own fault, Jeremiah lamented. He's too trusting of people, particularly old friends that purport to be men of God. Had he put a proper system of checks and balances in place, he might have caught Ormand's embezzling right from the start.

Jeremiah waved a folder of bank statements in the air. Just this morning, he had spoken with the account manager and obtained all the proof he needed. Mid-week cash withdrawals were made from the account he and Ormand had set up to hold donations between the Crusades—a hundred dollars here, five hundred there.

Jeremiah slapped the papers down on the table and pointed to a withdrawal dated June 29. I remembered that day clearly—how could I forget? Jeremiah and I went to breakfast and spent the whole afternoon and evening together. There was no way Jeremiah could have made that withdrawal. He only touched that account when he had to write checks from it on Sundays. Ormand handled all other money matters.

Jeremiah called himself a fool, and I immediately protested. One ought to be able to trust one's friends. An honest person assumes that others are honest, but that's not always the case.

Despite the dark circles under Jeremiah's eyes, his eyes burned as intensely as ever. In his preacher's voice, he exhorted, "Our enemies are numerous and sly. We must be more careful in our choice of ally. Wolves that come dressed in sheep's clothing will feast upon our good intentions if we let them."

Saturday, July 10

I blinked, and everything changed.

According to Jeremiah, that's the name of the game. It's a rough business in the beginning. We must go where the wind blows us, take our knocks, learn our lessons, build our following, and eventually, we will be the ones calling the shots.

We moved to Grapevine today, an upscale neighborhood on the

northwest side of Dallas. It's all porticoes, white shutters, and brick facades. The sidewalks are uniform, and the yards are austerely tidy. I imagine that everything inside and out must be vacuumed sealed in plastic to thwart the unsavory influences of gravity and decay.

The house belongs to Reverend Gideon Carlisle. He needs someone to look after it while he and his family summer in Maine. We're not staying in the main residence—Jeremiah has taken over the pool house, and I am staying in the small upstairs compartment at the back of the house. Our new accommodations are clean and self-sufficient. My little apartment is fully furnished, so I was all moved in and settled as soon as I plunked down my suitcase on the dresser.

This place is far more comfortable than a hotel. It has its perks, but still, my stomach churns. Perhaps the sterile nature of modern luxury disrupts my delicate biome. So ravenous have I become for dirt, microbes, and carbon-based decomposition that it was almost a relief when I found a dead bird this afternoon.

I went out to the garage to search for a lawn chair and immediately discerned the sour bloom of rot among the bouquet of ordinary outdoor scents. A brief search led to the discovery of a tiny feathered lump in one corner. Its plumage was black with a bluish sheen and a faint dusting of gold.

Where did she come from? Perhaps she lived in the rafters of the garage until she expired from old age. I prefer that story to anything more abrupt and tragic. It didn't seem right to leave the little body there to decay on the pristine concrete. I rummaged for a piece of cardboard with which to scoop her up and tossed her into the bushes. Nature should have her. Let the bugs and the bacteria take her home.

TUESDAY, JULY 13

Our financial situation is grim. If we don't establish a steady stream of income soon, our ministry will not survive much longer. Over dinner, Jeremiah apologized for putting me in this position. He wished he could afford to compensate me for all my service to the ministry. I have done priceless work and deserve to be paid a fortune.

"I have been compensated!" I cried. "The work we do enriches my life in ways that money cannot."

I told him how honored I was to be a part of this undertaking alongside the great Jeremiah Promise. The money doesn't matter to me, I insisted. Let's just focus on financing the ministry.

Jeremiah considered my argument for a few moments, then smiled with relief. He promised to do right by me as soon as he could. I was glad to be able to give him this reprieve. He's a proud and independent man with a plan. The humiliation of charity must weigh heavily on him, but he bears it as well as he can.

I spent the rest of my evening cranking out moneymaking ideas. There must be dozens of ways to build up a steady stream of income for the ministry. I used Jeremiah's laptop to researched grants, crowdfunding, guest-speaking engagements, and paid media appearances. Most of these options seem better suited for a point down the road when we are better established.

I outlined plans for paid private healing sessions and small group gatherings. I sketched a website design and listed merchandise that we could brand and sell. Perhaps the newsletter that Jeremiah started could be used to solicit donations? Our mailing list must be thousands of

names long by now. I hope that he thought to retain it when he parted ways with Pastor Ormand.

If I chip away at a problem long enough, the right idea will eventually come along. Just one or two brilliant solutions are all I need—something worthy of Jeremiah's notice. I would not trouble him with anything less. He rarely listens to my schemes, so I had better be prepared to knock his socks off. Jeremiah's challenging manner prompts me to hone my thoughts and manage my expectations. Intelligence and discrimination like his demand superior input. I cannot aspire to be his trusted advisor unless I rise to his standard of excellence. When he finally does adopt a design of mine, then I'll know for sure that it's a good one.

Thursday, July 15

The Crusades are on indefinite hiatus, but this gives us time to get our small group meetings and Jeremiah's private practice up and running. Pastor Krish has kindly permitted us the use of his church basement for all our after-hours activities. I spent the last week cold-calling folks from our contact list, and the results were encouraging. Jeremiah has ten consultations next week, and our first Grace Group was this evening.

The turnout was good, I think! Jeremiah would probably disagree, but his expectations are always high. Four women and one man showed up. We began with introductions and personal stories, and every one of them surprised me. People go through so much strife. Illness, loss, thwarted hopes and dreams, addiction, recovery, relapse—it just goes to show that you can never guess where a person has been or where they are now by looking at them.

Grace Thiessen joined us tonight. I apologized for not recognizing her from the Crusades, but she explained that she had never been to one before. A friend had referred her to our group. Grace Thiessen wore a scarf on her head because she had lost all her hair to chemo. Like me, she had been diagnosed with ovarian cancer, but she had been through two rounds of treatment and enjoyed two periods of full remission before the cancer returned a third time. Like mine, her mind had recently opened to ideas it had never conceived before.

The word *remission* came up repeatedly this evening. Grace Thiessen had a lot to say and a lot to ask me about it. I was embarrassed to have no answers ready for her.

I have never really considered myself to be in remission. My cancer miraculously disappeared without the usual battles or bloodshed, and I consider its continued absence the work of fate, faith, and robust determination. When confronted with someone whose same lot in life has taken them down a harder path—forced them to spend years grinding through the philosophy of life's frailty and injustice—it's not so easy to tout simple solutions, even if they exist. I was relieved when Jeremiah stepped in and steered the conversation toward the light. He made much of Grace Thiessen's fortitude and promised that God would take it from there. She was about to feel a whole lot better.

The meeting was scheduled for an hour, but it lasted closer to two. Everyone had a lot to say, and we had no set structure for this meeting. Bethany and Raj Chellethe turned out to be musicians. Raj played guitar, and Bethany sang hymns for us. Jeremiah read Bible passages. People raised their hands and prayed aloud when the spirit moved them.

Toward the end of the evening, Jeremiah encouraged everyone that needed healing to close their eyes and lift their hands to God. He touched every person's head and prayed aloud for them. I checked the

collection box after everyone left. There were about nineteen dollars in there. It's something! In a few days, we'll try again.

MONDAY, JULY 19

Mondays are our unofficial Sabbath. This is our unspoken agreement. On Mondays, Jeremiah and I hide from inquiry and obligation, and we rest. Sometimes we do it separately, sometimes together.

Today, I spread a couple of chaise cushions on the ground by the backyard pool and stretched out with my sketchbook and pencils. Jeremiah must have spotted me from the window; before long, he came outside to join me. He took a seat on the nearest chaise and dangled something before my eyes. His lucky agate hung from a delicate silver chain. He encouraged me to touch it, but Jeremiah swung the stone out of my grasp when I reached out. What a tease! He continued to swing it back and forth. Back and forth.

"You're getting very sleepy," he chanted.

"Good luck with that," I said.

"Relax, and listen to my voice."

I assured him that it wouldn't work, but he tried to hypnotize me anyway. Finally, he gave up with an exaggerated sigh.

"I told you!" I laughed. I described another time that someone tried to put me in a trance and failed. It can't be done. He'll just have to live with that.

Jeremiah peered down at my drawing and remarked that the face was familiar. He wanted to know whose it was. It was Emily Brunson, the last person he healed at our very first Crusade. She had had advanced esophageal cancer.

113

Jeremiah studied my drawing thoughtfully for a time. He remarked that I captured her well. Not just her appearance, but something more—her essence.

I felt compelled to tell Jeremiah the story of eleventh-grade Conceptual Art. On the first day of class, Mrs. Maple had us spend the entire hour sketching an arrangement of plain, geometric shapes. Most of my classmates finished their drawings with time to spare, but I found the period woefully insufficient. I could not abridge the complex gradients of shadow and light. The more I studied those basic shapes, the more facets they revealed.

I was embarrassed to turn in unfinished work at the end of class. I thought my teacher would lecture me. Instead, she smiled thoughtfully and said, "You see a lot." She handed the paper back to me and told me I could come in after class to finish it if I wished. So, I did. That semester, I stayed after school quite a lot.

When I stressed about deadlines, Mrs. Maple would say, "Great vision takes great patience." She'd permit me to hand my assignment in late without penalty. It was a privilege I never took for granted nor expected from any other teacher, but it was the respite I needed during those tumultuous adolescent years. That art class was my life preserver.

Jeremiah listened to this story without comment, and when I was done, he smiled and went limp. His arms hung over the edge of the chaise. One of his hands dangled so close to my knee that a slight movement would have caused us to touch. I swear I felt a tingle between us like a faint arc of electricity generated by sheer force of anticipation. Despite the temptation, I did not close the tiny gap between us. Our touches were too precious for ordinary use. I wanted to savor them.

Jeremiah explained that he lay like this to stretch his back. I told him that Cartwright the cat used to sleep that way. He'd doze on the edge

of chairs and slip off, then jolt awake when he hit the floor. Jeremiah promised to avoid doing the same.

Ping! There's one more private joke to add to our posy. I laugh aloud when I recall some of our others—the "gnome" that runs around inside my body, causing various aches and twinges, for instance, or the many examples of Jeremiah's astonishing clumsiness. In fact, we have developed a secret shorthand of meaningful looks and nods to acknowledge all his bumbles. Just the other day, Jeremiah pulled his phone from his pocket, and the thing spurted out of his hand like a floppy fish. It took him three swipes to catch it, and when he did, he scowled satirically and slid me a sideways look. Indeed, I had seen the whole thing. I added it to my mental tally of his many endearing stumbles, fumbles, trips, and slips (as well as the lingering looks and smiles that followed).

This afternoon, I fell asleep on the couch and dreamed about Jeremiah. He and I and several dozen others were gathered in the church basement. The room was crowded and noisy. Jeremiah pulled me aside and led me through a small door under the stairs. He wanted to show me his new secret technique for prolonging human life.

The door led to a small room that contained nothing but a table. Its surface looked like a giant chessboard. I was supposed to climb up, lie down on it, and let it fold around me like an eleven-pointed star. Jeremiah offered to demonstrate. He lay down on the table and invited me to lie on top of him. His body cushioned me from the table's hard surface and pinching hinges as the thing began to fold around us. In my dream, I didn't care about the contraption, what it was doing, or why. I only cared that Jeremiah was near me.

Thursday, July 22

Confession: I bought a lottery ticket.

I was out for a quick stroll on Tuesday morning when forces unseen suddenly yanked me into the gas station on Hall-Johnson. Perhaps it was the hand of fate directing me to the financial miracle we needed! In retrospect, those random numbers didn't *feel* like winners. There wasn't a single odd number among them, and, as we all know, odd numbers are best. Does one ever really "feel" their way to winning the lottery, though? Since its inception, many people have *felt* that they would win, but few ever have. Somewhere in the universe, there must exist a humongous dump heap of thwarted inklings and fruitless intuitions.

As if on cue, renowned psychic Melody Jermaine was featured on the news this morning as a Powerball consultant. One of the questions she receives most from clients is: what are the winning numbers? Alas, that is one of the few she cannot answer. Lottery number selection is a matter of random chance, Melody explained. God has no hand in it. Her psychic powers are attuned to the divine order, not to happenstance.

I used to think that good luck is something that I could *push* into being by focusing with all my might. I'd tense up, scowl with concentration, and will my desire into being. This was not a very reliable method of manifesting things. I succeeded about as often as I failed.

Perhaps I was going about it the wrong way.

Good fortune does not strike me as a difficult thing to move. When it does come along, it floats like a stray helium balloon and alights like a bird. On the periodic table, I imagine it fits somewhere between the elements of serendipity and pure chance.

What is serendipity? What—precisely—is the difference between the two? Neither luck nor serendipity can be harnessed by demand, but the latter seems more likely to prevail in times of need. It strikes me as a gentle sort of static that attaches to good intentions.

All right, then. I shall call today's big break "serendipitous" rather than "lucky." The lottery ticket did not pan out, but my research led me down a rabbit hole of moneymaking ideas until I stumbled out in the land of "paranormal proof" prizes.

Several organizations in the United States and worldwide offer cash awards to anyone who can demonstrate psychic, supernatural, or paranormal ability (including faith healing) in a controlled laboratory setting. All we'd need to do is submit an official statement describing Jeremiah's special powers, negotiate the terms and conditions of his demonstration, let the scientists observe and measure a live healing in a laboratory, and then collect the prize money.

There are several sizable cash prizes currently up for grabs. In exchange for verifiable proof, the Fayetteville Freethinkers are offering $5,000, and the North Texas Skeptics are offering $12,000. But why not aim higher? The Independent Investigations Group is offering $100,000, and—are you ready for this?—the James Candini Educational Foundation is offering ONE MILLION DOLLARS! For Jeremiah to win the million-dollar prize, he would have to submit to a very rigorous vetting process. Surely, he is up to the task! What *wouldn't* he do to free us from our financial constraints?

I contained my million-dollar excitement all day until Jeremiah returned, settled in, and answered my text. I *really did* think he would be pleased with my findings this time. In a way, he was—Jeremiah threw his head back and laughed. Yes, of course, he's heard of James Candini and the

Million Dollar Challenge. Who hasn't? James Candini is an infamous witch hunter who has wasted countless hours of airtime attempting to glorify the debunking industry.

Jeremiah asked if I happened to discover Candini's origin story in all my research. No? Then he should enlighten me. Like most public figures that make a living from picking on others, Candini has spent his life pursuing petty personal vendettas. Since childhood, it was his ambition to be a great magician, but he was not a particularly talented one. He was jealous of every gifted performer in his field that was more successful than him—practically everybody—so he made a career out of attending magic shows and ruining the performers' tricks. His resentment didn't stop there, though. He widened his debunking net to snare all manner of psychics, mystics, telekinetics, and faith healers. This guy was determined to claw his way to the spotlight one way or another—it's too bad he had to tear others down along the way.

As for the million dollars—who do I think provides the financial backing for so sizable a prize? Pharmaceutical companies! James Candini rigs these "scientific" tests to fail, then goes on national TV and declares that there's no such thing as faith healers. Five minutes later, there's a commercial break advertising XYZ antidepressant. *Feeling blue because James Candini disproved the existence of God? Ask your doctor about this medication today!*

Jeremiah shook his head and chuckled as he walked me to the door. No, ma'am, we won't waste our time pursuing impossible dollars.

Well, that was humiliating. Back to the drawing board.

SUNDAY, JULY 25

Jeremiah is becoming scarce again. The weight of the world is on his shoulders now that Pastor Ormand is out of the picture. When he's not busy with private healing sessions, he's networking with local religious groups and searching for investors. He's gone most of each day and is exhausted when he returns. Every day, I offer to help him in any way I can. He only wants me to do research, answer the phone, and schedule appointments. I'm a glorified office assistant. No—actually, there's nothing glorified about it.

I can't fault him for being gone a lot, but I still get restless. It doesn't take long for me to begin to miss Jeremiah, regardless of the reason. I've become a little too jumpy around the phone. Every ring and ding gets my hopes up, but the messages are rarely from Jeremiah.

This afternoon, I became so stir crazy and fed up with the beige walls of my tiny apartment that *any* distraction would be a welcome relief. Right on cue, I received a text message from Freddie Childress. Freddie has contacted me several times over the past few weeks, but I've been slow to respond. I've been conflicted. The birdhouse incident created a lot of tension between Jeremiah and me. At the same time, I did promise to meet up with Freddie someday.

When he contacted me today, I was eager enough for social interaction that I responded promptly. Freddie had just finished work for the day, was in the area, and wanted to meet for coffee. I agreed and picked a little European cafe down the street that I could walk to in under half an hour.

I arrived early, but Freddie was there before me. He looked half farmer and half gentleman: he wore overalls and a blue blazer, and his hair glistened with pomade.

We took our seats. Despite his exceptional height, Freddie seemed to peer upward at me. His black, deer-mouse eyes bore into me, and his delicate features twitched anxiously. I ordered hot tea, and he ordered a cookie. Freddie's long, chapped fingers quickly crumbled it to pieces on the plate.

I asked him questions about his life. What does he do for work? Does he have family in the area? As Freddie answered, I listened closely to his manner of speaking. I couldn't help but wonder if his stutter was *really* gone. Evidently, it was. His words would catch now and then, and he'd halt with hesitation, but overall, his words flowed smoothly.

I learned that Freddie manages all the candy and gumball dispensers on the north side of Dallas. Freddie's father started the business thirty years ago, and Freddie took over after his father passed.

I offered my condolences, but Freddie quickly changed the subject. He wanted to know *everything* about me—where I had come from, what my life was like before this, whether I had a family. It was difficult to resist the tug of his gentle curiosity, so I told him about my beloved garden and cottage, my former job at the library, and my daily walking adventures. Before I knew it, I was opening up to him about my family history as well. I told him about my father's car accident, Dave's overdose, Mom's stroke. I even admitted to him in a half-whisper that, deep down, I've always felt that I stumbled into a cursed existence the day we found my best friend's body in the woods. That freak accident. Poor Teddy. They said he didn't suffer much, but it was still an awful way to go.

Freddie rested his chin on both fists and listened to my stories with innocent awe. So enthralled was he with every aspect of my tale, wheth-

er happy, grotesque, or insignificant, that I felt compelled to elaborate more and more. Every detail seemed to impress him deeply, right down to the stained-glass panel in the front door of my cottage.

A couple of times I attempted to pass the speaking role back to Freddie, but each time he gently redirected the attention back to me and urged me on. When pressed, he'd smile and say that he'd never learned much of anything by talking.

Hours passed in the blink of an eye. By the time I realized how late it was, it was too late. Jeremiah was likely to return to the house any minute, and I didn't want to be gone when he arrived. I said a hasty goodbye to Freddie and promised to be better about keeping in touch.

Jeremiah pulled into the driveway just as I reached the house. My stomach clenched apprehensively. I wished I had paid closer attention to the time. He wanted to know where I had been, and I told him the vague truth: I had gone to meet a friend for coffee. Jeremiah seemed displeased, but he didn't inquire any further.

Monday, July 26

Last night, I dreamed that I worked in a corporate office. Outside the break room window stood a big, dead tree. It was just a smooth gray trunk with nubby limbs. Most of its small branches were gone. A tree trimmer had come to cut it down, and everyone in the office was crowded at the window to watch.

I recognized the tree trimmer—it was Alexa Bremen, a friend of mine from elementary school. She was dressed in a sleek unitard and wore circus makeup. With chainsaw in hand, Alexa climbed to the top of the dead tree with deft acrobatic flare. She wrapped her legs around the highest branch and started the chainsaw. Then she began to cut pieces off the tree with broad artistic swooshes.

I noticed that Alexa always cut toward herself as she worked her way down the tree. The blade passed dangerously close to her body, closer all the time. I tried to convince my coworkers that it wasn't safe, that we ought to intervene, but no one listened to me. They just wanted to enjoy the show.

Alexa continued to perform with a smile, but dark gashes began to appear on her arms, shoulders, and chest. Still, nobody noticed anything wrong with this. They were eager for the finale: Alexa tossed her chainsaw in the air, leaped to the ground, and put out her hand. With horror, I watched the saw fall blade downward. I woke up just before she caught it.

Last night, a storm blew through Luck and dropped a tree on my house. We lost the Sentinel, my granddad's oak, and part of the roof as well. I almost didn't find out, except it suddenly occurred to me to call Missy this afternoon to check on things. I felt guilty that I hadn't spoken to her in nearly a month, and even more guilty when I found out what had happened.

Missy said she had meant to contact me in a day or two, once she had all the facts. She didn't want to worry me. But since she had me on the phone, she might as well tell all. Her preliminary inspection revealed daylight coming in through the southwest corner of the attic. She'll have Mac take a look at it when he gets home on Sunday, and then we'll know more.

Oh, dear. My home. My tree. My aching heart. I shouldn't have assumed they'd keep while I put them on indefinite hold.

I paced and mulled over the best course of action. Homes and trees

have feelings like all things do, and mine were ailing. My first impulse was to rush home and attend to them.

Should I? I'm needed here, too. Jeremiah will miss me, and I cannot abandon the ministry at so critical a time. What little money I have left may be better allocated for repairs. It's a difficult decision, but I feel I must stay put for now.

Tuesday, July 27

Crusades will resume in another week or two, and Jeremiah has commissioned me to hit the streets with Crusade fliers once again.

My gusto is wanting. I seem to recall two bad discipling experiences for every good one, and this makes me reluctant to even begin. Perhaps this is a temporary state of mind. I have been degrading into a flu-like funk for the past few days, and it's difficult to feel driven and enthusiastic when I have no energy to spare.

This afternoon, my skin ached, my breath felt hot in my throat, and the gloomy skies had me squinting until the pain enveloped my whole head in thick, throbbing rotations. I almost fell asleep several times during the forty-five-minute bus ride back to Grapevine. The last thing I wanted was a lecture from Jeremiah when I got there—and that's saying something since ninety-nine percent of the time, I would gladly accept anything from him.

In retrospect, I can see the signs of agitation that led up to my talking-to. Something else was bothering Jeremiah, and he was poised to nitpick. As soon as the words "her God" slipped out of my mouth, he had the ammunition he needed to fire.

Jeremiah corrected me: I should always say "God," not "her God" or "your God." People absorb all the subtleties of speech. Even if they don't know what they heard, their brain processes it and passes judgments. Slip-ups breed distrust and distrust ruins faith.

I should always *appear* devoutly religious, Jeremiah lectured. People trust pious leaders. I may not (I may *never*) believe the same things as other people, but I must respect their beliefs if I want to be allowed into their world. People rely on appearances and results. Few may ever know the truth—or the difference.

This abrupt rebuke from Jeremiah fell on me from a crushing height. I suppose my impending fever weakened my defenses and made me vulnerable to censure. I collapsed on the couch and cried as soon as I made it back to my apartment. I'm ready to throw this day away. Thank goodness it's over.

Friday, July 30

Jeremiah has recruited three new crew members. I found out five minutes before our first staff meeting. I guess he couldn't wait a week for me to return from the brink of death so I could help him with personnel decisions.

Do I sound grumpy? I don't mean to be—well, maybe a little. I thought Jeremiah and I were supposed to make crucial ministry decisions together. But it's not like that rule is written down somewhere. Jeremiah can do as he pleases. He is free, and I am . . . I don't know what.

He pulled me aside right before the meeting to explain. Two of the three new recruits were personally recommended by Reverend Gideon himself. They were long-time members of his congregation. Taking them on was a no-brainer, and Jeremiah was sure I'd approve. The third

recruit was our new Director of Security. Jeremiah assured me that he had taken extraordinary pains to find and vet this guy, and he felt confident that I would approve of him, too.

I asked how in the world Jeremiah could afford to pay three full-time staff members when we barely had the money for food and gas. He chuckled. I needn't worry! He had worked out deals with all of them. One was interning for college credit. The other two agreed to some sort of prorated recruitment commission arrangement that—honestly, after a point, my attention fogged over, and I couldn't follow all the details. But it sounded alright.

It wasn't hard for me to guess who was who as I took a seat at our Arthurian round table. The woman must be Carmen Jenkins, our Director of Media. The recent college graduate that nearly leaped over the table to introduce himself must be Calvin Bixby, Jeremiah's new Personal Assistant. And the compact, keen-eyed man that sat ramrod straight in the chair directly across from me must be the security man, Jude Clements.

Jeremiah commenced the meeting by announcing everyone's names and roles. I expected no surprises here, so I was completely caught off-guard when he introduced me as "Vice Minister and Director of Human Relations."

Even with a stuffed-up head, I was pretty sure it was more title than it used to be.

Vice Minister?

Human Relations?

Not *congregation* or *ministry* or even *public* relations? Human—which presumably places every homo sapiens on the planet within my purview. I didn't and still don't know how to feel about this. How is one expected to relate to all humans? Is a degree or certification required?

What are the specific qualifications?

I expressed my concerns during our drive back to the house. Jeremiah told me not to worry about titles. They are assigned for the benefit of subordinates. He just wanted to make it clear to the others that I am his right-hand man, and they should come to me with public relations matters. That's all.

I ought to know by now that Jeremiah's wisdom precedes my own. I am gratified that he is now touting me as his "right-hand...*man*."

Friday, August 6

Carmen blustered into the meeting, waving a copy of *National Enquirer*, and proclaimed that it must be our lucky day. World-renowned faith healer Bernard Finn was caught on camera holding hands with an attractive young woman who was not his wife. The article offered juicy details of his illicit affair.

This was precisely the sort of moral lapse we needed to light an already-fragile fuse, Carmen enthused. In the ministry world, reputation is everything. The recent Senate inquiry regarding Bernard Finn's questionable use of ministry funds was the perfect setup. Even though the investigation was inconclusive, a bomb was ready to go off (tick, tick, tick). Just one more little spark of moral indiscretion, and—boom!

The timing *couldn't be better* for us to rush in and seize the spoils of Bernard Finn's self-destruction. His followers were on the verge of turning away in droves, and when they did, they would need a new spiritual leader. The impeccably principled, philanthropic, real-deal Jeremiah Promise would be just the ticket.

It's time for Jeremiah to tell his side of the Bartholomew Lambrecht story in a very public, very sympathetic way. According to Carmen, our efforts to quietly distance ourselves from the scandal are the exact opposite of what we should be doing. We should be talking about it constantly. Leave nothing to the imagination. Make it clear that Jeremiah was ignorant of his former ministry's misuse of funds and that he was an innocent victim of that evil man's wrongdoing, just like millions of other good, honest folks.

Carmen has friends in high places, and one of those places is the Christian Broadcasting Network. She's already negotiating an interview on the national Christian news program *The Christ Club*.

Furthermore, Jeremiah should be giving as many statements as possible to newspapers, magazines, and blogs. The sensational details of his story are sure to attract a lot of attention to our cause. We need to work double-time behind the scenes to establish our "brand" so that it's ready to go the moment we hit the big-time. We need a website, a weekly newsletter, mail campaigns, ad campaigns, social media. We need to pave the way now for long-game items like book series, box sets, live-streaming subscriptions, and podcasts. If Jeremiah can perform the Gift of Healing, then surely, he can teach it, too. He should offer online courses that could eventually be built into a certification program, a school, and a nonprofit foundation.

This laundry list of flashy marketing schemes made me cringe on the inside. I watched Jeremiah for signs of skepticism, but I saw none. He went on and on about hiring a professional film crew to document our Crusades. In the long run, he'd like to create an official rags-to-riches documentary about his *Journey Back to Grace.*

He was thrilled with all of Carmen's ambitious marketing ideas and enthralled with the woman herself. The two of them excitedly discussed details as if they were the only people in the room—and I felt what it

was like to be on the chilly periphery of his dynamic duo.

It looks as if Jeremiah Promise has met his match in Carmen. Nothing but piss and ambition seems to flow through her veins. It's my (petty) consolation that she sports a big, sparkly wedding band on her left hand. Their enthusiasm for each other must be purely professional.

Sunday, August 8

Crusades have recommenced, and attendance is more robust than ever.

The energy was strange today. Ever since we left Pastor Ormand's cozy little microcosm, things have ceased to be uniformly harmonious and upbeat. But I suppose discord is bound to appear somewhere in a large and growing group of people. It's impossible to control the dynamics of so many.

I spent most of the hour before the Crusade today trying to console an inconsolable woman. She did not appreciate my attempts to soothe and quiet her. She yelled at me for not listening to her and only grew louder each time I attempted to respond.

"You don't *know* me!" she cried angrily. The people around us stared. I was embarrassed and shaken. What in the world does one say to that?

Nothing.

Eventually, it occurred to me to just shut my mouth. I was so intent on avoiding a scene that I wasn't listening to the woman. She had something to say, and by God, she was going to say it. The woman vented her feelings loudly, and I didn't attempt to interfere again. People stared. Let them stare.

Once the story was all the way out, I couldn't blame her for being upset. The woman's son had just been assaulted in prison, and she wasn't

allowed to visit him. What mother wouldn't be out of her mind with fear and anger?

Tonight, I couldn't get that woman or her jarring story out of my mind. I want to fix her distress, but I can't. I want to say that I understand, but I don't. Even if I could use an experience of my own to relate to her, I still couldn't *know* for sure what she's been through, what she thinks, or what she feels. Each person alone has the authority to understand herself.

I've been thinking a lot lately about the word *perspective.*

Every person's point of view is unique. It's formed from a lifetime of experiences, thoughts, choices, and feelings, and no perspective is right or wrong. Sometimes I'm tempted to deny things I haven't seen with my own eyes. But I'm starting to realize that some people are endowed with the gift of exceptional sight—whether it be foresight, insight, vision, or experience. Some (like me) are privileged to behold the world's wonder and beauty, while others are obliged to witness more than their fair share of ugliness.

It's unwise to deny perspectives that differ from my own. If I hope to be believed, I must believe others. Best to seek out those who see differently than I do and listen to what they have to say. Learn from them.

Monday, August 9

We spent the entire day at the church, and I was not prepared for so long a stretch away from home base. I forgot to pack my sketchpad and didn't bring nearly enough snacks to get me through the day. I ended up raiding the vending machine and blearily trying to focus on the one book that I had brought with me. It was a rigorous, research-based publication that examined the biological and sociological components of anger—an interesting topic, to be sure, but a bit dry.

The day was chock-full of appointments and meetings, but Jeremiah and I still somehow managed to sync up for a quiet half-hour this afternoon. He came into the pastor's office and asked what I was reading.

I explained that I was working on a hypothesis about anger, and this was research. Jeremiah promptly rejoined that he had a hypothesis about anger, too, but he wanted to hear mine first. Eager for any opportunity to talk about it, I launched into a discourse about the anger response and why it may not be a *real* emotion. It seems to be something else entirely—something that masquerades as feeling. Anger often presents as a secondary response to another, primary emotion: fear, shame, guilt, or worry. That's why it's so easy for anger to escalate to rage. But anger only serves one real purpose in our lives: to combat injustice.

Jeremiah nodded and agreed that anger is a useful tool. It enhances strength and enables humans to accomplish superhuman feats. When focused—like a laser—it can be a powerful force, indeed. Jeremiah revealed that he used to struggle with "anger issues." In his youth, he had quite a temper. He didn't like being told what to do. Sometimes he'd put his fists through walls and wouldn't even feel the pain.

I pointed out that he was perhaps grappling with *perceived* injustice. Whether it was the result of real unfairness or youthful misconception, his anger was probably authentic.

"That's a gift," I affirmed. To be able to focus and channel energy like that is akin to a superpower. It's a good thing Jeremiah found an outlet for his passion.

We agreed that it's vital to differentiate genuine anger from false rage. One can be highly productive and the other highly destructive. How do we know the difference?

"Consider the origin," I proposed. Become familiar with the physical nuances of each. And perhaps—in the case of a leader responsible for the well-being of many people—become accustomed to seeking outside counsel.

I think Jeremiah knew what I meant by that, though he didn't acknowledge it directly. He graced me with that odd little half-smile of his and said it was time for him to get on to the next meeting.

Saturday, August 14

I have not been as friendly toward the new recruits as I ought to be. Sure, I have been polite and civil. We have sat through meetings together, and I have shared pertinent information, but none of these actions could be mistaken for warmth or friendliness.

I'm jealous! There, I said it. And I'm sorry.

After having Jeremiah Promise to myself for many weeks and enjoying the bonds that developed naturally through mutual strife, I viewed the newcomers as threats. I already had to share him with hundreds of congregants per week, and I didn't like having to divide the remainder of Jeremiah's attention into three additional portions.

I was wrong to think in terms of scarcity. Can I not trust by now that Jeremiah and I have our special connection? Must I also have his constant attention and reassurance?

Today, I embark on a campaign to endear myself to Carmen, Calvin, and Jude. I'm fortunate that at least one of them has never seemed to mind my standoffishness. Calvin, the Personal Assistant, has been relentlessly pursuing every opportunity to become my new best buddy. Though he has an unfortunate obsession with gossip, I am grateful to have someone around that's easy to talk to. I shall just have to be careful what I say around him.

Carmen and Jude are tougher nuts to crack. I suspect that our aloofness may be mutual. Carmen seems content to mostly ignore me; Jude is deferential, but he does not speak to me unless I get in his way. When our paths cross, he says, "Miss!" with a curt nod and veers around me without missing a beat.

Despite their reserve, both individuals belie a wealth of intriguing subtexts. Both exude masculine confidence, but Carmen is more aggressive. She seems to approach everything and everyone as a competitor that must be defeated. Jude, on the other hand, is the picture of absolute impassivity. His operational frequency eludes my radar. More than once, he has sneaked up and startled me with his Ninja-like stealth.

Calvin has informed me that Carmen used to work for a big-shot marketing firm in Fort Worth before taking time off for personal reasons. Like a boxer returning to the ring after a significant hiatus, I imagine she's eager to prove her might.

Jude's backstory is vague. Calvin claims that he was a weapons specialist in the Marine Corps for a dozen years or so. Why he left and what he did for the next dozen years is less clear. What he likes, what makes him laugh, what he does for fun—also unclear. That's okay; I like a challenge.

I have a plan. I will study these people, and then I will befriend them, whether they like it or not.

Sunday, August 15

Jeremiah continually improves on his showmanship. He outdid himself at today's Crusade. Everyone was swept up in his fiery passion—there was a standing ovation! I'm impressed by the sensitivity with which Jeremiah attunes himself to his flock's needs and customizes his strategy accordingly. Like a skilled conductor, he brings together collections of diverse elements and arranges them in symbiotic harmony. When I gazed out at the audience today, I briefly beheld a single complex organism looking back at me.

I wonder if divine gifts are not isolated phenomena but rather ecosystems of faith. Perhaps the healer *needs* the believers to have faith in him just as much as the believers need the healer to heal them. They are symbiotic entities that sustain each other, and neither can thrive without the other.

It makes sense that Jeremiah would balk at my previous suggestion to pursue cash prizes by performing miracles in sterile labs. Miracles don't happen in vacuums! He needs his network of true believers, not a tribunal of skeptics (anti-believers). Just look how powerful he is in a room filled to the rafters with faith. Just imagine how much more powerful he could become if the room were bigger.

Jeremiah saved a lot of souls today. The floor was littered with braces, crutches, and wheelchairs. At this rate, we may need to negotiate some sort of weekly pick up deal with the Red Cross.

TUESDAY, AUGUST 17

Missy called last night to let me know the cost to fix my cottage. Insurance will cover the roof, but I'm going to have to pay out of pocket to have the tree removed. Mac put in the lowest bid possible, and even that's going to cost me nearly everything. All my savings. There will be very little left over to pay the monthly expenses. Missy said she'd do what she could to help.

But.

I may lose my home if our financial situation doesn't improve soon. Jeremiah's supreme confidence in God's grace is looking pretty good right about now. I wish I could sustain that tranquil mindset. It took only half a day for the locusts of angst to descend upon me. It's been a rough night. I hope tomorrow will be better.

WEDNESDAY, AUGUST 18

Jeremiah stopped by in the early afternoon to see if I wanted to run a few errands with him. Of course. Any excuse to spend time with him. We drove to Fort Worth to pick up a few things here and drop off a few things there, mostly paperwork. Neither of us was in the talking mood today, but that was alright. We don't always have to talk.

The drive back to the house was the best part—Jeremiah took back roads the whole way. It's as if he *knew* that I wanted to savor the journey. The heat of Texas summer was as oppressive as ever, but the cold blast of Jeremiah's AC cut the humidity. Everything the sun touched

was tinged with pre-autumn gold. I pressed my forehead against the car window and gazed at the passing shapes with dreamy satisfaction.

Suddenly, it seemed silly of me to go on any longer, denying how I feel about Jeremiah. He and I, together, make all the sense in the world! We get along so well; we have so much in common; we're as close as can be. Emotionally, that is. It would take only a minor quantum feat for us to find ourselves on the same side of the looking glass, finally free to embrace.

How would it be done? With magic words? Magic spices? Exchanges of heart and soul? We have talked many times, but never about "us." Maybe we should—but how to begin?

After dinner, Jeremiah sat by the pool for a bit, and I went down to join him. I sketched the reflections I saw on the water while Jeremiah processed paperwork. With a furrowed brow, he paused and murmured something aloud. This opened up a conversation between us, which led him to ask me what I thought of Carmen.

I wasn't sure what kind of answer he was looking for, so I conservatively said she seems to be good at her job. Jeremiah agreed. He would like to delegate more of his work to others, and he's optimistic that someday that would be possible. It takes him a long time to trust someone else to do a job right.

I recalled what he said about *trusting* me to take care of ministry business when he appointed me Director of Human Relations, and I felt a rush of pride. This seemed like the perfect lead in to the conversation I dearly wanted to have with Jeremiah. Then something else occurred to me, and my heart sank. In what other scenario is trust highly prized? When there is an ethical obligation to maintain only platonic regard for one's close friend and ministry partner, perhaps?

I stammered to a halt before any of the wrong words could escape my lips. Instead, I said, "I trust you, Jeremiah."

He nodded and said he sure hoped so, by now.

Soon after, Jeremiah turned in for the night. I remained behind. Restless, I paced around the pool in the dark. Even in his absence, his gravitational pull put a kink in my orbit. At one point, I followed that tangent to the pool-house steps and raised my fist to knock at his door.

I care for you very much, Jeremiah. I want us to try for something more.

But I left without knocking.

I can't do it. I can't risk destroying the solid foundation of friendship Jeremiah and I have built. Perhaps these feelings are not what they appear to be, considering how my circumstances recently changed. For as long as I could afford to live a life of adventure, I could remain patient and let things unfold in their own time. I was content to focus all my energy on future hopes and dreams and demand little from the here and now.

Then a tree fell on my house and, like an ax, cut down my world of possibilities. Difficult choices lie ahead. The gods of time demand a sacrifice.

I cannot bear to ask Jeremiah for money, not when I have seen the meager offerings left in the Grace Group coffers, not when he has put aside his pride to confide in me about our finances. To ask would be so crude. I do crave some sort of assurance that things will be all right in the end, though. Some guarantee that I won't have to sacrifice absolutely everything for him—and if I do, then at least it will be for the worthy cause of true love.

It's no use to try to cram my relationship with Jeremiah into a box with prescribed meaning. It's not one definite thing or another, because it's already much more. I know that our connection is extraordinary, regardless of what it's called or what it means to anyone else. That ought

to be enough. These feelings I'm having are whimsical. They will pass.

FRIDAY, AUGUST 20

Last week, Calvin Bixby was on a course to become my new best friend. I have since become wary of his wiles. His manipulations are starting to show. I get the sense that he's using me to get closer to Jeremiah, and I don't like it.

If Calvin were a hard worker, I could at least respect him. But he's a loafer. Lately, there's been a lot of, "Where's Calvin?" and, "Did he do that thing I asked him to do?" and (sigh), "When you see him, send him to my office, please."

He has not been fulfilling his duties, and he seems disinclined to do the hard work of building authentic rapport with Jeremiah. Thus, Calvin is not a difficult bud to snip. All I need to do is pinch off his information supply and watch him wither on the vine.

A part of me relished the twitch of irritation that I saw in Jeremiah's face when Calvin didn't show up to the crew meeting today. I'm glad he's aware of his assistant's shortcomings.

The moment that Jeremiah stumbled upon yet another order of business that Calvin had neglected to attend, I leaped at the opportunity to pick up his slack.

I glanced smugly around the room and caught the pointy end of a hard stare from Jude. He does not look at me often, but his dark eyes seem to spear me with palpable reproach when he does. What's his deal? Does he judge me for judging Calvin? I may not be innocent of this, but it's not like I've done anything to sabotage the kid.

SUNDAY, AUGUST 22

I have taken on a new hobby: the Getting Jude to Talk to Me game. Going forward, he and I will be working together closely at the Crusades, and I like to think this will make the hours we spend together more bearable. He's markedly averse to conversation, so that makes me try harder to engage him. When we have downtime together, I ask him questions. He never answers, beyond a curt nod or conclusive, "Miss."

I am sorely tempted to start filling in his side of the conversation with my best impressions of John McClane from *Die Hard*.

SUNDAY, AUGUST 29

Today was challenging. An incident at the Crusade pulled me twenty years backward, to an age I don't care to revisit. For this, I'm finding it hard to forgive.

The man's name was Dennis Horton. He came stumbling in during the welcoming hour, obviously inebriated. I don't know how I managed to spot him so quickly. As soon as he stepped in the door, I made a beeline across the room. A shocked woman was shoving away his groping hand just as I arrived. I slapped on a smile and persuaded Dennis Horton to follow me outside, away from our precious flock.

He told me garbled stories about his cruel wife of twenty-eight years who was withholding his rightful fortune from him. In soothing tones, I called him "poor dear" and asked to see a picture of her, hoping he'd pull out his wallet. I caught a glimpse of the home address on his li-

cense. Bingo. Call him a cab, send him home, problem solved.

I waited for the cab with him to make sure he didn't wander off. As I helped Dennis Horton down the sidewalk, he suddenly contorted and tried to kiss me on the mouth. I managed to dodge his brown-toothed leer, but while I was off-balance, he took the opportunity— ugh, it hurts to even write it—to grab my crotch with his gnarled claw. I stumbled backward, tripped on the curb, and went down hard.

Jude suddenly swooped in out of nowhere and tackled the man. He twisted Dennis Horton's arm behind his back and hustled him out of sight. I heard a door slam and a car drive off. That was the end of that.

I picked myself up, dusted my dress, and sat down on the nearest bench. Jude came to check that I had sustained no sprains, breaks, or nasty scrapes. My elbow was a little bloody and my knee bruised, but that was all.

"Next time, call me," he said. Then he returned to the church. I remained on the bench for a while. The Crusade began, but nobody came looking for me. Jude must have filled in the others on what happened.

Oh, how I wanted Jeremiah right then. I wished for his sympathy and reassurance so badly that it hurt. I imagined him sitting down beside me, putting his arms around me, and demanding justice on my behalf. But he was busy.

Finally, I collected my thoughts and went back inside. The Crusade was halfway over. I felt like a sleepwalker as I went through the motions of catching the anointed and helping them to their seats. As soon as the service was over, Jeremiah slipped out the back. I stayed to talk to congregants for a couple of hours, as usual. Usher Anabel Lightly was kind enough to drive me home.

I took a long shower, but the soap was insufficient to wash away the residue of the day. When I reached for the conditioner bottle and found it empty—that was the final straw. I raised that plastic expression of my frustration high over my head and slammed it down on the edge of the tub. Again, and again I slammed it down until it was a crumpled, oozing mess.

Dear Dave, darling brother, ill-fated addict:
Thanks for the memories.

Ah yes, Dave, the innocent escapist. Always some shade of drunk or high and game to entertain little sis with his inebriated antics. It was all in good fun until somebody got hurt—but even then, the question of who was to blame was always inconclusive.

I kept the secret all this time. Did you?

Mom was convinced that he was harmless. And he was. Just a lost little boy that needed to be loved into the light. We kept him at home instead of forcing him into treatment. Mom and little sis looked out for him, cleaned up after him, and excused his lapses in judgment.

Easy for you. You're dead.

I'd like to know who answers for the damage done by lost little boys that never find the light. Does the blame just float off into the ether? What about the ones that get hurt—are they expected to forgive? To forget?

I tried; I really did. I buried the memory of that day. But it's still there. Mom, away visiting a friend. Dave, high as usual. Late-night pizza run. Little sis left behind at the gas station. The fishy old man forc-

ing his calloused claw up her dress. The weight of her brother's guilt smothering her own mortification, politely entreating her to entomb that hard rock of truth in silence. Gone. Buried. Forgotten. Until today.

MONDAY, AUGUST 30

I lay in bed for quite some time, picking at the wounds of yesterday. I didn't realize that my business with my brother was unfinished. Memories of two decades past ought to have crumbled to dust by now. I guess that's not how memory works.

I've been waiting for some sort of apology or vindication that's never going to come. Dave is gone. He can never become the brother I wanted him to be, nor can he apologize for what he did or who he was. This avenue of closure ended a long time ago.

It occurs to me that everyone leaves behind a legacy. My brother's gift to me was a series of lessons about personal responsibility. Being pushed into a caretaking role early taught me to be more aware of the burden I place on others. Watching Dave flounder in chaos taught me to continually seek clarity and control. If I could control the bad stuff, I could prevent it from happening again.

This mindset made my world very small for a long time. It was debilitating to know on some subconscious level that it wasn't possible to foresee and prevent every unwanted possibility. I was unhappy, and bad things happened anyway.

I have always blamed myself for the assault at the gas station. Who else was there to blame? Dave? Even when he was present, he was hardly ever there. The old man? He's long gone.

I blamed myself for Dave's overdose and for Mom's illness, too. Never overtly—always in the form of if-onlys and I-should-have-dones. If only I had connected the dots sooner, if only I had helped them both more, if only I had given them less trouble, etc. Subtle failings, all.

Compassion is something I have advocated for many times but never fully understood. Perhaps it is not just for other people, but also for oneself. As is forgiveness. I thought my opportunity to forgive died with Dave. It did not. Somebody alive today needs it more than he does—me.

It's a relief to simultaneously say aloud and hear the words: *I forgive you.* For lacking the power and foresight to stop these bad, sad things from happening, I release you from blame. I also forgive you for harboring secret resentment that grew in the dark, like cancer.

All these years later, there is little to be done about the past. There is no point in looking there except to learn something new about myself. Painful as it can be, a long-awaited resolution is well worth the trouble. When I wrote "thanks" yesterday, I meant to be ironic. I see now that it was the beginning of insight.

I *am* thankful.

Dave was a key influence in my life. He helped shape me as a person, even if he did so by modeling what *not* to do and be. Dennis Horton was an agent of revelation. Obnoxious as our encounter was—and don't think I won't file a police report—his offense was a blessing in disguise. I'm grateful for the opportunity to explore the limits of compassion and forgiveness. Until these limits are tested, I don't know what they are. Until I know what they are, I cannot exceed them.

Meanwhile, Freddie continues to impress me.

He called this afternoon just to catch up, and all my tip-of-the-brain realizations came tumbling out. He listened attentively and encouraged me to go on as long as I liked. Talking things through with

him helped crystallize my understanding. It was wonderful to express my ideas aloud and feel heard and understood. He's turning out to be a splendid friend.

SATURDAY, SEPTEMBER 4

"Smooth" is the word I would use to describe every aspect of our trip to Virginia. Smooth is everything that is not coarse or challenging. It's easy and consistent and free of lumps and bumps. But it's also flat, regular, uncomplicated, and impervious to inspiration.

It was a short trip, just long enough for Jeremiah to make his debut on *The Christ Club* and do a little peripheral networking. When we weren't in the production studio, I spent my free time moping in my fancy hotel room. Jeremiah and Carmen were occupied with back-to-back coffee, lunch, and dinner engagements. I was glad to leave the socializing to them, though the separation from Jeremiah was painful. I couldn't put my finger on the problem exactly, but I sensed the distance between us growing in more ways than one. Nothing would relieve the dull ache in my gut or my vague sense of foreboding. Even the magnificent rose garden right outside my window could not draw me out. I was too depressed to enjoy it.

The show taping was scheduled down to the minute and structured for optimal efficiency.

8:00 am - Rehearsal.

8:30 am - Makeup.

8:56 am - The three of us shake hands with host Rob Patterson.

8:57 am - Jeremiah makes a clever joke.

8:58 am - Jeremiah asks to review his cues.

8:59:53 am - Jeremiah flashes me a zealous grin.

8:59:54 am - My heart stops beating.

8:59:57 am - My heart surges back into action.

And 3, 2, 1 . . .

The studio was smaller and darker than I expected. Everything that was not part of the film set was painted black. I watched the live filming from the dark, chilly bleachers. One of the film crew noticed my shivering and kindly lent me her coat.

Jeremiah gave a brilliant interview. He was enthusiastic but composed, paced, and articulate. His tones undulated like a silken tide. He told several shocking tales from his term with BL and explained how he had repented, submitted to the Holy Spirit, and been reborn free of contamination from his former business. He now surrounds himself with those that walk in God's grace, and he's grateful for every minute of his new life.

There was one brief hitch in the interview when Rob Patterson asked Jeremiah for his thoughts regarding September 11, the upcoming anniversary of Apostle Bartholomew's martyrdom. BL prophesies that he will be released from prison on that date and rocket back to fame by the end of the year. Comments?

Jeremiah chuckled and adjusted his jacket. He said that he felt sure God's will would be done, and everyone nodded. Right answer.

The host urged him to share the story of his humble beginnings, and here's where he took me by surprise. The story he told on national television was not the same one he told me.

He talked about living in a small house beside an apple orchard when he was a boy. It was his dream to climb to the top of the biggest tree and pick the most beautiful apple he'd ever seen. During his climb, he lost his grip and fell. He hit his head, and God came to Jeremiah and

told him that He'd save him if he promised to go forth and heal other broken people like himself. Thus, his name became his Promise to God.

Try as I might to put it out of my mind, one niggling technicality would not leave me alone: Jeremiah lied to one of us—either to me or to everyone else.

I worked myself up to ask Jeremiah about the discrepancies in his story later that evening. Jeremiah explained that the purpose of telling an origin story is to communicate the moral, not the facts. No one cares how *exactly* he came by his healing powers. They don't want to be disappointed by a dull or unrelatable story. Rather than bore people with a lot of backstory about the ferry system near his childhood home, he opted to tie in well-recognized Biblical symbols—the tree, the apple. People trust that which is familiar, and trust is an essential ingredient in healing.

I suppose he's right. Storytelling is a powerful agent of inspiration. Stories are the building blocks of understanding, so the more emotionally impactful they are, the better. To what degree does it matter if stories are fiction, so long as they convey meaningful lessons?

Perhaps my fidelity to truth is too idealistic. The straightforward principles of my provincial life are struggling to survive outside that protected sphere. The world is complicated. Sometimes, exceptions must be made. Trouble is, I'm starting to lose count of them.

Monday, September 6

I can't shake this cold. Seems like I'm always sick these days. What's wrong with me? Nothing major, I hope. When my period was late a second time, worry began to creep in. *Can't be. Not possible,* repeats the voice of reason over and over until it takes the shape of a mantra. Jeremiah Promise didn't just treat my cancer—he *cured* it. Surely lightning can't strike me twice.

Frequent colds and angst—these may be the phantoms of sleep. Insomnia may be the real culprit. Night after night, I approach the pillow with hope, but as soon as the lights click off, I am wide awake and ready to get back to work. Sometimes my mind spins with thoughts and impressions from the day, but not always. Sometimes I'm simply alert, watchful, waiting for something to happen. What is it?

SUNDAY, SEPTEMBER 19

Jude has become ever-present at the Crusades. He's always within my line of sight. The shift in his behavior was so subtle that I almost didn't notice it. At first, I thought I was imagining things. About half a dozen times, I felt this inexplicable itch to speak to him, looked up, and there he was.

Does it have something to do with the Dennis Horton incident? Jude's hovering seems to trace back to that day. If it's concern that has provoked this change in his behavior, then I appreciate that. It's also entirely possible that he has flagged me as a liability and intends to keep a close eye on me. I'd like to thank him for rescuing me the other day, but I have been too shy and too ashamed to do it. The situation was embarrassing and awkward, and he was right—I should have asked for his assistance. He's the security expert.

Last week, I tried baking my thanks into a batch of cookies and presenting them to him in a fancy tin. But Jude wouldn't accept them. He took one look, shook his head, and continued setting up the microphone. I left the cookies near his backpack. He never touched them. They remain right where I left them.

Jude perplexes me. He doesn't seem to like me, but still, he hovers.

MONDAY, SEPTEMBER 20

Somebody (unknown, possibly an usher) captured behind-the-scenes footage of the volunteers consolidating the offering baskets and counting out the money. The video was posted on YouTube and received two hundred views and a few nasty comments about the "religious-industrial complex" before Carmen had it removed.

Jeremiah announced the new policy today that everyone must turn in their cell phones before the Crusade. No more secret backstage photos or videos. Jude will outfit us with radios and earpieces.

TUESDAY, SEPTEMBER 21

The Crusades are starting to blend together. I see lots of new faces but hear many of the same stories. Arthritic hands, malignant tumors, birth defects, lost jobs, learning disabilities—I fear that I am slowly growing insensitive to the plight of the individual. I try to remember all the names, faces, and conversations, but no matter how many of them I hold onto, even more scatter from my memory. No matter. Thoughtful touches and personal details are less important than confidence and diplomacy, I've learned.

Good posture is the key to projecting confidence. Sure, I've heard this plenty of times before, but practice makes perfect. It's helpful to see the difference in strangers' reactions when I stride up to them with chin up and shoulders square. People are more comfortable sharing personal information with me when I act like the one in charge.

I've discovered that the best way to appear confident is to *believe* that I am. Never mind that errant hair or dark fleck of something stuck to the tip of my nose. As long as I feel good, I look good. Most people are more willing to believe the self-image that I project than they are to believe their own eyes.

Jeremiah has been coaching me in techniques for building rapport with strangers as quickly as possible. Though he's never called it this, I believe the method he employs is something known as "cold reading."

If I see that a woman's fingers are swollen or bent, for instance, I should ask her about her arthritis. She's usually delighted that I noticed and more than happy to tell me about it. If I see a man with a walker who favors one leg, I should ask him about his hip pain. If it's his back rather than his hip that troubles him, he'll correct me without calling attention to my mistake. People can be wonderfully lenient.

People often give subconscious cues to their discomfort. A tilted head or jutted chin may point toward a subtler malady. A touch or tap may reveal a point of agitation, whereas a protective hand may cover a source of pain. When all else fails, there are probabilities to fall back on. Heart troubles and diabetes are statistically favorable presumptions.

At first, I found this practice uncomfortable. It felt wrong to base our work on so many guesses and assumptions. But Jeremiah explained that it's the only way we can help as many people as we do.

"In this fast-paced environment, it's not possible to discern and con-firm every single data point," he said. His connection to God requires considerable energy and focus. He cannot afford to tire quickly during the Crusades, so sometimes, we must use our ordinary powers of per-

ception to approximate the truth and keep things moving. I suppose Jeremiah is right.

Constant practice improves my intuition and powers of observation. The old adage is proving false: books *can* be judged by their covers. People reveal more about themselves than they think. Every detail, from shoes, clothing, accessories, and haircut, to posture, carriage, eye contact, expression, and age, is part of the story that people wish to tell.

Alas, most of these stories fly in one ear and out the other. I have no time or energy to contemplate them all.

FRIDAY, OCTOBER 8

Bartholomew Lambrecht was released from prison today.

In an interview on the news this morning, his lawyer explained that several critical pieces of evidence were obtained illegally. Without these, the prosecution had no case. They called a mistrial. Just like that, it was over, and Bartholomew Lambrecht was free to go.

I sprinted barefoot to Jeremiah's door. Even from a distance, his distress was palpable. I wanted to be there for him, to listen, to talk, to rant, or to sit together in silence—whatever he needed.

I knocked and knocked but received no answer. I waited and waited, but the pool house windows remained dark. Had he risen early and left? His car was in the garage. I could *feel* him close by. I sent him several text messages, but he didn't respond. Finally, I retreated back to my apartment to wait. I will wait all day if that's what it takes.

When my phone dinged in the early afternoon, I was disappointed to find a message from Freddie, not Jeremiah. Freddie wanted to meet for coffee, but I declined. What if Jeremiah resurfaced while I was gone?

I couldn't stray far. We've been working so hard to put that part of his life behind him. This must be quite a shock for him. What now? Will BL try to contact Jeremiah? Will he seek retaliation for Jeremiah's testimony at the first trial?

I've gleaned only slivers and shreds of the rumors surrounding BL's case (we've been avoiding news and updates as much as possible), but the bits that I've pieced together are frightening. Supposedly, he has laundered money with the mafia and has ties to the KKK.

Rather than succumb to hysteria, I did some research online. I learned that BL was indicted on eight counts of wire fraud and twelve counts of mail fraud. That's all. There's plenty of hearsay circulating on the Internet, but these twenty instances of fraud are the official units of truth.

I don't know how to feel now. Sick? Sad? Relieved? I wish I could comfort Jeremiah. Draw out the poison. But he must need his space, so I will let him be.

Monday, October 11

His eerie silence continues, despite yesterday's Crusade.

I was glad to have confirmation of life, at least. Jeremiah's whole face was marked *Do Not Disturb*, so I didn't dare. His sermon was tepid, and his anointing was robotic. He seemed to be going through the motions, waiting for it to end so he could retreat into the gloom.

Freddie invited me to lunch today, and I was more than happy to accept. It was a relief to see a friendly face. Seldom have I felt so at ease opening up to another person—particularly one I haven't known for long. I'm used to being the one that listens attentively while others pour their hearts out. Freddie's sincere interest and nods of encouragement made it easy to elaborate on my every thought and feeling. I talked so much that two-thirds of my salad still remained by the time Freddie's plate was clean.

He took advantage of a short pause in my story to slip a small, black pouch out of his jacket pocket and excuse himself from the table. When he returned, he noticed my curious glance and flushed self-consciously. It was insulin, he explained. He gave himself a shot after every meal.

"But I thought you said I healed you!" I exclaimed.

"Of course, you healed me—of the *stutter*," Freddie smiled. That's the wish he held foremost in his mind when we first shook hands. That's how that works. Maybe some other time, we could shake hands again, and I could heal his diabetes.

Sometimes I question whether Freddie is serious. He's a bit eccentric, and his demeanor can come across as childish, but once in a while, I catch a glimpse of a mastermind crouching low.

For the time being, I shrugged and changed the subject. It was Freddie's turn to talk while I finished my meal. I expected him to be glad to have the floor, but he wasn't. He sat further back in his chair, fidgeted with his napkin, and gave only brief, uncertain answers.

"Just fine, thanks."

"Not much."

"Oh, yes, I agree."

It bothered me that he was so reserved after I had just spent the last hour pouring out my heart. My agitation quickly came to a head, and I rushed our lunch to its conclusion by drawing his attention to the time. Freddie's eyes widened with alarm. He tried to keep me talking by switching back to a previous topic, but I was determined to go.

Now that I am back at the apartment, restless and alone, I wonder why I was in such a hurry to get here. We were having a good time at the restaurant, weren't we? I puzzled over the incident for some time. It was a welcome respite from my incessant worry about Jeremiah Promise. I guess I felt . . . unsafe . . . when Freddie wasn't equally as frank and open as I was. That put me off-balance. I thought something must be wrong. It didn't *feel* wrong—it felt natural and peaceful, but it defied my expectations.

It occurs to me that Freddie probably isn't accustomed to speaking at length, considering that he's had a stutter all his life. While others practiced the skills of self-expression, Freddie developed the art of attentive listening. He means well—better than most, I'm inclined to think. Sometimes, I get too wrapped up in the feelings of the moment and forget to consider others' perspectives.

TUESDAY, OCTOBER 12

At the last minute, Jeremiah decided he wasn't up to facilitating Grace Group and dropped the responsibility on me. That was a bit of a shock, but it was ultimately for the best.

Eight people showed up. A robust turnout. It took quite some time to get the group on task, as all my efforts to direct the discussion were thwarted by questions and speculation about Jeremiah Promise. Where was he? What was he doing? Had I heard this or that about him? What about the mistrial? Will he and Bartholomew Lambrecht reconcile?

At first, I was puzzled by this indefatigable obsession with the Man Himself. Everyone in the room seemed to have a grade-school crush on our fearless leader. We might as well have spent the hour doodling his name in our notebooks and attempting to sort out whom he intended

to take to the dance.

As I looked around the room and considered each person, I realized something. Seven of them were married; four had spouses present. Three were seniors. None of them were likely romantic candidates for Jeremiah, yet they all seemed to be, well, in love with him. Perhaps it was a different kind of love, like that of a baby duckling imprinting on its mother. Even in his absence—especially in his absence—these folks seemed to have an unshakable urge to follow in his every footstep.

Is this how I behave around Jeremiah?

THURSDAY, OCTOBER 14

Jeremiah came back to Grace Group tonight. Thankfully, his hiatus was brief. This freed me up to experiment more with active listening.

Freddie-inspired reflections have led me to several hypotheses about tip-top attentiveness. For starters: pure listening is possible only when I empty myself of self and become an open vessel. There must be room inside me for others' thoughts, attitudes, and feelings before I can imbibe them. Also, self-consciousness is an obstacle to self-emptying. When I'm too focused on myself, that preoccupation depletes the finite quantities of energy and attention I have to share with others.

Attention is a precious resource, often in short supply. People want to be seen, heard, and understood. When I meet this demand with my own eyes, ears, and mind, there is no limit to our depth of connection.

I practiced this new kind of listening today. It was challenging. I could only sustain that level of concentration for minutes at a time, but even that much was revealing. I discovered that with the earnest urge to connect comes a peculiar, sometimes painful sensation of dilation in my heart and mind. Tunnels seemed to open through which raw feelings and ideas flowed directly to my core.

Kendra Viks was my primary subject of interest tonight. I spent extra time with her before and after the meeting, absorbing her story like a sponge. With each minute I focused on her, I seemed to drift farther from myself—like a child loosening her grip on the swimming pool edge and preparing to let go.

Kendra Viks was a pale, youngish woman with short, curly hair and big dark eyes. She arrived pushing a walker ahead of her. The doctors didn't know why her pain was so bad. Most days, she could barely walk. They kept trying to diagnose her with arthritis, but she was sure it wasn't that.

She prayed every day for God to end her suffering. She didn't think she could bear the burden of it much longer. Jeremiah delighted in this woman's faith and assured her that she would feel much better after all was said and done. He made her the centerpiece of the group, laid hands, and prayed over her with gusto. By the end, she was able to walk across the room without assistance.

Something about the whole thing just didn't sit right with me. I couldn't put my finger on it. I didn't doubt Jeremiah's success in healing Kendra Viks. She walked unassisted; we all saw it.

Yet, it felt as if I had vacuumed up a tiny speck of something—dirt, sand, broken glass—when I focused on Kendra with all my might, and it was irritating my innards.

After the meeting, I folded up Kendra's walker and sneaked it out of the room while no one was looking. I caught up with her as she limped down the front steps and implored her to take the walker with her, just in case. Maybe she would never need it again. I hoped so, but . . .

There was a reason Kendra's story hit me particularly hard, but it

took some time to figure it out. In her, I saw not only the visage of my mother—same curls, same dark eyes—but I also heard the echo of a very familiar story.

I don't remember a time before Mom's mysterious suffering began. She was always in pain, spent years visiting various doctors and clinics, but never received any definitive answers. She submitted to surgeries and pills with unpronounceable names, but none of them fixed her. Sometimes she would spend days confined to bed, moaning and apologizing.

According to my mom, she was a very vigorous woman. She loved telling stories of the horses she had ridden, the trees she had climbed, and the boys she had beaten at softball, and I believed them all. We all wanted to believe her, even though her account didn't quite line up with reality. By the time I graduated from high school, she walked with a cane. We talked about things like this as if they were temporary setbacks, and yet Mom's troubles were the fragile furniture of my life for thirty-something years.

"What happened?" I once overheard her ponder aloud as she gazed at herself in the mirror. That question went unanswered, as did others— for instance, what kind of God would allow so much suffering?

A doctor once recommended that Mom make an appointment with a psychiatrist. She never did. Her troubles were physical, she declared. It was a waste of time and money to chase down shadows of things past. But I wasn't so sure. I couldn't help but wonder if somewhere beneath her tenacious facade lay a tangled heap of grief.

Friday, October 15

I wonder if a degree in astrophysics would help me calculate the pattern of Jeremiah's shifting moods. Lately, they've been utterly inscrutable. I spend a lot of time wondering what I did wrong.

"Where were you?" Jeremiah demanded to know when I returned from lunch with Freddie a few days ago. He obviously had his suspicions, but I couldn't imagine why they were so severe. I told Jeremiah about Freddie, and Jeremiah retorted that "bad company ruins good morals." He chastised me for fraternizing with a member of our flock.

This seemed like an overreaction. Why did Jeremiah assume Freddie was bad company? What did he think we were doing together? I told him that it was *just* lunch, but Jeremiah didn't believe me.

On Wednesday, Jeremiah scheduled a meeting with a potential investor at the same time as Grace Group. He left me to facilitate once again. I chose to see it as a good thing that he considers me capable of handling the group, but it felt more like an ambush than an honor.

Thursday evening group was a completely different story. Jeremiah was bubbly and charismatic. He showered me with confiding smiles and secret glances and finished the event with a rousing speech about God's unwavering love.

Then back again, the other way, he bounced during today's crew meeting. We should rename it the Jeremiah & Carmen Quibble Show. The two of them spent the entire hour arguing. To be fair, it's usually Carmen that starts it. Her frequent interjections are approaching an unprofessional level. Her brash remarks seemed designed to provoke him, and eventually, he bites back.

Something seems to be "off" with her lately. Whenever she's in the vicinity, I can sense her like a coming storm. Last week, I heard a snippet of a phone conversation between Carmen and her husband. She was vehemently defending her right to work long hours and take business trips. Perhaps tensions at home are bleeding into her work life.

After the meeting today, I stayed after to chat with Jeremiah.

I asked him, "How are things?"

"How are things? Good! Great, actually!" he exclaimed. He ticked off several upcoming ministry developments on his fingers, all of which he was excited about (none of which he had mentioned at the meeting).

I attempted to engage him in further discussion, but he just propped up his side of the conversation with, "Yep . . . yep . . . yep," until he received a phone call and had to leave the room.

I don't understand him. I'm trying hard to stick to the rose-colored conjecture that it's not personal. Jeremiah is under a lot of pressure and may still be processing the Bartholomew Lambrecht situation. I wonder if either of them has attempted to make contact—that might explain some of this weird tension.

MONDAY, OCTOBER 18

So much for our special Sabbath. It's slowly slipping out of existence as Mondays fill up with meetings, consultations, and ministry miscellany.

TUESDAY, OCTOBER 19

I was hunched over the keyboard, wholly absorbed in a series of infinitesimal kerning adjustments on our ministry poster, when Freddie called. He had two tickets for a musical performance in Austin, and he wanted me to join him.

I initially declined. All this work to do, so little time. Freddie persuaded me that I deserved one night off. Besides, Jeremiah was gone. Where did he get off to? He never tells me anymore. I guess that means I don't owe him any explanations, either.

We had a few hours to talk during the drive down to Austin. Freddie said more than I've ever heard him say before. He told me about his various collections—antique gumball machines, vintage magazines, Christmas village figurines, and so on. He also revealed that he has an exceptional fascination with birds. All kinds of birds—large, small, pretty, and plain. He could recite the genus and species of just about every type of bird in Texas. Quite a few birds live in the tree outside his home, and he likes to watch them. Sometimes he talks to them. Sometimes they talk back. I glimpsed that mischievous gleam in Freddie's eye again, and it made me wonder how much of what he said was earnest and how much was teasing.

We went to a small venue on East Sixth Street. The headliner was Ross Strickland and Co. I'd never heard of them before and had no idea what to expect. Freddie refused to tell me. He said it was always better to approach art without preconceptions.

The band assumed positions and began playing for about fifteen minutes before the frontman ambled up on stage and tuned his guitar. When he was ready to go, he introduced himself as Ross Strickland and said he had a story to tell. He wanted his audience to know where he had come from and why he was there.

Ross had been an addict all his life, dependent on everything imaginable—drugs, alcohol, gambling, love. The people that knew him ex-

pected him to turn up dead any day. *Oh, that guy is still alive?* They'd say. *Unbelievable.*

About eighteen months ago, with the help of Jesus Christ, he was saved in Houston and finally sobered up for good. Now his pain is our pleasure. He plays his soul out at every performance because every performance is his second chance at life.

He warned us that his stage antics might seem extreme. People might think that his performance was a display of conceit. Indeed, he tended to get caught up in the moment. Sometimes he even cheered himself on. But he didn't do it out of arrogance. He was really cheering for God because he's God's instrument now.

The music that followed *was* extraordinary. It began with slow, throbbing blues and ended with some of the wildest rock and roll I've ever heard. Ross Strickland ended up sprawled on the floor, spinning in circles and playing so fast that it wasn't hard to believe he was channeling a force greater than himself.

The words of Ross Strickland that resonated with me most were, "My pain is your pleasure."

To think: pain could be a useful thing. I've only ever thought of it as an unwanted side effect. I thought it evidence of weakness, but perhaps it is a sign of strength. Maybe even a form of power.

Freddie and I discussed the performance as we walked back to the car. He admitted that he was personally acquainted with Ross Strickland. They had met at the Houston Revival summer before last. It clicked. *Oh!* That was the same time that the musician said he sobered up. At a Revival? Had he been healed by faith? Freddie smiled and shrugged. *Maybe.*

We had one more stop to make before we headed back: Barton Springs. It was a large outdoor pool fed by a natural spring. Half was rectangular, and the other half gradually petered off to irregular, rocky shallows. The bottom of the pool was carpeted with aquatic plants, and the water flickered with salamanders and tiny fish.

At that late hour, we had the place all to ourselves. We took off our shoes and socks and dangled our feet in the calm, clear water. The minnows darted curiously at our toes. I couldn't stop giggling, and Freddie was amused by my delight. When I looked at him, my heart surged with gratitude. I reached for his arm and squeezed it.

When ten o'clock rolled around, I was struck by a frenzy of yawns. Freddie made a nest of coats in the back seat and suggested that I take a nap while he drove the three hours to Dallas.

As the steady hum of the highway lulled me toward sleep, I gave silent thanks for Freddie. He has a gift for popping up when I need him.

Thursday, October 21

Grace Group is officially mine. This time the role change is permanent. Jeremiah claimed that he doesn't have time to facilitate so small a group for so little money. He would prefer to focus on private healing sessions while I counsel the "regulars."

At this point, I'm okay with taking the lead. It has bothered me to notice how little engaged Jeremiah has been lately. His attention and passion seem to be directed elsewhere. I asked to borrow his Crusade blazer on meeting nights, figuring that if people could see it, touch it, and pray with it, they might find the absence of the Man Himself more tolerable.

Group went smoothly this evening. The difficulty of the day lay in what happened beforehand. I accidentally perceived too much.

A woman named Cora Jamison showed up fifteen minutes before the meeting to privately discuss her concern about her young daughter, Isabel. Cora believed that Isabel was possessed by the demon Asmodeus and that this demon was causing the girl to have terrible nightmares and exhibit "naughty" behaviors. She was reluctant to be more specific, but I gleaned that these naughty behaviors were of a sexual nature.

Cora confessed that she could not afford a private healing session with Jeremiah, but she begged me to put in a good word with him. God willing, he would call Isabel to the stage at the next Crusade and cast out her demon. Would I please tell him that the girl's mother desperately missed her sweet little girl?

As we spoke, I observed Cora closely. She was a short, soft-spoken woman with greasy brown hair that hung in a braid over her shoulder. Something about her face was slightly off-kilter. There was a bluish tint at one corner of her mouth. Was that the stain of something she ate? The side effect of a medication? A trick of the light?

When she turned her head, her braid shifted to reveal a part of her neck that had previously been covered. I saw several faint brown lines on her skin. Bruises in the shape of a handprint.

On the hand that brushed loose strands from her face: a wedding ring. A few minutes later, her husband came into the church and complained that she was taking too long. She flinched when he touched her shoulder. Poor Cora. Poor Isabel. It would seem the whole family was ill, possessed by something dark, indeed—but not demons.

Here is where assumptions lead me into trouble. I see more and more things that are none of my business, and then I jump to conclusions so quickly that the line blurs between conjecture and proof. I struggle to withhold judgment, but intuition won't be denied. If I try to ignore it, the suspicious details scrub round and round in my mind, abrading my

psyche like steel wool. What am I to do with these inklings? Should I take action? Should I tell someone? I've tried talking to Jeremiah about this a few times, but he just warns me away from gossip.

Friday, October 22

I dreamed that Jeremiah and I were standing near the pulpit of a big, beautiful church. No one else was around. We were talking and laughing—and then he kissed me. He *kissed me!* At long last, we'd arrived at that blissful place where nothing else in the world mattered.

Then I remembered that I had forgotten my sketchpad in the coat room. I had to have it, but I didn't want to lose Jeremiah. I pleaded with him to come with me, but he refused. He'd wait for me at the pulpit, he promised.

As I walked up the aisle, the carpet turned to grass, and the pews flattened into stepping-stones. Trickling tributaries of blue-green water flowed between the rocks and formed a rushing stream. The current caught my foot and swept me away.

I awoke in distress. Why, oh why haven't I told him how I feel? What am I waiting for? All those long, meaningful looks and deep conversations are slowly fading away. I assumed he must know by now how I feel, but maybe he doesn't. Perhaps my prince is under a platonic spell that can only be broken by speaking the magic incantations aloud. What are they? I'd dearly like to know. I suspect the fully-formed words are bunched up inside the lump that catches in my throat from time to time. It's the source of many aches, both above and below. Enough! It's time to speak—to come clean, know the worst, and move on.

WEDNESDAY, OCTOBER 27

Jeremiah returned very late last night. Fragments of headlights slid across my ceiling as he pulled into the garage. I started to put on my shoes, meaning to go over to the pool house to talk to him, but I thought better of it. He might interpret this as an intrusion of his privacy, and I didn't want to press on our already-fragile connection. I decided to leave him be and speak with him in the morning.

I waited until ten o'clock, hoping Jeremiah would emerge into broad daylight on his own. He didn't. Eventually, I had no choice but to knock at his door. I needed the car keys. Several days ago, I asked to borrow his car (to visit Freddie, but I didn't tell him that part), and he agreed. But then he made a show of scheduling today as his "solitary contemplation" day—in other words, he didn't *want* the car, and he didn't want to be disturbed, either.

The Jeremiah that came to the door was not one that I had seen before. His hair was disheveled, his chin bristly. There were dark circles under his eyes. I couldn't imagine what had effected this change, but a thread of intuition tugged me away from that line of inquiry. I did not want to tempt him to pry by prying myself.

I told him that I had errands to run. He looked at me ominously and handed me the keys as he quoted Matthew 7:15, "Beware of false prophets, who come to you in sheep's clothing but inwardly are ravenous wolves."

This was excessively grim, and it threw me for a loop. I spent a quarter of an hour sitting in the car, mulling things over.

Jeremiah has this uncanny ability to know when I'm going to see my

friend and make me question myself. Does he know something about Freddie that I don't? Freddie *seems* harmless enough. He feels alright to me. I enjoy his company. So far, he's been nothing but a good friend. I concluded that *maybe* Freddie hides some deep, dark secret—maybe everybody does!—and I'd just have to trust my own judgment and proceed with caution. Then I shook my head to clear it, started the ignition, and headed out.

Freddie lives in the smallish town of Fate, Texas; past long rows of warehouses and broad stretches of farmland. I eased off the highway onto a frontage road fit for a giant, doubled back through a portal beneath, and was greeted on the other side by a colonnade of telephone poles ready and waiting to escort me the rest of the way. I drove slowly on the sun-bleached asphalt, careful to avoid the deepest of its jagged cracks and fissures. A sagging fence trotted alongside the car like a shaggy mongrel. Children's toys and lawn ornaments were strewn about various yards. Sparks flew as a welder leaned low over a piece of sheet metal propped on sawhorses.

I was supposed to take the first right and follow that road until I found him. I was doubtful of these instructions, but Freddie assured me that I'd know his house when I saw it.

Indeed, I did.

Freddie had not exaggerated when he told me that "quite a few" birds lived in the tree in front of his house. I could hear the cacophony of chirps, chatters, and caws well before I could see it. From a distance, the tree appeared to be overladen with fruit of every size, shape, and color. As I drew near, I saw that the tree was ornamented with dozens— perhaps hundreds—of birdhouses. I parked the car and hopped across the yard to get a better look. The creak of a screen door alerted me to Freddie's approach. He came and stood beside me, his eyes shining

brightly. This was his masterpiece, he told me. He was honored that I had come to see it.

We walked around the tree while he pointed out his favorite bird-*homes*. He had a story for each one and for the birds that inhabited them. He could name any bird to which I pointed.

"Oh yeah, that's Dante," he'd say. "Dante and Lightning hatched three chicks this year."

Freddie invited me inside for lunch. A spread of crustless bologna cheese sandwiches and canned peaches awaited us. I was transported back to summer days of long ago when I made lunches like these and ate them standing over the sink. After lunch, Freddie excused himself to go take his insulin shot. When he returned, I had questions for him. How long had he been doing this? Did he tire of it? Did it hurt?

Freddie explained that he'd been taking shots every day since he was ten years old. It didn't bother him—he hoped it didn't bother me.

I asked him if he'd ever had serious problems with it. Freddie shrugged. Sure, once in a long while, his sugar levels would get wonky, but he could usually feel it and make adjustments before anything really bad happened.

Freddie lit up. "I know! How about if you cure me right now?" He put out his hand. I shook my head. Heck no! Sorry, Fred, I can't cure anybody of anything. That's Jeremiah Promise's job.

He said that's okay and chuckled. He knew I could do it if I *really* wanted to. In fact, he's convinced that I healed my cancer, not Jeremiah Promise, but I would have to come around to that notion in my own time. He could wait.

Freddie lit up again and said he wanted to show me some things, but they were in other rooms. He led the way down a dim hallway, past staggered stacks of old magazines and newspapers. They were coated with dust. These belonged to his mother, he explained. She liked to collect things.

He pushed aside a stack of cardboard boxes to get at the door behind them. This must have been a sitting room in some past life. Now, it brimmed with antique candy dispensers of every shape and kind. He intended to fix them up. Once they were back in service, he could double his territory, easy. Expand the business, maybe even hire some help. Freddie pointed out an angular, chrome-finished behemoth in the corner with a dusty display window and a perky array of pinball plungers. That one was the first machine that his father had acquired in 1962. Freddie intended to oil that one up, fix a couple of springs, and set it up in the Galleria next month.

I crouched down to examine a glass globe that still contained a few stale gumballs and asked him how long he'd lived here. All his life, he said. He was born here, lived here with his mama for many years, and took over the house after her passing.

We retreated to the front steps to drink tea and chat for a while. A shadow seemed to have slowly come over Freddie. His shoulders hunched forward, and his laugh seemed forced. There was a distance in his eyes that I could not account for.

Finally, he said something to the point. "Do you think we are friends?"

I affirmed that we were.

"Do you think we are good enough friends to share secrets?"

I said I thought so. I guess it depended on what it was.

"I have a secret," he said. "Some people would say it's a bad thing, but I don't think it is."

He was ready to show it to me, but I had to go with him to the bedroom to see it. The bedroom? Oh. I cautiously followed him inside, prepared to bolt if anything went sideways. Freddie's bedroom must

have been the smallest room in the house, barely big enough to fit a twin bed and a dresser. I wondered why he would choose to stay in there when he had the run of the house.

Freddie squeezed around the bed and went to open the closet door. He disappeared for a minute. I waited just outside the room and peeked around the doorframe. Curiosity tugged at my collar, and apprehension tugged at my sleeve. I'd like to say that I knew the man well enough to defend his character in front of God and everyone, but when it came down to just him, me, and the moment of truth alone together in his rustic rambler, all bets were off. I couldn't rest easy until I knew the nature of this secret.

There were rustling noises, and then a puffy purple, prom-looking dress appeared.

"What do you think?" he asked.

I wasn't sure what he meant. I said the dress was very striking. Freddie held it under his chin and smoothed the fabric against his chest.

Oh.

It took a moment to understand.

Oh!

"The color looks nice on you," I ventured.

"You think so?"

"Yes. Do you?"

Freddie wasn't sure. There was no mirror in the room, and he was not allowed to take the dresses out. His mother had been very clear about that. The sweat on his brow dripped on the fabric as Freddie looked down at himself and then back up at me. His eyes had become very large, and his mouth had become very small, and I feared that in another moment, he might burst into tears. I couldn't bear that, so I offered to retrieve a mirror from somewhere in the house and bring it to him. In fact, that was an excuse to walk away for a few minutes and pull myself together.

Freddie told me where I could find his toolbox. I went to get a screwdriver and took down the mirror from his bathroom. When I returned, Freddie had put on the dress. His face was a mush of emotions. I smiled warmly at him to set the tone, and chanted, "Mirror, mirror, on the wall."

The room was so cramped and Freddie so tall that it was difficult for him to see much of his reflection. I hugged the mirror to my chest and contorted at various angles to provide a better view. We figured out that if he stood in one corner and I knelt on the bed in the diagonal corner, he could see everything from the knee up.

Freddie gazed intently at the glass. He turned this way and that to view different angles. At first, I felt acutely uncomfortable with the way his eyes traced every detail of the figure before him. He appeared to be looking at me—but I was only the mirror bearer, and when I glanced down, it was Freddie's body that I saw.

"You look very nice," I said.

Freddie explained that this dress was special because it was the only one he had gone out and bought on his own. The lady at the thrift store in Austin had helped him pick it out. He had told her he was buying it for his sister. He was pretty sure she knew the truth, but she helped him anyway. Her kindness meant the world to him.

He had other dresses. He opened his closet door wide to show me a whole rack of them. The rest had belonged to his mother. She had been a large woman. Though they had never discussed it openly, his mother knew about his preference and was quietly sympathetic. Twice a year, she used to fill a box with clothes to donate to the church rummage sale. That box always sat out on the back porch for a week or longer. Why

would she let it sit for so long if she didn't want him to sneak a peek and take out a few pretty things to keep? If she noticed pieces missing, she never said a word.

Freddie's smile faded. "Daddy wasn't keen on it, though," he said.

When he was about thirteen, Freddie's father found the collection of women's clothing that he kept hidden under his bed. He forced Freddie to cut up the clothes with his hunting knife and throw them in the fire. "Sissies are sinners in God's eyes," his father chastised him. He made Freddie pull down his pants and lean over the kitchen table while he pressed a hot iron to Freddie's backside. This was to teach him about sissy hell, his father said.

I hugged Freddie and told him I was so, so sorry. He didn't deserve that. No one did, not from a father. Freddie said it was okay. The past didn't trouble him. He had forgiven his father a long time ago.

He was eager to turn the conversation back toward dresses since he didn't often get to discuss them with anyone else. We took turns describing celebrity gowns and dream dresses in considerable detail. Freddie's delight was as contagious as a dry brush fire.

His laughter abruptly ceased, and after a timid pause, he asked if he could kiss me. Flustered, I shook my head and patted Freddie's arm.

"Because I'm wearing a dress?" he asked.

No, it wasn't that. I told him there was only room for one in the romantic part of my heart, and that space was already occupied. But Freddie was and always would be a dear friend, and he had a place in a different section of my heart.

Freddie guessed who that "one" person was, and I confirmed it.

"Does he make you happy?" Freddie asked.

"Yes, sometimes," I said.

I suddenly felt listless and cold, as if a dense cloud of condensation had just vacated my body. Freddie and I lay shoulder to shoulder on his bed and drifted off into silent contemplation.

I thought about the intimacy that Freddie and I shared. Intimacy, now there's a word with a wealth of underutilized dimensions. It is often reduced to an ordinary euphemism, but its greater worth may be found in this riddle: name the means by which one embraces tightest without touching and plunges deepest without spilling a drop of blood.

I don't know if the word is paradoxical by nature or if we humans make it so. It seems that most of us want to shun the emotional closeness that we crave. It's rare to float comfortably in a state of intimacy without fearing for one's safety—but that's where *being* becomes the essential part of being there for another person.

I may have briefly dozed off. Sleep is such a simple thing around Freddie—I don't know why it's so unattainable most other times. Around midnight, Freddie roused me by telling me that I was the most peaceful person he'd ever met. Now there's a truly great compliment.

Friday, October 29

A beautiful galaxy of understanding has clicked into focus. I was wired all night because my mind was busy dashing through the avenues and alleyways of epiphany.

It's huge. Massive. Life-changing! I have figured out the secret of *why people like me*.

Because I'm a "good" person, right? That's what I've spent my whole life believing. I have spared no expense pursuing excellence. The better my character, intelligence, and accomplishments, I thought, the more people would like me.

Yet, no matter how hard I worked to improve myself, I couldn't win everyone's favor. There were always stubborn outliers, and their distaste for me hurt me deeply. I just assumed I must be transparent to those people, and they could see some horrible flaw deep inside me that others couldn't. Silly notion! Human bodies are opaque. When we look at each other, our eyes explore the surfaces, not the depths. We search for what is familiar and favor it over what is foreign. In fact, we tend to look for *ourselves* in the reflections of other people. We are a bunch of walking, talking mirrors that gravitate toward the ones that show us favorable impressions of ourselves and recoil from the ones that expose our shortcomings.

I have encountered more than a few people over the years who didn't seem to engage with reality. I envision them wandering through life as if it were a funhouse mirror maze, always reacting strongly to others' perceived judgments without realizing that they were merely reflections of themselves.

This reminds me once again that self-consciousness has no place in ideal social encounters. Preoccupations and insecurities only muddy the reflections we share with others. Perhaps we prize confidence so highly because it bounces brisk, refreshing self-assurance off everyone around it. Does Empathy play a role in this? Empathy is a universal language of sorts. Being extra sensitive to the feelings of others enables a person to perceive truths about other people that they can't or won't express any other way. Understanding a person's emotional ailment enables another to discern the remedy and reflect it back to them.

It saddens me to think that most people I meet in life may never look past the mirror image. They may seek affirmation or solace from others and be satisfied or dissatisfied with what they get, but still not think to look beyond what they see. Not care about the live person they're

projecting onto—who *I am*, what I've done, where I've been.

I wish I could use this discovery to help people! But knowing something about human nature doesn't change it. People are set in their ways. Best to understand and accept that they are this way. Only a few will ever look past their own reflections. Those few are worth their weight in gold.

Thursday, November 11

I dreamed that I was picking apples while the sun went down. The apples grew inside thick, thorny brambles that tore at my hair and clothes. I had to get down on my hands and knees and crawl through narrow tunnels in the shrubs to reach them. But I pressed onward, determined to fill my bucket before sunset.

Friday, November 19

A man named Carlton Percy came to the group tonight seeking deliverance from addiction. I told him that Jeremiah was unavailable to lay hands on him, but I'd be happy to schedule a private appointment. After the meeting, Carlton pulled me aside and told me that I'd "do." He only wanted to confess, and he could do that here and now if I was willing to listen. He didn't mind that I was neither a priest nor a pastor, so I heard him out.

Why did I do such a foolish thing? I could claim that I was overeager to throw my heart wide open, listen impartially, consider different perspectives, and improve lives by affirming others. But let's be hon-

est—the real reason was vanity. The man's flattery was a trick, and I was an easy mark.

Carlton Percy was a man with tastes for some very dark and twisted deeds. His pale blue eyes locked onto mine as he described his proclivities to me. When my mind dilated with compassion, volumes of suffering and shame poured into me. I absorbed every drop of his darkness, and it stayed with me long after he was gone. I could not close my eyes without conjuring up visions of sliced flesh and smashed fingers and . . .

Other, worse things.

What creates such strange desires? Do they result from trauma? Nature? Nurture? I want to understand. Sometimes the source of a person's suffering is buried so deep inside that he can't reach it or see it himself. Outside perspectives may be of use in such cases. Empathy normally helps.

Unfortunately, I did not gain much insight into Carlton Percy's source of suffering today. He blinded me with pain before I crossed the threshold. I suspect that this was his intent from the beginning. I perceived the sickly-sweet tinge of rapture in his aura as he narrated the particularly awful details of his story. He had come to share, not to confess. It took me hours to realize that the deep despair I felt wasn't even mine. This made me feel a little better, but it didn't banish the bad things. Once darkness sets in, it isn't easily expelled.

I am utterly exhausted. It takes an enormous amount of energy to keep my heart open after a violation of this magnitude. Must I *feel* everything? Can't I choose what to feel and what not to feel? Is this what Jeremiah goes through week after week? If so, I can't blame him for wanting to run away and hide after every Crusade.

Sunday, November 21

It's been a challenging week. The tough cases keep coming.

Part of me is beginning to dread the Crusades. I know that our mission to help people precedes all other earthly considerations. My feelings on the matter are moot. But when the tides of suffering keep rising higher, buffeting me endlessly like a dinghy on the open sea, I begin to doubt the integrity of my vessel.

Today, I had to intercept a family of seven as they rushed the stage with a wheelchair. I hastily recited the spiel about Jeremiah Promise needing to rest after the service. Then I handed them a pamphlet and quoted his rates for private healing sessions (five hundred dollars per hour, or a sliding scale for qualified candidates).

Zong, the eldest son, dutifully translated for his father. The father, Tsai Fang, shook his head, and with tears in his eyes, he explained that his teenage daughter Hua (the young lady in the wheelchair) had advanced muscular dystrophy.

I bent down to shake Hua's hand. Her curled fingers were rigid, and her arms were thin as sticks. Only her eyes moved; there, I saw sparks of feeling and intelligence.

Tsai Fang lamented that the hospital bills had become insurmountable. He simply could not manage Hua's care anymore, and he would do anything to have Jeremiah Promise lay hands on her. But he couldn't afford to pay. They barely had the money for gas to get here. The whole family spent two weeks living in the van lent to them by their church in Wisconsin. They had come all this way for a chance at a miracle.

Wisconsin! I remarked that this was my home state. That was a mis-

take. Tsai Fang grinned and grasped my hand, desperate that this point of connection might gain him a few extra crumbs of favor. I cleared my throat and tried to look busy as I searched my clipboard for Jeremiah's scholarship forms. For some reason, I couldn't find them. I started to explain that we could, in theory, reduce Jeremiah's private rate by half if they provided proof of financial need. The father shook his head before the son was done translating. No, they could not afford half of Jeremiah's fee. Not a quarter. Not a penny.

There had to be another way. I told the family to sit tight while I went to speak with Jeremiah. Perhaps he would make an exception just this once.

I spotted Jude standing guard outside the pastor's office. Lucky break! Jeremiah was still in the building. He looked up from the Bible spread open on his desk and reluctantly allowed me to explain myself. He then asked if I was referring to the Hmong family that had camped out down the street for the last couple of weekends. He knew them!

Good.

To his credit, Jeremiah did take a minute to think it over. But then he shook his head and declared that it was not his place to subvert God's will. If twice they came to the Crusades, and twice God elected not to call them to the stage, He must not want to heal the child. There was nothing Jeremiah could do.

"That doesn't make sense!" I cried. Didn't Jeremiah heal everybody in the beginning? He just shook his head and turned his attention back to the Bible. I stared at him, but it was as if I had already left the room. It took the last of my strength to go back out there, deliver the bad news, and watch the light dim in seven sets of hopeful eyes. I took down their contact information and said I'd let them know if anything changed. We all knew it was a hollow offer, but there was nothing else I could do.

MONDAY, NOVEMBER 22

Heavy clouds, heavy thoughts, heavy eyelids.

I miss home. It hit me hard this morning, like a cannonball to the gut. Seven months, I've been away. That's a long time to go without a piece of my heart. Missy had more bad news for me last night. She had gone over to check on things and found my basement flooded. A pipe had burst from the sudden, hard freeze. Boxes of Mom and Dave's things had been sitting in water for days, probably ruined.

I had restless dreams last night and woke in the dark with a migraine. Today, I'm weak and exhausted. Can't focus. Is this what a hangover feels like? I spent the whole morning and afternoon on the couch wrapped in a cocoon of blankets. My first choice would have been to sleep the day away. But on and on, night and day, eyes open, eyes shut, all but the few essential hours of rest continue to elude me.

I tried to watch television but found it unsatisfying. I tried to draw, but the pencil wobbled on the paper. There seemed to be nothing to do but close my aching eyes and think. In the early evening, I summoned the strength to get up, get dressed, and take a short walk around the neighborhood. On the way, I passed a few people on the sidewalk and exchanged greetings. This lifted my spirits a little and helped to draw my attention outside my pathetic self. I felt a bit better.

When I returned to the house, I found Jeremiah sitting beside the pool, waiting for me. He confronted me with that familiar refrain, "Where were you?"

I said I went for a walk. Jeremiah feigned amazement. Did I do this often? He told me that the urge to seek external pleasures was a sign of

the Devil's influence. He personally found such time better spent clois-
tered in quiet, solemn reflection.

"Okay," I said.

It seems I can do nothing right.

SUNDAY, NOVEMBER 28

Jeremiah's growing preoccupation with hellfire and damnation has become disturbing. His messages of faith, compassion, and persistence are
losing out to condemnations of sin, demands for aggressive evangeliz-
ing, and calls for financial sacrifice. When did this shift begin? How
long has it taken me to notice?

I attempted to speak to Jeremiah about this before the Crusade. He
shrugged off my concern and insisted that this was what the people
came to hear. He had to be strict to keep them on the righteous path.
The people needed tough love. We were here to save people, not coddle
them, and so on and so on. He said all this very calmly.

Jeremiah then went on stage and delivered a ferocious homily about
Sin's bet with Doubt that she (*she*, he said) could beat him in a race to
the Devil's doorstep. I was surprised the congregation accepted Jeremiah's castigation so readily. They moaned, they wept, they hungered for
his ferocity, unaware that there might be a gentler path to righteousness.

Halfway through the sermon, I tuned it out entirely. My eyes unfo-
cused as I gazed at the audience, and it struck me that a lot of other
things had changed since we first began. The church lights were dimmer.
The music more stirring. The atmosphere hotter.

All those bodies packed into one room created a dense, jungle-like
atmosphere. Fever mingled with fervor. Foreheads grew damp, smiles

softened, and cheeks glowed. People swayed and prayed and lifted their hands skyward, their undulations guided by a primal pulse. I leaned forward to look closely at the faces in the front row and saw languorous expressions and heavily lidded eyes. These people were no less than half-asleep, steeped in the ecstasy of some unseen dream.

Strange, I hadn't noticed this before. It came on slowly. Or did it? There was always ecstasy and exultation; I remember that. But there used to be more liveliness and disarray, more light, in the beginning.

Friday, December 3

My soul is cold. It aches like a frozen finger that has been gripping the slippery lip of sanity for too long. My mind burns. It is infected with the fevered friction of my thoughts. As the tremors of fatigue intensify hour after hour, every muscle fiber forewarns that a great ripping and tearing and rending of flesh lies just ahead.

What? What's wrong with me?

I grab my phone to check the time and find a text message from Jeremiah: *Not coming to the meeting? (Frowny-face)*. A pinprick of elation, then vexation when I consider how dependent I've become on his meager scraps of attention. My heart is hung up on a thorn—able to neither move nor remain comfortably in place. I wish I could cut myself free, but the snag is beyond my reach. My bond with Jeremiah has endeared, inspired, coerced, punished, and resigned me to remain near him no matter what. But it's becoming more and more difficult. Our friendship ails. He neglects it entirely, and I don't know how to fix that.

I have felt many times that some force greater than us smashed Jeremiah and me together. But it's times like these, in the dark, when I'm

weak, that I deeply, ruinously question the purpose of this journey. Is it meant to deplete all my joy and drown me in sorrow? Because that's what's happening. A few hundred lives have been saved—that's something! It really is! But it's not enough. Not when I have to go out every week and face the teeming masses of people that Jeremiah's God did not tell him to save. The costs are becoming too steep to justify my staying. A decision is fast solidifying that, even a week ago, I couldn't imagine making. I think it may be time to go home.

SUNDAY, DECEMBER 5

My mind is made up.

I only need to raise the money to buy a ticket home.

Easier said than done. My few good friends (Missy, Freddie) have already done more for me than I can afford to repay. I can't bear to ask them for anything more. I dare not ask Jeremiah for money after all the conversations we've had about ministry finances. Besides, I don't want him to know until the arrangements are final. I have a feeling he won't react well, and I don't want to give him the chance to object.

I resigned myself to the humiliation of taking up a collection from the ushers and film crew after the Crusade. This was awful for two reasons:

1. I have not taken the time to get to know them well enough to ask them for anything.

2. They're accustomed to collecting donations, not giving them out.

    I had to explain myself anew to each person.

I can only imagine what they thought of me. News flash: *Vice Minister of Wholesome Healing is Too Broke to Handle Her Affairs.*

I gathered a few tens and twenties, not enough to pay for any kind of ticket home. Tears welled up as I counted out eighty-three dollars. But then, a voice behind me.

"Miss Believer."

I turned to find Jude standing there. He shoved five hundred dollars into my hand and strode off before I could object or thank him or anything. Five hundred dollars! From Jude Clements, of all people.

Monday, December 6

Tonight, I book my flight home; until then, I must remain silent on this subject. I'm afraid my resolve might falter if I allow Jeremiah to interfere. He approaches most things as if they're negotiable, but this one is not.

For the next twenty-three hours, I shall compensate for my guilt by gifting him small favors. I offered to make dinner tonight. With a somber half-smile, he acquiesced and went away to relax while I cooked. He remained silent all through the meal. I wondered what he was thinking but was afraid to ask. Were my intentions transparent to him? Was he evaluating my ethics? My judgment? My loyalty?

When at last he spoke, it was to tell me stories from his childhood. They were heart-wrenching tales of neglect. About his mother—who loved him, he was sure—but who was not a nurturing sort of person and rarely expressed kindness. About his father—who did care for him in some capacity, he was sure—but who hid him shamefully away at boarding school and rarely ever visited. Here I'd spent half the evening fretting about Jeremiah's attitude toward *me* when he was wrapped up in troubles of his own. My stomach twisted with guilt.

I must never be ungrateful and forget that he *saved* me. At no time should I let thoughts of myself eclipse my compassion for him. I longed to reach out and touch him, hug him, break down this inexplicable barrier that had grown between us. But though my hands crept across the table toward him, an invisible boundary seemed to prevent me from making contact.

This has happened before. I don't understand it. You would think something as simple as touching another person should be easy.

Thursday, December 9

I panicked at the thought that this might be my last and final chance to tell Jeremiah Promise how I feel, and still, I didn't take it. I DIDN'T TAKE IT.

I love you. You're everything to me. Let's try for something more. These simple phrases have rolled around in the back of my mind for months, wearing smooth like worry stones. They ought to slide off the tongue easily enough. I meant to say something after the Crusade on Sunday, but the opportunity didn't arise. On Monday, I was mute, and on Tuesday, no second chance arrived. On Wednesday, I didn't see him at all. Serendipity and I are locked in a mutual chokehold.

I know it sounds like I'm manufacturing unnecessary obstacles to a relatively easy solution. It shouldn't be this hard to just do it. Just pick up the phone and call, text, any time of day or night. Believe me, I tried. My hands shook. The send button stuck like a gun with a bullet jammed in the chamber. I tried calling, but he didn't pick up.

Today was my last chance to see him in person. I had to break the news that I was leaving, but he kept interrupting me.

"Did you transcribe the notes from the meeting?" he asked as he thrashed through a stack of papers on his clipboard.

"Yes, of course. Speaking of meetings, I won't be—"

"Has the shipment of prayer cards arrived yet? We're going to need them this Sunday."

"They're due tomorrow, but you're going to have to get someone else to—"

Jeremiah stopped moving papers around and squinted. "Is this a typo? You've got to be kidding me. We just order ten thousand of these, and there's a typo."

"I fixed that before sending it to the printer. But I—"

Around and around we went with these tangents. Did he know? Was he upset? Was he trying to snub me in the name of grief or dismay? Right up to those final moments, I couldn't guess whether he'd miss me or forget me as soon as I was out of sight. His apparent indifference boasted that he didn't care. Only my mess of unsubstantiated feelings hinted otherwise.

When I was finally able to tell him the part about me going home, Jeremiah wanted to know the precise duration of my absence. "A week? Two weeks? Two and a half weeks?" he demanded.

"I hope not long," I said. I dared not tell Jeremiah that I had bought a one-way ticket.

"Fine," he said coldly, then reminded me of several tasks I ought to finish before I go.

I feel sick about leaving him. I fear what will happen when I go. Will it tear out the vital part of me that is connected to him? Will something unnatural grow in its place? We didn't even say goodbye. Perhaps that's for the best. Farewells are trivial in the grand scheme of things.

SATURDAY, DECEMBER 11

My pen-holding hand is heavy.

The sound and fury of life have ceased, and the silence is oppressive. It's eerily quiet at home. I remember all the things as they should be—how to play house, how to be content, how to live alone—as one remembers lyrics to songs after the music is lost.

I've been gone half a year, but it might as well be half a lifetime. Everything looks different. Smaller. Darker. The carpet and walls are duller. Yet, aside from a few new scars and a coating of dust, not much has changed here.

SUNDAY, DECEMBER 12

When I first opened the pantry, I was flabbergasted. It was full. The upper shelves were lined with neat rows of canned tomatoes, pickles, peppers, grape juice, and three kinds of jam. The lower shelves were stocked with crates of purple potatoes and mesh bags of onions. Bunches of garlic and herbs hung from hooks. My tiny deep-freeze was full of blanched corn, peas, and beans. A handwritten note taped to the pantry door informed me that the carrots and parsnips were still in the ground outside.

This was all Missy's doing. She must have spent a solid month harvesting and preserving my crops, and she didn't even mention it during our phone calls. It took me a full day to muster the strength to thank her. I insisted that she keep the food for herself, but she wouldn't take it. After all my mother had done for her over the years, she said, it was the least she could do for me. Tonight, I took a portion of every savory thing that Missy had saved for me and made a soup of it. I set one place at the table and sat down to a proper home-grown meal. I swallowed two spoonsful of soup; the third one came back up. I caught it in my napkin, along with a sob.

All at once, I was struck by the humbling fact that I had failed. I was foolish! My ambitions were too bombastic. Fanciful dreams: stupid. Mission to save the world: stupid. Idealism doesn't cut it. A person needs far more strength and resilience than I have to thrive in this world.

Monday, December 13

Doubt grows louder when it's quiet.

Did we meddle with Fate?

Did we make enemies with the Powers that Be?

Perhaps the people that Jeremiah Promise delivered from death were not meant to be saved. For that, there would have to be consequences. Defiance of the natural order wreaks havoc on body and soul.

Tuesday, December 14

I walked to town through the snow. As I studied the gentle, rolling fields and forests tucked beneath their soft winter blanket, I felt grateful to be home. When last I was here, I spent my days dreaming of faraway places. But when I was far away, I wished I could better recall the precise colors and smells of the soil, leaves, waterways, and country roads.

I went to Sheldon's diner for lunch and was amazed by the reception I received.

"That's our girl!" he exclaimed when he saw me walk in the door. Sheldon didn't even grumble when I went around the counter to hug him.

Several friends and neighbors came over to welcome me home and ask about my travels. Gail and Maureen from the library were at the end of their lunch breaks, but they made me promise to stop in and visit the old gang a little later. A couple of gentlemen in overalls stopped by to get the scoop. I didn't know them, but they expressed genuine interest in my story. It's then I realized just how much I'd missed the camaraderie of my small town.

I had no proud tales to tell and was reluctant to say much, but the diner folks coaxed out a few of the facts. Because it's the nature of details to weave tightly together with one another, my friends and neighbors soon had hold of enough threads to tug out the rest of them. I told them about Dallas, Jeremiah Promise, and the healing Crusades. Their awe embarrassed me. *It's not as grand as you think!* I wanted to say.

By the time I returned home in the early evening, I felt like twice the person I was this morning. Where did this infusion of vitality come from? Hours of conversation and laughter with old friends should have been tiring, but instead, they left me feeling more alive than before.

These few extra ounces of energy have inspired me to consider the laws of social dynamics. In general, I assume that socializing saps my strength and that I must regenerate alone or in nature. But this is not always the case. People don't affect me equally. Some seem to *give* energy, while others deplete it. Perhaps it's a matter of choosing my company more carefully.

Even gregarious people that strike me as powerhouses of vigor and vivacity can sometimes have a draining effect. Meanwhile, certain quiet, steady folks don't have to do or say much to revive me when I'm low.

WEDNESDAY, DECEMBER 15

It feels right to go for a long walk every day. I missed this.

Today, I took a novel route with the hope that it would prompt novel thoughts. The road I chose was broad and straight, so I expected to see few eccentricities along the way. The simple fields and cloudless skies were reason enough to contemplate the profound silence of winter's sleep.

A mile down the road, I came upon an abandoned property. Its eerie outhouses called to me. I tramped through the snowdrifts to examine the skeletons of a greenhouse, a shed, and a chicken coop. My presence must have disturbed an owl. It hooted at me from its hiding place.

A flash of insight stopped me in my tracks.

This place—this is where I was formed. I come from a land where the harsh cycles of death and rebirth live deep in one's bones. Winter's children know that no end is truly the end. Come spring, the sap will rise, and life will rebound once again.

THURSDAY, DECEMBER 16

I spent all day cooking, cleaning, shoveling snow, and being otherwise productive around the house. This afternoon, I made a fire in the fireplace, and now I'm lying on the floor surrounded by books and sketchpads. When I was little, I used to spend all my time on the floor. It's a

grounding place.

I am home, and home is me. We exist reciprocally within each other. I'm the fabric of the couch cushions and the pattern of the wallpaper. I extend to the top of the rafters and the bottom of the baseboards. I'm the door frame with the gouge where movers accidentally rammed Mom's stand-up piano. I'm the three and a half steps up to the porch (mind the first one!), the stained-glass panel in the front door, and the opposite wall of rainbow light.

Freddie is the one that comes to mind now when I gaze at that stained-glass panel. He was so fascinated with my description of it when we first met for coffee. This morning I snapped a picture of it and sent it to him. He responded with prompt delight. Shouldn't friendship be light and easy like this? I'm grateful that Freddie keeps in touch, but I'm hurt that he's the only one.

I stretch, exercise, eat good food, talk to good people, dive into distractions, but nothing will undo this knot in my gut. That's because it's tied around Jeremiah, and try as I might to evict him from my world, he won't let go. I keep telling myself that the ache will lessen with time—but so far, it has not. Deep down, I don't think my business with him is done.

FRIDAY, DECEMBER 17

I've decided that Jeremiah's healing powers must be a part of the natural order. No mortal possesses the strength to bypass the laws of creation. If he performs miracles, it's because miracles are natural. Nothing can be done that is not within the realm of feasibility.

The elaborate designs of Fate are difficult to decipher when one is

ensnared within them. I envision Fate as a network of waterways whose currents carry us in set directions. We can resist the water's flow and create anomalies in our paths along the way, but we cannot change the water's general course or destination. Perhaps we only imagine we defy destiny from time to time, when, in fact, every surprise we encounter along the way has already been decided.

Anyway. I'm not convinced that every instance of illness we encountered at the Crusades required a healing miracle. Most did, some didn't. Many people came to us in crises so dire that nothing but an act of God could save them. That begs the question: why?

In some cases, I believe it came down to unfinished business. Some people put off their duties or dreams until they're told they can't have them anymore. Only in that final hour are they seized with the desire for more time and the will to make the most of it.

In other cases, it seemed to come down to self-neglect. Perhaps it's just easier—ironically—to let the minutia of daily life blot out looming threats and serious dangers until we find ourselves fatally cornered in a tower of denial. (But that's my specialty, isn't it? Plodding on and on through a tolerable existence, convincing myself that everything is fine until it almost kills me).

At the Crusades, I saw plenty of ailments that ought not to have existed. Overgrown tumors, advanced cancers, minor infections that went septic—all things that might have been avoided with the aid of awareness and regular self-care. There were compelling stories behind every malady, and each one painted a discernible picture of some mental, emotional, or spiritual deprivation. I saw infections of the mind and tumors of the soul that ravaged the body in ways no physical ailment could. I saw families that had been turned upside down by addiction, anxiety, and depression.

Why?

Because we do not seek help when we need it. We shrink away from our fellow humans and isolate ourselves for safety's sake until our bodies give out. We, the living, are connective creatures with an innate desire to merge. Separation is unnatural. It's not even possible, really, any more than it's possible to separate one wave from the rest of the ocean.

I could go on for pages describing categories of people, but I could never capture a complete picture of all humankind. To these rules I just jotted down, there are exceptions, exceptions, exceptions. Every story is full of nuance, every situation unique, every life valuable. No one deserves to be cast aside or have their life deemed less meaningful than another.

Trouble is, I feel like that's the way our work was headed. It was all about the "worthy" and the "chosen." What made them worthy? How did God choose them? I know that there were too many of them for one man to save. Jeremiah *could not* help them all, but that didn't make it right to pick and choose, either.

SATURDAY, DECEMBER 18

I wonder how the ministry is doing. No—I wonder how Jeremiah is doing. Does he think of me? Does he miss me? Still nothing from him, not a peep. My mind plays quiet tricks on me. It whispers: *He's too proud to reach out. He has to protect his heart, and silence is the only way he knows how.*

No. His silence speaks louder than words. It's the dreaded response to the question that I couldn't bear to ask. In most cases, the simple answer is the right one—and when one appears not to care, it's because he doesn't.

I'm tangled in a net of unequal love, and the struggle to extricate myself is exhausting. I've lost track of my reasons for struggling in the first place—what am I trying to do? Break free of the net? Destroy it? Conquer it?

I have become so consumed by the romantic twist of my fairy tale that now I can't disentangle myself from it at will. Fine. I surrender. I am trapped in a net, and that's that. Is it really so bad? Honestly, I was looking for an escape from pastoral complacency, but I never took steps to leave until Jeremiah Promise came along. Even when I was out there, entrenched in the wide world, I considered turning back many times before now. Jeremiah gave me a reason to keep going. No matter how difficult things became, I pushed through because of him. Because I believed in him and our mission. Is this not still the case?

So romantic love isn't feasible. So what. That fact alone hasn't reduced me to rubble or torn me to shreds. I continue to live, and one day follows the next much as it ever did. I'm growing used to this constant ache in my heart. I'm learning to bear it.

There's no denying that Jeremiah and I do have some special sort of bond. It's real—I need only flip back through the pages of my sketchbook to see it written down. Our bond is that of idol and acolyte. I've learned much from him and developed feelings of deep gratitude toward him. I must have made the mortal error of mixing up eros and agape. It would be unethical for us to form any sort of romantic connection. Jeremiah knows that better than anyone. He's wise to keep strict boundaries. Even if I could, would I be willing to trade all the insight and ambition that he has inspired in me for something so commonplace?

No. I would not.

This evening I made another fire in the fireplace and watched it

crackle. Now and then, I added a few sticks. My impulse to recoil from the flames sparked ideas about the function of fire.

Blazing heat is an appropriate thing to fear. At some point, we all discover the consequences of touching it and learn to keep our hands to ourselves. We carry memories of painful burns with us for years—for lifetimes, even.

But fire does so much more than inspire fear. It is also an essential tool. It feeds, sustains, and furthers life. It enables us to forge the complex metals with which we build our world and the complex mettle from which we build ourselves.

As I sat before the flickering blaze tonight, I thought about the endless cycles of elation and disappointment that I've been through with Jeremiah over the last year. He has heated, cooled, trampled, and twisted my heart so many times that it has begun to transform into a new sort of metal—an alloy of hope and discouragement more durable than either on its own.

Perhaps suffering doesn't want to be pitied or suppressed. Like heat and flame, pain serves a purpose. It is an agent of change. Fire may be fearsome, but it is also bright. It's a guiding light that shows us what the darkness tries to hide.

SUNDAY, DECEMBER 19

Freddie and I had a long talk today. He thinks I should come back. I told him my reasons for leaving, and he said he *still* thinks I should come back. He has seen my ambition with his own eyes and is convinced that it's authentic. Jeremiah may have provided opportunities for me, but the zeal with which I applied myself was all mine.

What I do next is up to me, of course. Other outlets for my passion are bound to come along. Freddie wants me to be happy—but he reminded me that happiness is not the same as joy. I suppose he's right. Ease and exultation are fleeting, but satisfaction and peace of mind are built to last.

What do I want to do with my life? That's the question. What is my aim, apart from Jeremiah's? Maybe it's not as grand as his. I have fixated on this idea of changing the world and been disappointed with the dismal magnitude of my impact. But if I were to focus on my real locus of control, which is considerably smaller, it might be enough to align my daily actions with my values. I cannot help everyone, but there is still plenty of good to be done.

If I were to return to Dallas, and this time maintained the strictest possible focus on individuals we can help rather than the teeming masses we can't help, I think I *could* be happy.

Tuesday, December 21

I spent my last couple of days at home packing boxes and stacking them in Missy's basement. She will try to find a tenant to help cover the expenses. Otherwise...

Well, never mind that. It's time to face forward. My mind is made up, and my ticket to Dallas is punched. An hour ago, I separated from Midwest soil. I don't know when I'll see home again.

These hours in the clouds are my final stretch of limbo. When I come down on the other side, my resolution will be complete.

Wednesday, December 22

Eleven days of absences have bought me eleven ounces of Jeremiah's enthusiasm upon my return. He seemed pleased to see me again and acted as if nothing was amiss. He didn't ask about my trip or how I'd been, but instead launched into a ministry briefing. I suppose that's fair. It's not like I had exciting tales to tell about it anyway.

While I was gone, Jeremiah initiated a new direct mail campaign and started recruiting "spiritual liaisons" from the congregation. They will earn private healing sessions with Jeremiah by bringing in so many new disciples per month. He also fired the entire film crew and found replacements. Just like that, Caroline and Eddie are gone. That's too bad. I liked them.

Christmas falls on a weekend this year, and Jeremiah has arranged for back-to-back Saturday and Sunday Crusades at an auditorium with over two thousand seats. Quite a step up. Jeremiah is convinced that he can pack the place to capacity, and I don't doubt it. Things are really taking off, and I am happy for him.

I talked to Freddie on the phone this evening, and he promised to come to the Christmas Eve Crusade. It feels like forever since I last saw him. I am eager, though a little uneasy. He said he would have a "surprise" for me, but he didn't give me any details. Oh, Freddie! Your intentions are solid gold, my friend, but I wish you would understand that surprises tend to bring more trouble than delight.

Thursday, December 23

Criminy! I forgot where I was for a moment. The disorientation of sleep had me thinking I was still at home. My own bedroom door never wanders open in the night, so I didn't expect it to be in my way when I walked toward the bathroom. Bam! Fireworks in the dark, followed by a clap of pain. Say what? It almost sounded like a shout, but I couldn't make out the words.

Head wounds tend to swell quite a bit, so I'm icing it. I pace into the bathroom every five minutes to check myself in the mirror, and my forehead just keeps looking worse. *No, no, no! Not the day before the Christmas Crusade!*

Right smack in the middle of my forehead throbs a flashing neon arrow. It seems to point with angry, red purpose toward . . . what?

Saturday, December 25

Freddie is dead. It's all my fault.

195

AFTER

Bits and pieces.

The funny shape of his mouth.

Bad dreams—the same ones every night. The boa constrictor hiding in the bushes. Me yelling at the top of my lungs, my voice barely rising above a whisper. People looking at me like I'm crazy.

It was contorted and flecked with foam at the corners.

The endless pacing. The urges to pick up the phone and dial his number. "Did you hear, Freddie? It was awful, just awful."

Jude was pumping his chest and listening for breath. He seemed to know what to do—big whoosh of relief. Moments later, a riptide of believers swept him out of reach.

Critical details rapidly disappearing into the folds of time. Falling in line with feelings and echoes that can never quite rise to that level of clarity again.

Wednesday, December 29

His reprimands cut us to the bone. We were lucky that we were not in jail. He had gone to a lot of trouble to prevent our arrest. Some of the

others were not so fortunate. He couldn't do much for the usher that broke the EMT's nose, nor the dozen or so disciples that attacked the police officers after they pried open the doors.

Jeremiah went on listing disastrous details while I buried my face in my hands. But these weren't the worst of it. "The worst is that you *both* betrayed me," he seethed.

Ours is a delicate and dangerous business. He cannot tolerate the presence of traitors in our midst. It's the sacred duty of all ministry staff to maintain absolute faith in the healer and implicitly obey his commands.

"Betrayals are like mice!" Jeremiah declared. "Where there's one, there are always a dozen more." He pounded his fist on the podium and demanded to know in what other ways we'd been undermining his holy mission. How long have we been corrupting his ministry? Obviously, one or both of us must have been consorting with the Devil.

I could feel the white-hot rage smoldering in the folding chair beside me. Jude did not say a word, nor did I. No explanations, no excuses, no mumbled apologies could repair the damage that had been done.

Freddie waving at me from the valley of salvation-seekers, his face flushed and gleaming. Was something off about him? Maybe—just a fleeting impression. His smile was miles wide, so I decided he must be alright.

Jeremiah pointed an accusatory finger at each of us and said that we were the ones that brought death into his house. He could have saved that man's life had we not gotten in his way. For our sins, he was tempted to throw us both out. But he wouldn't be so brash. He would pray on it. In the meantime, we had better stay out of his way.

Jeremiah left us alone, and Jude sprang to his feet and hurled his

chair across the room. It nailed a cart of folding chairs, all of which crashed to the floor in a thunderous cascade. He, too, stormed out, leaving me stunned.

Friday, December 30

Damage control, that's what we're calling it.

According to Carmen, time is of the essence. We fell off the horse, and now we must scramble to get back on. It's unfortunate that we had to cancel the Christmas Day and New Year's Eve Crusades, yes, but we will prevail. Big, exciting plans in the works. Details to come. Dismissed.

I barely recognized my colleagues today. Half of them were strangers to me. The other half looked gaunt beneath the fluorescent glare. Sickly light slashed across their features, and shadows pooled in every hollow.

His nose and mouth were black, gaping holes. Eyes wide, watery, and imploring, he made inhuman sounds. I wanted to understand him, but I couldn't make him out.

The conference room cleared out, and only Jude remained. He apologized for throwing the chair, then turned to leave without waiting for a response.

"That's it?" I called after him. No discussion? Nothing else to say?

"You don't like me, do you," I said.

"Like or dislike, it's a non-issue," said Jude.

I asked him to explain, but he advised me to reconsider. His answer would be honest, and I wouldn't like it. Those words struck fear into my heart, but I invited him to go on.

He was blunt, indeed. He told me that he had no respect for blind allegiance, and mine was evident from the start. He's watched me follow Jeremiah around for months, indulging his whims and ignoring his shortcomings. Someone has now *died* because of Jeremiah's arrogance, and still, no one is holding him accountable.

My defenses flared, but with great effort, I smothered them. Jude's words were painful, but I could hear the ring of truth in them. I accepted his reproach without objection. Jude softened a fraction of a degree. He said he understood that the dead man had been a friend. At least I did the right thing in the end by calling emergency dispatch.

As he walked away, I glimpsed the dark patch of hair on the back of his head and felt a sickening thump of pain. I winced as a microphone squeal cut across the phantom ricochet of Jeremiah's voice. *Satan knocks! Don't let him in!*

Jude was the one that had dived into the crowd by the main doors. Someone had to unblock them so the paramedics could get in. He might have succeeded, had he not been attacked by half a dozen disciples and bashed over the head with a crutch.

Saturday, January 1

Official cause of death: heart attack induced by diabetic shock.

Natural causes, case closed.

Never mind the knotted gut and fevered thoughts. Never mind the questions that will never be answered now. Whose fault was it? Was it Freddie's fault for skipping his insulin shot? Was it Jeremiah's fault for not saving him? Was it Jude's fault for failing to pry open the doors? Was it the congregation's fault for getting in the way? Was it the EMT's fault for arriving too late? Or was it my fault from the very beginning?

Most involved parties were reacting to the circumstances they were dealt. But I should have known better. I should have warned Freddie off, stayed out of the way, dialed the paramedics sooner, had more faith. I should have known the combination of all these failings was lethal. I should have seen the danger. If the fault belongs to anyone, it's me.

Friday, January 14

Demon exorcism? Psychic surgery? Wholesome Healing Parochial School? His ideas are becoming more outrageous every day.

"We shall have an army of faithful followers!" Jeremiah declared. This army will require a well-trained hierarchy of command to oversee our holy missions. In the long-run, he wants to build an entire city dedicated to the study and practice of faith healing. It would be fashioned after Jim Bakker's Heritage USA and Oral Roberts University—but bigger, done right this time. He would erect monuments depicting biblical healings, and the amphitheater would play nonstop clips of live miracles captured on film. The university would offer bachelor's, master's, and doctorate degrees in the Holy Healing Arts. He would build a hospital dedicated to divine miracles. No scalpels, drugs, or rat poison, just the good old-fashioned Grace of God.

These dreams may be a long way off yet—but Jeremiah has mighty ambitions. If it's a multi-million-dollar venture he undertakes, then we shall raise millions. If God wills it, then it is as good as done. He ordered me to start researching permits, accreditation, and charter-school requirements. I should look into available tax breaks while I'm at it—oh, and by the way, Grace Group is canceled.

I balked. What? Why? That group was *my* means of making a difference! I was eager to get back to it and build upon the meaningful connections that had already begun to take shape. Bethany and Raj, Vero and Trisha, Markus, Gina, Bryan—week after week, they kept coming back. It must have been good for them. It must have mattered to them. Jeremiah claimed that the members had been exploiting us for free therapy without making any progress. It wasn't an effective use of time and resources.

"Problem?" he glared at me. I lowered my eyes to the meeting minutes and said nothing. I was on probation and dared not draw attention to myself. Best to tiptoe around him, lest the sound of my footfalls should remind Jeremiah that a traitor walks among us.

This is not like him—I know Jeremiah, composed, sensible, and shrewd. His increasingly erratic behavior must be symptomatic of deeper disturbances. He's like a thrashing lion driven wild by the thorn stuck in its paw. I wish I could help him, but I dare not venture too near.

The death must be tearing him up inside. I can only imagine what a blow it is to someone so passionate about saving lives. No time to stop and process. The show must go on. A lot of people depend on him. His following continues to expand by leaps and bounds. They have twisted Freddie's death into a miracle by saying that he sacrificed himself to become an angel. The rumor was picked up by several Christian programs, including *The Christ Club*, and now it's everywhere. Carmen is loving this. Jeremiah's fame has arrived whether he's ready or not.

Things are getting out of hand, and it's my fault. He charged me to hold him to a higher standard. He *implored* me to challenge him if I saw him heading into error, and I should have started calling out his cavalier tendencies sooner. Who else would? Carmen eggs him on. Jude says nothing.

What now?

If I speak up, he may cast me out for good; if I don't speak up, I fail.

TUESDAY, JANUARY 25

I lay on the couch most of the day, lingering in the twilight of sleep, unable to evade the cold fingers of Grief.

You again.

The question: can I do this yet again? Can I climb out of the wreckage and carry on once more? I guess so. There's no other choice. The only way to escape the loop of madness is to keep moving. I can bear most hours of the day if I stay busy. I wash windows, scrub walls, polish trim, extract dirt from the floorboard cracks with a safety pin.

Messages are piling up. They're my lesson on letting go. No need to rush to anyone's aid; if the call is important, the caller will try again.

I went shoe shopping this afternoon for the first time in a long time. My present soles are worn down to the quick and have begun to tear in the middle. My feet get wet every time it rains (not that it rains often in Texas).

Even at the mall, I was not free of Freddie's influence. I found myself wondering what colors and styles he would choose for me—only those that were far brighter and less practical than I would prefer, I'm sure. It was just wishful browsing, anyway. I had no money for shoes.

MONDAY, FEBRUARY 7

Jeremiah is leaving. He will be gone for two weeks, something about snake handling in Kentucky. I look ahead with dread. Two weeks without Jeremiah sounds like pure torture, but I know it shouldn't be. My personal feelings for him ought to have dissolved by now. They are not wanted, they don't make sense, they're due to expire. Still, I can only pull so far away from him before the elastic of his sticky, stretchy web snaps me right back. Perhaps two weeks apart will help to loosen his hold on me.

Jeremiah encouraged everyone to enjoy this hiatus, as it will be our last for a while. In March, we're going to hit the *national* Crusade trail. We will have back-to-back bookings for several months to come, and more opportunities are popping up every day.

On his way out of the meeting yesterday, Jude handed me two keys. One was for the ministry office and the other for a post office box. He commissioned me to check both while he was gone and provided a list of instructions for handling mail and so forth.

Where was Jude going? I couldn't imagine him taking a vacation. Nor could I imagine him with a family when he said he had family matters to attend to. He did not elaborate, and I did not pry.

Apparently, everyone is leaving town but me. They all expect me to stay behind and take care of business while they're gone. Being abandoned, once more—this is what I most fear. They expect me to sit alone in my cell day after day and wonder if Jeremiah will come back.

Friday, February 11

I have been provided food, shelter, and modern conveniences for my confinement, but few comforts or distractions. The stillness here is different than it is at home—here, alone, it grinds on me like bone against bone. Patience stagnates and time decays as I await his return. He didn't

say where exactly he was going. He won't answer his phone. As usual, he's scarce at the time I need him most.

I strive to crowd out my fears with justifications. He's just busy. He's just out of range. He's just conflicted. He just needs time to find himself. I shun the niggling voice of conscience that warns me away from the thin ice of excuses. I shame it.

You are weak.

You are a disappointment.

You have serious trust issues.

The slick walls of my beige cell give me nothing to grab onto as the turbulent waters of desperation consume me. I will struggle like this for hours before succumbing to exhaustion. That's when the visage of Freddie slips past my slumbering guards and comes to speak with me. Its eyes crinkle and its head tilts sympathetically. It reminds me to be kinder. I push it away.

Freddie once told me that he had prayed for me. He said that he recognized me when he saw me on the sidewalk that day—not by sight, but by feel. He knew I was the one he had been waiting for. At the time, I assumed Freddie was prone to fanciful exaggeration. Now, I'm starting to see its significance. It begs the question: if he called me into his life, then which of us was the principal and which was the pawn? Has everything I've experienced, felt, and believed up to now been a function of Freddie's prayer? Was his death predestined? Was it pivotal for some reason yet unknown?

The idea of order and the reality of chaos pull my mind in separate directions. I don't know which to believe. Despite every senseless thing that has happened, I am still filled with anticipation. Forces greater than me seem to push and pull me, sometimes gently and sometimes roughly, in a specific direction. I'm not so sure I want to go that way. I

scream and kick and dig in my heels, but momentum compels me. Who is responsible for this? Whose hand set these things in motion? How much of the fault is mine?

Friday, February 18

I went away for a while.

The forest was dark and dense where I went. The chasms were deep. Some reckless instinct propelled me off the path and plunged me into the thorny thicket without a thought of return. I promptly got lost. Then I got stuck. I struggled a little, but it was no use.

I sighed. Surrendered. Made a nest of fallen leaves and lay down to sleep. Just as I closed my eyes, the wilderness decided against me. It spit me out.

I have come back. Back to my beige chamber.

Saturday, February 19

This morning, I hobbled out of my hollow like a newborn fawn. Thankfully, the sun was bright and invigorating. I ate a big breakfast and sat by the pool, allowing its glittering refractions to chase away the shadows.

Can it really be that easy? Perhaps it all comes down to perspective—a thing that must be regularly refreshed. I forget to step back and consider just how small a speck I am in all of space and time. The whole world is crowded with parallel lives, each with its own set of woes. From the outside, most problems don't look that bad. It's a relief to step out of the windowless confines of the mind and see that the sun is still shining, the world is still here.

This evening, I roamed the streets. I walked without a destination, but I didn't need one. As I unshuttered my senses and aired out my grief, I was greeted by the pleasures of simple things and in-between places. The gusty breeze challenged me to remain present and alert. It thrust novel scents, sounds, and sensations upon me at every turn, insisting that I pay attention. No more space for rambling ruminations or detached sentiments.

SUNDAY, FEBRUARY 20

I dreamed that I was home on a crisp, clear spring day. I went outside to check the back garden with a wicker basket under my arm. There beneath a massive juniper tree, I saw Mrs. Maple in her paint-covered smock, beckoning me. I went to stand beside her, and together, we gazed up into the sparse and shady interior of the tree. From there, we could see all the way to the top. Yellow and white onions hung from the boughs like Christmas ornaments.

Mrs. Maple told me to choose an onion. I could have any one that I wanted; she would have it brought down to me. I pointed out the one that hung on the highest branch, and Mrs. Maple went to whisper instructions to a waiting lemur. The lemur bounded up the juniper tree, plucked the onion, and dropped it. The onion came down slowly, growing larger as it fell. By the time it reached the ground, my prize was taller than me. Mrs. Maple took a picture of me standing next to it.

Tuesday, February 22

Jeremiah and Jude are due back tomorrow.

I cracked open my planner today for the first time in weeks and realized that I had let PO Box 245 slip silently into neglect. Whoops. I hopped on a bike and zoomed off to the post office, expecting to find the ministry mailbox stuffed to the gills with responses to Jeremiah's latest direct mail campaign.

I found only a dozen or so envelopes waiting for me. More surprising still, a letter from Pastor Ormand Kenneth sat at the top of the slim stack. What in the world could he have to say to Jeremiah Promise? The envelope was thin, perhaps containing a single folded sheet of paper. I resisted the urge to hold it up to the light.

Next stop: the ministry office on William D Tate Avenue. I had only been to our headquarters a couple of times. Glamorous as it sounds, there's not really much to it—a room with a window, a small desk, and a chair. I doubt anyone spends a lot of time there. Jeremiah probably retains it for the snazzy-sounding street address.

The office door was jammed, and it took some serious pushing and shoving to get it open a crack so I could squeeze through. Once inside, I discovered the reason for this: a mound of mail was wedged under and piled up behind it. Ah-ha! Here were the results of the mail campaign— it finally made sense.

I searched the recycling bin out back for a cardboard box, cut it to the right height, and secured it behind the door to catch future mail. This project so thoroughly distracted me that I forgot why I had come. I was supposed to leave the PO Box mail on the office desk, per Jude's instructions. But I went all the way back to my apartment, ate lunch, took a nap, and read a few chapters before I discovered that the mail was still in my backpack. I considered going all the way back to the office to complete this task tonight, but decided that it was unlikely anyone would notice or care if I dropped off the mail tomorrow instead. As a reminder, I set the mail on the window ledge by the door.

As I turned away, the whole stack chased me off the ledge and dropped to the floor with a *plop*. I bent to picked them up, and in so doing, I noticed that several of the envelopes had bank logos on them. *North Dallas Bank & Trust. Chase Bank. Wells Fargo.* Three banks? That was odd. I shuffled through the rest of the mail and found two more envelopes with different logos. *Five* banks.

The statements were all addressed to someone named Hrithik Mukherjee. I wracked my brain, but the name didn't ring any bells. Perhaps it was a case of misdelivered mail. Perhaps the former owner of the post office box forgot to update his address. Perhaps a dozen perfectly reasonable explanations. That was almost the end of it. But.

One of the envelopes was unsealed. It looked as if it never had been—there was no shiny paste on the flap. An accident of the production line, I suppose. A twinge of conscience warned me that it was wrong to look at someone else's mail, but curiosity got the best of me. I used my fingernail to carefully slide out the paper inside and unfold it. It was a Financial Statement of Accounts for January. I skimmed down the list of deposits and came to the balance at the bottom: $68,767.22. Wow! Who the heck is Hrithik Mukherjee, and what's the secret of his success?

Here's a thought: what if Hrithik Mukherjee is Jeremiah?

It doesn't make sense. But it does. He told me himself that Jeremiah

Promise is not his real name, but he never did tell me what his name used to be.

What about *all that money?* Where did it come from? What's it for? Just the one account balance represents much more than one week of Crusade donations. Even on our best day, we never break ten thousand.

Could it be private donor money? Direct mail money? Investor money? Grant money? He keeps me mostly in the dark these days. Whatever he's into, it must be lucrative. There are four other accounts, all with the same name—I can only imagine what they contain. Why so many? Could there be some business or tax advantage to spreading money around? I'm not well-versed in financial practices.

But perhaps all this speculation is based on errant assumptions. Perhaps Hrithik Mukherjee is someone else entirely—a friend, an associate, a stranger.

One thing is for sure: I can't ask Jeremiah about this. He would be furious if he found out I was nosing around. I shall try not to fret about this anymore. It's probably nothing.

Wednesday, February 23

I swear that I did nothing, absolutely nothing, to warrant such a severe back spasm. I just reached up for a box of cereal, and zing! Every muscle in my lower right quadrant wound up and sucker-punch me from the inside. The timing couldn't have been worse. Jeremiah was due back in the early afternoon, and I meant to run downstairs and welcome him home as soon as I heard the car in the drive. Instead, I spent the morning laid up in bed.

Fortunately, Jeremiah figured out that something was amiss and

came to call on me. He was surprisingly sympathetic to my pain and offered to lay hands. He helped me turn over in bed and then walked his fingers up and down my spine like a giant grasshopper. Once he located the tenderest spot, he pressed his cool palms there and prayed out loud. When he was done, I smiled and thanked him, and then we went to the kitchen to sit and talk for a while.

It was easy. Fun. Relaxed. Our connection was almost as natural and effortless as it was in the beginning. This renewed version of Jeremiah was tinged with sage and dusty mountain roads. He painted pleasing abstracts of the places he went and the people he met. It was wonderful to see his glow again. I folded up my curiosity about Hrithik Mukherjee and tucked it away. Things were finally good between us, and I wanted them to stay that way.

Jeremiah and I talked until the early evening, at which point he went to go unpack. After he left, the back spasm returned. Oh, who am I kidding. It was never really gone.

FRIDAY, FEBRUARY 25

I would have preferred to sit by Jeremiah on the plane, but he's stuck with Carmen somewhere near the back. I ended up with a seat next to taciturn Jude. That's fine. Now I have plenty of time to reflect.

It's late. The plane is dark except for a few scattered rays of light here and there, and the atmosphere of sleep imposes a general hush among the passengers. Jude is reading a crisp copy of *Paradise Lost*, and I'm doodling onions. An annoying sliver of brightness winks at me from the empty seat between us. That's where the pools of our overhead lights overlap. It reminds me of the thanks I owe Jude, long overdue.

Jude is shifting in his seat now. His agitation tickles my senses. Now he's closing his book and tucking it into the seat pocket in front of him. I suppose I should ask him what the matter is.

I asked Jude if he disliked flying. No, flying was fine. I ask him about his trip to Wyoming. His trip was fine, he said. Mission accomplished.

I had hoped that chit-chat would present a natural inroad to the topic I wanted to cover, but Jude seemed determined to dead-end the conversation. Finally, I had to awkwardly blurt out, "Thanks for loaning me the money to go home. I really needed that."

Jude nodded. "Don't mention it," he said. It wasn't a loan. I didn't have to pay him back. At that, we ran out of things to talk about. I uncapped my pen and resumed doodling.

After a while, Jude spoke again. "I can't sleep."

"Me neither," I said.

When he was in the military, he could sleep anywhere, anytime—on concrete, in mud, propped up against trees, or for brief blips between mess hall shifts. He would loosen his bootlaces, pull his hat down over his eyes, and it was lights out for ten, twenty, sixty minutes. Work and training could be physically punishing at times, but they kept him on track and clear-headed. Sleep wasn't a problem until he left the military.

Jude's inexplicable willingness to speak made me eager. I overreached. My next couple of questions were perhaps a little too personal, and he shrugged them off. The discussion ground to a halt once again.

We ran into turbulence, and my pen squiggled off the page. With a sigh, I closed my sketchpad and exchanged it for a book. Luckily, I had traded my copy of *Don Quixote* for Tam's copy of *A Room of One's Own* shortly before takeoff. Jude asked me if it was good. I said yes, but I had only just started it.

He said he didn't care much for poetry (referring to Milton, I presume) and could only take so much of it in one sitting. I asked him why he chose that book, and he said it was recommended to him—though, he wouldn't say by whom.

We discussed literature. Evidently, Jude is an avid reader. He sticks mostly to history and philosophy, though he's versed in the classics. He also reads user manuals from cover to cover.

Before I knew it, the plane was descending into Chicago O'Hare. The stir of sleepy passengers gradually outstripped our conversation as everyone prepared for landing. Perhaps I was mistaken, but just before we stood up to deplane, I thought I heard Jude mumble, "Thanks."

SUNDAY, FEBRUARY 27

(Chicago, IL)

Jeremiah was on fire. With his words, he cast spells. With arms like scythes, he cut swaths through the fog and drew signs in the air. He raised the people to their feet and then dashed them to their knees in roaring praise of Jesus. The air grew thick with roiling tangerine tendrils of holy rapture. Jeremiah seemed to grow broader, taller, brighter with each surge of reverence that overtook our impressionable flock. When the moment was right, he swapped great strokes with precise ones. His decisive incisions sliced the collective fervor to the quick. And then! A subtle flick of the wrist unleashed a legion of donation buckets as he murmured the instructions for universal absolution into the microphone.

So begins our march across the nation.

Monday, February 28

(Chicago, IL)

First thing this morning, I was startled by a sharp rap at my door. It was Jeremiah. He was very agitated. He had come to notify me that the airport was shut down, and all the flights were canceled. "They" were trying to sabotage our tour, but we weren't going to stand for it. I should call the charter company and book a bus to Fargo.

When I opened my curtains, I saw nothing but white. A storm had descended on the city overnight. It continued until late morning; by then, everything was buried under two feet of snow.

I called several charter companies. Nothing is available before Thursday. We'll likely be able to book another flight by then. Either way, we're grounded for a day or two.

Jeremiah has been pacing the hallways like a caged animal. I can hear him through the door, exclaiming, laughing, bantering on the phone. The noise he's making is almost frantic, boastful. He needs to be seen and heard. What is he afraid of? Does he think that without an audience, he will disappear?

Tuesday, March 1

(Chicago, IL)

Ugh.

I feel sick.

Sick, sick, sick.

The Salisbury steak lost its appeal long before it began to congeal. Ironic—it's the meat's fault I don't want to eat it. Well, technically, it's the room service guy's fault. If he had remembered to include silverware with my meal, none of this would have happened.

It's also my fault. Had I left my room ten seconds earlier or later, none of this would have happened. I was on my way to the hotel dining room when I ran into Jeremiah in the hallway. His jacket was slung over one shoulder, his hair disheveled, his collar unbuttoned, and he was just leaving a hotel room that wasn't his own. Three things happened at the same time: Carmen's voice slid through the crack in the door, the door clicked shut and locked, and Jeremiah caught sight of me from the corner of his eye.

Tick, tick . . . boom.

So. It was Carmen's room. Bold, brassy, unhappily married Carmen.

Was that lipstick on his collar? Seriously?

He paused to make a quick calculation, but too late. He was trapped. The look on his face was worth a thousand words, but I didn't want to think of a single one of them.

I hurried past him quickly and turned the first corner. I took the long way back to my room and spent many minutes staring at the plate of cold meat. A wave of nausea wiped out my appetite in one sweep.

Maybe it's a misunderstanding. Maybe he was there to heal her—like he tried to heal me the other day. There wasn't any funny business between us just because I was lying in bed. But in this case, it just happened to be late in the evening because that's when they were both free, and it got a little overzealous because it was an especially tricky case and oh who am I kidding *there was lipstick on his collar.*

WEDNESDAY, MARCH 2

(Chicago, IL)

The sour stench of dishonor soaked into the bedclothes and draperies overnight. I'm trying to breathe exclusively through my mouth, but I can still taste it.

Jeremiah and Carmen, together. Since when? For how many weeks and months have I been carrying a torch for him in vain? I probably should have seen the signs: their weird bickering and all the time they spend together. The worst part is that I sensed him slipping away, bit by bit, like dirt through my fingers, but I didn't know why.

I feel like a fool. All the ideas I had about his superhuman nobility. The exquisite admiration I had for his enormous self-restraint. *That's* what I've striven to emulate and believed I could never attain. Like a clap of thunder, clarity informs me that no magnitude of patience nor miracle of fate was ever going to make him mine.

Not that it matters now. I've given up on all that. But for some reason, it still hurts.

SUNDAY, MARCH 6

(Fargo, ND)

Still nothing. No explanation, no discussion. Not even a guilty passing glance, but that's probably because he doesn't look me in the eye at all. Apparently, we're just going to pave right over the incident and carry on. I'm getting awfully tired of all this pretending.

Monday, March 7

(Fargo, ND)

The thought of Jeremiah+Carmen only becomes more persistent the harder I try to put it out of my mind. I toss and turn, trying with all my might not to listen for footsteps in the hall or squeaks from their respective hotel rooms. I don't care, I tell myself over and over as if my conviction might slip from memory the moment I cease to repeat it.

I turned on the light and moved around, hoping action would propel me on past all this. The troublesome thoughts just sped up to keep pace with me. Around eleven o'clock, I got dressed and went down to the hotel bar in search of a not-so-lonely place to sit and draw. There, I found Jude. He sat in a booth alone, reading a slim volume: *Animal Farm.* He glanced up as if alerted to my presence by some preternatural sense.

I froze and smiled sheepishly. No point in pretending to be strangers. I went over and asked to join him, and he nodded to the open side of the booth. I told him I couldn't sleep because of an ethical dilemma. He put down his book.

The words just spilled out of me, though I kept the details vague. I told Jude about my "friend's" covert affair with one of his married coworkers and my struggle to understand how he could even consider it. I explained how this behavior clashed with every fiber of his moral character. It pained me to speculate aloud that he must be in love with her. Love was the only admissible reason that I could think of to compromise one's religious and professional boundaries.

The two of them may bicker and snipe. They may appear to be unhappy with each other and choose to spend only half the night together,

but it's not my place to judge their feelings for each other. Love works according to its own dictums. Exceptions to rules are made every day.

Talking it out relieved my mind a little. Jude asked me how much of this story was confirmed and how much was conjecture. I admitted that it was based on a few facts and a lot of surmises. He advised me to confront my friend, learn the real story. Best to get the truth straight from its source. If my friend was a true friend, he would be honest with me. Whatever his response, it was bound to reveal something more of his character.

I know that Jude is right. I just needed to hear someone else say it out loud. I don't want to confront Jeremiah, but I have to. It's the only way to settle my mind.

WEDNESDAY, MARCH 9

(Fargo, ND)

I was determined to speak privately with Jeremiah after the crew meeting this evening. Part of me homed in on today as Do or Die—and this made me want to skip it altogether. But I couldn't. Once I decided what to say, I was doomed to distraction, sweaty palms, and racing heart until I had it out.

First, though, we had to get through the hour-long meeting. The combative dynamic between Carmen and Jeremiah was as apparent as ever. She would antagonize him, and he would clench his jaw and try to ignore her until he couldn't anymore. Around and around they went.

For days, I've been waiting to see which way the ax would fall. Would informed observation reveal a well-concealed depth of feeling between them or a lack thereof? I still don't know if this fresh evidence of dis-

cord is a disappointment or a relief. Is it worse to find out that their affair is loveless and his morality flawed, or that his heart belongs to someone so obviously wrong for him? Impossible to say.

At the end of the meeting, I bided my time while the others packed up and headed out of the conference room. The moment came to speak to Jeremiah, I almost had it within my grasp. Thirty seconds into a bit of introductory small talk, I sensed a rain cloud darken the doorway behind me and saw Jeremiah's face fall half a degree. Sure enough, Carmen had come back.

"Oh, it's *you*," she remarked dryly, as if I was some ordinary interloper. She wedged herself between Jeremiah and me and handed him a cup of coffee as she complained that it wasn't hot enough. I turned on my heels and strode out, enraged that my opportunity to unburden my mind had been so easily disrupted. Fortunately, I calmed down quickly and reasoned that I had every right to speak privately with Jeremiah. I turned around and went back.

Jeremiah was still in the conference room with Carmen. I went up behind him, tapped him on the shoulder, and told him that we needed to talk. It couldn't wait. It would only take a minute. He submitted to my request with surprising ease and followed me out to a secluded recess in the hallway.

"What's up?" he asked.

"I take it you and Carmen are a thing," I said.

He simpered, laughed, and looked kind of . . . I don't know what. Sheepish? He said yes, it was true, but it wasn't a serious thing. They were keeping it casual, very low-key for now—at least until her attitude changed.

Her attitude? What did that mean? I wondered if he really believed that Carmen's attitude *could* change, considering that she had exhibited an aggressive and quarrelsome disposition since the beginning.

I told him point-blank that his relationship with Carmen was un-ethical and had created a weird and uncomfortable dynamic at the crew meetings. We could not be productive when the two of them spent two-thirds of the time bickering. And let's not forget the splash that Bernard Finn's affair made in the tabloids last year. They raked that famous faith healer over the coals just for holding hands with a woman that was not his wife. Imagine what *another* scandal might do to Jeremiah Promise's reputation if this sort of indiscretion came to light.

Jeremiah took my warnings well. He listened intently and leaned against the wall with his arms crossed. He asked if anyone else knew about this. I said no, not yet. He said good, let's keep it that way for now. He needed some time to consider my feedback. With that, the conversation ended.

That was not something I ever wanted to do. It felt all backward and wrong to chastise Jeremiah Promise for his personal choices. I'd rather he simply maintain a high standard of integrity at all times, but perhaps that's unrealistic. Perhaps I've been too hard on him. I forget that he's not yet thirty. Still so young. His old soul is at odds with his youth-ful fallibility. He was bound to err sooner or later—and if he was an ordinary man, he could afford to. But he is an extraordinary man, and his actions are open to public scrutiny. If I can catch him doing ques-tionable deeds, so can other people. Others might not be so forgiving.

A profound sense of calm rushed into my body immediately follow-ing our talk. The shift was so abrupt that I hardly knew what to think or do. I just wanted to keep moving, so I went for a walk around the city. The world seemed to have changed since I last saw it. The dif-ferences were subtle but deeply rooted. I sensed a tectonic shift in the collective energy around me. Strangers stared as I passed by. What were they looking at? I glanced at my reflection in a storefront window and saw nothing out of the ordinary. No streaks on my face nor hairs out of place.

Had they overheard my conversation with Jeremiah? Did they wonder at my audacity? Impossible. Strangers see only what they want to see—or what we show them.

The darkening sky drew my gaze upward, and what I saw there stopped me in my tracks. A net of thin, cottony gauze was cast across the entire expanse. Each puffy cell was rimmed with shades of pink and purple from the waning sun. There was one irregularity, and it was directly overhead: a hole was opening in the clouds. It was shaped exactly like an eye.

I dug a scrap of paper and a pen out of my bag and sketched what I saw. Within minutes the cloud opening buckled and vanished, but I was satisfied that I had seen what I needed to see. I headed back to the hotel.

As I approached the revolving doors, I saw Jude coming up the sidewalk from the opposite direction. He did a double-take. Did he see it, too? That inscrutable something that kept snagging strangers' glances? Jude stood back from the door and gestured for me to go in first.

TUESDAY, MARCH 15

(Portland, OR)

I dreamed that Jeremiah and I were driving along the coast of Africa toward our vacation destination. The windows were down, the warm breeze ruffled our hair, and all the blues, greens, and yellows were saturated to the max. Our conversation followed the gentle, meandering curves of the coastal road, and our hearts brimmed with joy.

Upon our arrival at the tropical hotel, we went to our separate rooms to unpack. Carmen came in dressed as a maid and insisted on helping me change the sheets on my bed.

"You win," she said as we fluffed the top sheet and smoothed it down. I didn't know what exactly she meant, but I felt relieved. Then I woke. I tried to hold onto that delicious feeling as long as I could, but it dissipated as all dreams eventually do.

Sunday, March 20

(Portland, OR)

I miss my friend. I miss *having* a good friend.

Sorry, Freddie—I don't mean to imply that you're not enough. You're always with me, you know, but I miss the experience of talking to a friend and hearing a friend talk back.

Though I have striven to maintain good, strong rapport with at least seven of my nine traveling companions, I have struggled to cross over into friendship with any of them. An immutable distance exists between them and me that I cannot seem to overcome.

I have nothing in common with either of the head ushers, though George and Jason are well suited to each other. They always seem to be discussing golf or fishing when I pass by, and I can never follow their conversations for long.

The film squad seems to have started its own exclusive club with its own language and customs. Sonja, Tam, Andre, and Frank rarely leave their metaphorical blanket fort, and though they are cheerful and polite to me, they always seem eager to dispense with business and return to their clique.

Jeremiah is always busy, standoffish, or embroiled in some insufferable spat with Carmen these days, so that leaves but one candidate for friendship, and that's Jude.

Jude and I have managed a few civil—dare I say, stimulating—conversations, which is more than I thought possible. This makes me optimistic. I keep hoping to stumble upon the secret spring that unlocks his sense of camaraderie.

It's nearly impossible to learn through experimentation what motivates or excites Jude. His every outward expression is restrained. This makes it challenging to get on his good side (or his bad side, for that matter, or to know which is which), but I don't mind a challenge. What do I have, if not time, an analytical nature, determination, and desperation to make a new friend?

I peg Jude as a relentless loner. He keeps to himself and is slow to recognize me as someone he's spoken with before. He does not seem to take offense when others ignore or condescend to him. He encourages people to underestimate him, I think. Through painstaking observation, I have discovered that Jude's disposition is not as impervious as it seems, however. He may best be described as a non-Newtonian fluid—a substance that abruptly stiffens when stressed but yields a bit when approached in an indirect manner.

My efforts to ingratiate myself with Jude were rewarded today when, during clean-up, he made a dry, offhanded remark that struck my funny bone like an arc of static electricity. I couldn't do the joke justice by repeating it here, so I won't even try. Suffice it to say, the sudden arrival of Jude's sense of humor was so understated and surprising that I laughed almost to tears.

Did he mean to elicit such a response? At first, he seemed baffled. But after a suitable delay, a twinkle appeared in his eye, and the corners of his mouth curled a bit. Yes, he meant to be funny.

MONDAY, MARCH 21

(Las Vegas, NV)

We have arrived in the lavish land of Las Vegas, where no expense is spared, and no square inch of real estate will settle for less than the best. It's miles of Number One as far as the eye can see. Every shop, every hotel, every performance battles for top billing.

Jeremiah, Jude, and Carmen will be tied up in meetings with investors and producers for the next four days. The film squad has been commissioned to go out and record stock footage for the documentary. That leaves me mostly on my own this week with lots of city to explore.

I could see the tip-top of the Eiffel tower from my hotel room window. It called to me, so I took my first trip to Paris today. From there, I intended to walk down one entire side of the South Strip and up the other, but my plan was spoiled in less than one block.

There's no such thing as walking straight on the South Strip. Crossing a street isn't a thing. The corners are fenced, and the only way to move between blocks is to ride up an escalator and zig-zag through the skyways. I was funneled through every major hotel and casino along the way—City Center, the Monte Carlo, New York, New York. The turrets of Excalibur enticed me from a distance long before I could reach them. I had to zig through MGM and zag past Tropicana to get there. My journey came with a series of jarring transitions from blasting sunshine to murky darkness. The inner halls and caverns of Las Vegas existed in perpetual twilight, uninterrupted by windows or clocks. The ceilings were covered with murals of dusk-rimmed clouds. They

seemed to encourage evening attire and attitudes at all times of the day.

I arrived in Las Vegas with a tiny ambition to gamble. I thought I could perhaps be the one that whips out the last twenty-dollar bill to her name, feeds it to a machine, and hits it big. I could be the one that swoops in with my eleventh-hour luck and secures a bright future for us all. But I lost my taste for slot machines within the first hour of my journey through the Strip. I passed thousands of them—surges, swells, eddies, and tsunamis of them. They blocked me at every turn, demanding my attention with their garish glitter. Where there were slots, there were button-pressers of a sickly, sallow tint, with eyes glazed by the flashing, electric lights of enticement. I watched the insatiable metal boxes gobble up bill after bill and thought about how quickly and thanklessly my twenty would disappear into one of them. I remembered what the psychic said about there being no God in random chance. Is there a God in Las Vegas? I fear that there is, and He's the kind that conspires against His flock.

Morning advanced to afternoon as I made my way further south along the Strip. The crowds thinned, and the streets quieted. I passed vacant, glassy pools and glided through empty corridors. I roamed in and out of ghostly ballrooms and banquet halls, seldom encountering other living souls. Once, I turned the corner of an upper story in Mandalay Bay and found a woman playing fetch with her dog in the long gallery. My presence must have spooked her. She was gone when I passed that way again.

Around dusk, I turned back just in time to witness the city's electric dawn. Lights dazzled the eye from every nook and cranny. Dance music set the cadence of my walk from block to block. The nocturnal crowds stirred—they were bright-eyed and famished. Some laughing guy came up to me and asked if I wanted my photo taken with a *real* model. I said

no thanks and left him bewildered in my wake. He must have been expecting a different answer.

Many shades of extraordinary bombarded my senses with sights, sounds, and smells. They imposed a hefty tax on my faculties, and I soon had to stop and sit down on a fountain edge to rest. A show had just ended at a nearby theater, and the audience cascaded out of the exit doors. Sparkling Vegas performers stood by like live mannequins to greet their fans as they passed. Everyone smiled ecstatically, shook hands, posed for photos, and chatted. The glossy scene did not become any more intriguing or thought-provoking as it unfolded, and I was soon restless to flip the page.

When I stood up to carry on, my limbs seem to have been swapped out for sandbags. It was such an exertion to walk that I was out of breath within a few steps. Alarmed by this sudden change, I pulled out my phone and considered calling for help. But who? Jeremiah? A part of me automatically longed to be rescued by him, but my heart sank lower with each unanswered ring. Unavailable. I didn't leave a message.

Jude? My thumb hovered over his name for a moment, but I scrolled on past him.

I called Missy, hoping that a few words with a friend might be the ticket. We discussed her efforts to find a tenant for my house. She thought she had a line on a relative of a friend that needed a place to stay. The uplifting news lessened my fatigue, and I was able to finish my trek back to the hotel.

As soon as I got back to my room, I closed the curtains, climbed under a stack of blankets, and buttoned myself in for the night. That's more than enough Vegas for one day.

Tuesday, March 22

(Las Vegas, NV)

I woke jittery and parched, impatient to continue my exploration of the Strip. I had not yet seen the northern half, and I was anxious to do so today.

The north side is not as controlled as the south, but it's just as opulent and overwhelming, if not more so. I wandered through the Flamingo, the LINQ, Harrah's. I visited the Venetian and meandered along an indoor canal crowded with gondolas and striped gondoliers. In the Forum Shops at Caesars, I examined replicas of ancient ruins, rode a corkscrew escalator, and admired a dazzling fountain full of Roman gods. Every step of the way, I thought, *oh look, more dazzling glamour, more intricate beauty, more impressive feats of engineering.* I wearied of it all over again and felt even more drained this time.

There's something deeply unsettling about a place that leaves nothing to the imagination. In Las Vegas, where everything is bigger, hotter, and brighter than life and every fantasy is realized, I need not labor to find inspiration in small details or poorly-lit crannies. It's too easy to grow numb to sights and sounds that would otherwise shock and amaze me. I feel an unhealthy craving creeping into my bones. It threatens to leach the satisfaction out of simple pleasures.

WEDNESDAY, MARCH 23

(Las Vegas, NV)

I need only watch them quarrel-flirt for thirty seconds to confirm that they're still seeing each other in secret. Apparently, nothing has changed. I thought I could steel my nerves and put aside my personal feelings for a few hours a day. Not so. My whole body aches with frustration.

I'm angry with Jeremiah for letting this dalliance drag on. I've never been *angry* with him before. It's unsettling. Doesn't he see that it's about more than him, her, or me? It's the ministry leader's job to foster peace among his staff. It's the spiritual leader's job to set a good example for his flock. He persists in playing with fire that has the potential to burn us all.

THURSDAY, MARCH 24

(Las Vegas, NV)

That's it. I'm going to strangle him!

Carmen thinks she might be pregnant, and I had to hear it from Sonja, the sound tech. Not only has Carmen been talking to others about her relationship with Jeremiah, but now she might be pregnant and poised to bring down a load of drama on all our heads. Apparently, she's afraid of what might happen if her husband finds out it's not his.

Were they not on the same page about the secrecy of their trysts? Did he even bother to have that conversation? There's nothing like having an affair *with his own publicist* to ensure that a scandal like this reaches

epic proportions. It seems we've veered into a daytime soap opera!

Perhaps it's for the best that he didn't answer the door when I stomped over there to scream at him. Better that I spent my initial frustration pacing and stewing privately so I could come to the realization that my rage was really hurt. I'm hurt as heck that Jeremiah did not heed my warning to be careful. Did any part of our frank conversation get through to him? But perhaps by the time we talked, it was already too late.

I have ground through far more contemplation than this matter deserves, and I have concluded that I must calm down to a level at which I can speak frankly with Jeremiah once again. As much as I want to chew him out, that probably won't resolve anything.

Saturday, March 26

(Las Vegas, NV)

Jeremiah's moods are unpredictable. Just when I expected him to fly at me in a rage, he crumbled beneath the burden of my dismay even before I lowered the full weight of it upon him. He knew what I wanted to talk about before I opened my mouth and was quick to assure me that he had slept very little and prayed a lot over the last week. He asked God to make things right as He saw fit, and this morning, Carmen's blood finally washed away the evidence of their sin. *Praise Jesus, hallelujah!*

He swore that it was over between them, and he would adhere more strictly to the moral precepts of his office from now on. If I would entrust him with my faith once more, we could carry on our mission more vigorously than ever.

My stomach twisted pitifully with each phrase that came out of his mouth. I'm fairly certain he's an unwell man, but still, I balked at the blatant manipulation that slithered beneath his words. I listened uncomfortably as he went on and on about his desire to return to the righteous path and how much he needed my help to do it. God sent me to show him the way, he said. So let's put the little things behind us and focus on the ministry. That should be and would be our sole focus all the time.

Right. As if my focus has been anything *but* the ministry this whole time. What "little" things did he want me to put behind us? His "little" lies? His "little" affair? Or Freddie's "little" death?

The more he talked, the more distant his voice sounded. My chin dropped, and I sank down into a deep, dense stupor. Though my mind continued to process all that I saw and heard, I could neither move nor react. It was as if my every conflicting thought and feeling had slammed together, resulting in catastrophic overload. I was stuck in that state until Jeremiah said something offensive enough to yank me out of it. He told me to hurry up and work out my "bugs" so that we could go on to do great things together.

"My bugs?" I snapped, leveling my gaze at him. "No, I will *not* hurry up and work out my bugs. I will figure out what to do in my own time, and it will take as long as it takes."

SUNDAY, MARCH 27

(*Las Vegas, NV*)

I caught a glimpse of Jeremiah and Jude arguing backstage. I couldn't hear what they were talking about, but I saw malice flash between them

like high carbon steel.

It was interesting to observe how well they were matched in grit and intensity. The two stood locked in conflict like rams butting heads. One flared with acrid gesticulations, and one glowered with clenched fists and planted feet, but neither dominated the other.

When the two separated, I hurried over to speak to Jeremiah. He brushed me off. I chased after Jude, but his lips were sealed. No hints, no acknowledgment, no reassurance from either of them.

Argh! Enough with the secrets. I am sick and tired of being kept in the dark, left to stumble over devastating surprises. I guess I will just have to find this one out on my own. Reticent men, beware. If I can discover Jeremiah's secret affair by accident, just imagine what I could do with a bit more focus and determination.

Monday, March 28ᵀᴴ

(Las Vegas, NV)

At sunset, the mirage falls away beneath our feet. I watch from the window as a line appears on the sand where the oasis ends and the desert begins.

The transition between landscapes seems abrupt from so far away, but I know that it's not as absolute as it appears. The firm boundaries that keep the desert at bay do not prevent its influence from seeping through. For all its dazzling fountains and lush greenery, Las Vegas is still, in its very nature, a desiccating place. Thank goodness we're not staying. We're heading west now, toward blue ocean and Mediterranean climes, to a place where figs and pomegranates grow on trees.

SUNDAY, APRIL 3

(Gardena, CA)

The entire auditorium is a stage, and all the men and women are actors. The line between audience and performer has blurred to such a degree that I can no longer tell them apart.

For this show, no rehearsals are required. Even the most minor parts are etched directly onto the performers' hearts. They know what to expect and what is expected of them—shout here, moan there, grimace, fall to the floor. Before they walk through the door, they sign an invisible agreement to come broken and leave whole.

Jeremiah does not have to prove his power anymore, nor does anyone need convincing. Each and every one of them wants to be the miracle. But there will be no miracles tonight unless everyone's faith—from the intern's to the infant son's—is absolute.

SUNDAY, APRIL 10

(Gardena, CA)

A man leaped from the audience and accosted Belinda Kleven, our check recipient, as she returned to her seat this afternoon. Jude and two ushers rushed to intervene. They grabbed the man and hauled him outside. A trail of rants followed him out the door: something about corruption, the 99%, and the religious-industrial complex. Jeremiah quickly got the Crusade back on track.

When Jude returned to his station a little while later, his forehead

was damp, and there was a small scrape on his cheek. I asked if he was alright. Of course, he was.

"I feel sorry for the guy," I remarked.

"I don't," said Jude.

I explained that I sympathized with the man's desperation, even if his public display was inappropriate. Jude argued that the man wasn't desperate—he was an exhibitionist who wanted to publicly complain without affecting real change. Just look how quickly everyone forgot about him once he was gone. He wasted time and energy and accomplished nothing. There are ways to influence people, but that wasn't one of them.

I was surprised that Jude seemed more irked by the man's poorly executed protest than he was by the trouble it caused him. That the man could have done a *better job of it* was not a critique that crossed my mind.

SUNDAY, APRIL 24

(Anaheim, CA)

First, the bank statements. Now this.

It's officially safe to say that something doesn't add up. Somewhere in the numbers, there exists a sizable discrepancy. Have the congregants been writing bad checks? Have the ushers been exaggerating? Or is it possible that Jeremiah—?

About three weeks ago, something odd happened. During Sunday evening cleanup, Jude radioed and asked me to come backstage to help him with some two-person job. When I arrived (less than five minutes later), the task was complete. He asked me to wind up electrical cords instead. This seemed like pointless busywork, but okay, I complied.

As I worked on the cords, I overheard snippets of conversations between the six ushers as they waited to be let into the counting room. Taysha, our most vivacious usher, loudly whispered to the others about a *ten thousand dollar* check that a congregant had dropped into her donation bucket. She knew she wasn't supposed to talk about it, but how could she not?

"Imagine—being able to drop ten grand just like that!" she enthused with a snap of her fingers.

I imagined it, alright. All week long, I imagined it. Come the following Sunday, I almost choked on my gum when Jeremiah Promise called Breanna Pearson to stage to accept a check for nine thousand. That's a lot of money, of course—but it was only half the amount I expected.

That evening, I timed my exit to sync up with the last usher on her way out. I casually steered our conversation around to the experience of counting a bucket full of cash. What was it like for her? Did it take long? Was it mostly small change? Ones? Fives? Twenties?

"Oh yeah, tons!" she exclaimed. It was mostly paper cash, a few checks, and "a lot more twenties than you'd think."

That night I sat down in my hotel room with paper and pencil and sketched out a reasonably conservative hypothetical.

I knew we had filled all 4,800 seats that week—that much I could see with my own eyes.

Let's say 70% of those people donated. That's 3,360.

Let's say 90% of those people donated $25 or less.

Let's say 50% of those people donated $5-$10, with another quarter giving more than $10 and the other less than $1.

I drew a grid with various combinations and denominations of cash and assigned a probable quantity of donors to each category. Then I did the math. The number that resulted blew away all margin of error.

My calculations showed that an assembly of that size could easily have amassed a total cash donation of $63,823. Even if only half—even if a mere quarter—of the congregants were donating, we should be taking in more than Jeremiah is giving back. Yet even on our best days, we've never broken twenty thousand (according to him).

Where is all that money going? The obvious answer is that Jeremiah is doing something with it, but that doesn't make sense. It was his idea to give the money back in the first place. Jeremiah was the one that caught Pastor Ormand skimming off the top. That ruined their partnership. And besides, Jeremiah doesn't handle the money. He made a rule that neither of us should oversee donation collection or counting because it was a conflict of interests. That's what Jude is for. Jude brings all the ushers into a secure room and stands guard while they count the cash twice. He watches to make sure nothing finds its way into stray pockets, and then he locks up all the money someplace overnight until he can transport it to the bank in the morning...

Jude. Of course. Now, *that* makes sense.

Tuesday, April 26

(*Phoenix, AZ*)

I tried biding my time, but finally, I couldn't wait any longer. I went looking for Jude.

He wasn't in the hotel commons. I doubted that he'd go out on such a hot and windy evening, so I went to his room. A short, sharp knock brought him to the door. His eyes showed a hint of surprise, though he had already observed me through the peephole, no doubt.

"We need to talk," I declared.

The way that Jude glanced at my forehead made me think he could see the storm clouds gathering there. He retreated into his room and came back a minute later with keys and wallet.

"Let's go," he said.

We darted to the café across the street, took the booth in the back corner, and ordered coffee. As soon as the server turned away, I blurted out, "I know what's going on."

I took the page of calculations out of my pocket, smoothed it, and pushed it across the table toward him. Jude did me the courtesy of looking it over from top to bottom before narrowing his eyes and asking me what I thought was going on.

"The numbers don't add up," I said.

"What numbers?" Jude tossed the paper on the table.

"The money," I said.

"What money? This is sloppy conjecture."

"Maybe so," I argued, "But I've heard the ushers talk about their takes plenty of times. I heard about the five-figure donation someone dropped in the bucket. The week after, Jeremiah wrote out a four-figure check. That's a big discrepancy—even for sloppy conjecture."

Jude stared at me. The corner of his mouth curled with contempt, and this prodded me closer to the precipice of anger. As far as I was concerned, the case was already solved, and Jude—or rather, Judas— was the villain of this piece. He was the only other person close enough to Jeremiah and the money to exploit them both. It made sense.

I summoned up every ounce of ferocity and accuse Jude point-blank of skimming ministry funds. "You're not going to get away with this," I added with a theatrical flourish.

"It's not—" Jude paused. "I advise you to check your facts," he snapped in a tone sharp enough to cut glass.

What facts? Didn't he just dismiss all my "facts" with one sweep of the hand?

"Hrithik Mukherjee," Jude said.

That name again. From the bank statements—the ones in the mailbox that Jude asked me to check. He gave me the key. Did he expect curiosity to get the best of me?

I fished for more information, but Jude's lips were sealed. On all pertinent matters, he was contractually bound to silence. As in, he signed a non-disclosure agreement and had a legal obligation to keep Jeremiah's secrets. In the end, however, he did not need to breathe another word of it to me. I talked myself through it with Jude as my witness, and his pointed looks and stiffened jaw as good as confirmed it all.

Question: Why would Jeremiah skim his own donations if he didn't have to give up the money in the first place? He could have kept it all right from the start, and no one would have faulted him.

Answer: because that's Jeremiah's shtick. He's the holy Robin Hood—except in his version, he takes from the poor to give to the poor. His followers make offerings for the sake of gratitude and miracles, but they offer *more* when there is a chance of getting more back. It's ingenious, really. A holy Ponzi scheme of sorts. He creates anticipation where there is none and uses virtue to elevate himself above the mortal man.

Even I . . .

Even I believed it.

Question: why would Jeremiah go to such lengths to deceive me? Had he been honest with me, I would have understood, sympathized. I wouldn't have judged. Or would I have?

Answer: because try though I might to dodge the facts, Jeremiah is not the man I think he is, nor does he keep his secrets well. He's master enough of human nature to know that I might allow my faith in him to

crumble, but I would not let it collapse. He knows I cannot afford to lose *everything*. As I forge ahead on this path, the gates are closing behind me. My survival now depends on my willingness to ignore danger.

Question: how long has Jude known? A week? A month? Three? Six? I studied his eyes as I presented each guess. Though his face has never been easy to read, I have gradually calibrated to the minuteness of his expressions and learned that the truth lives mostly in his eyes.

Answer: more than a month, less than six. That's the length of time that Jude has *known*. My heart sank when I recalled a few dubious details that predated Jude's arrival. Things didn't just stop adding up when I took out a pencil and did the math. They haven't been adding up for a while.

What about that abrupt break with Pastor Ormand and his church? Jeremiah's accusations look a bit duplicitous from this angle. What really happened? Was it the other way around? That might explain our hasty departure and Jeremiah's clandestine confrontation with his partner. His righteous indignation was a nice touch.

I asked Jude why he would go along with this. Why not try to stop him? Jude said that it's not his place to stop Jeremiah. He's paid to do a job; he does it.

Wait a second—Jeremiah *pays* Jude? That part hit me harder than expected. Did Jeremiah pay the others too? Everyone but me? Mortified, I stammered that this made Jude a mercenary. A hypocrite! He criticized me for practicing blind allegiance, yet he sold his loyalty to the highest bidder!

"I do not *sell* my loyalty. I sell my services," said Jude.

"Corrupt services."

"I do nothing corrupt."

"Do nothing—that's right! Shame on you. Can't you see that Jeremi-

ah is weak? He needs help. He needs guidance. I thought you Marines were all about leadership, honor, integrity, and stuff."

Jude's jaw tightened, but he didn't respond. I blathered on for a bit about Jeremiah's enduring value as a symbol of hope for the masses. He might be more human and more fallible than I want him to be, but there is still an image of him worth salvaging.

"At least he heals people," I added, with the implied chaser: *that's more than I can say for you.* That's when Jude opened his wallet and took out a folded sheet of paper. He pushed it across the table to me. I opened it and found a list of names and phone numbers. Some of them looked familiar; some were crossed out.

As I studied the list, I remembered some of the faces that went with the names. Peter Carpenter: a slender man with white hair and sparkly brown eyes; recipient of the Crusade donation back in October or November. Kurt Bennigan: a large man with a limp; donation recipient in March. Cynthia Volker: long, silver-streak hair, metastasized lung cancer; star of our Chicago Crusade when Jeremiah convinced her to dance out of her wheelchair and toss her oxygen tank into the audience. She declared that she was cured of cancer right there on stage in front of God and everyone. Her name was crossed out. I raised my eyes questioningly to Jude.

"Deceased," he said.

I started to argue with him, but he held up his hand and told me not to take his word for it. I should call those numbers, talk to the friends and families of the people on that list, and let them tell me what became of Jeremiah Promise's supposed miracles.

When I returned to my hotel room this evening, I placed one phone call. Favour Ilan. She had come to us last fall with a brain tumor, and Jeremiah had dissolved it with a single thwack to the forehead.

Favour's sister answered the phone. She told me that Favour had stopped all medications and treatments for the tumor shortly after the Crusade. She died three weeks ago.

"Will we never be free of this curse?" Favour's sister lamented. "How many more sins must we atone for? I don't understand why God continues to punish us!"

Favour's sister confided that just before Jeremiah "healed" Favour, he told her that her family had been cursed for four generations. When he laid hands on her, he lifted the curse and promised her a long life with a husband and three children. So much for that. I wish I had comforting words to offer the grieving sister, but I had no words at all, so I hung up the phone. That was enough revelation for one day.

WEDNESDAY, APRIL 27

(Phoenix, AZ)

Missy may have found a renter for my cottage, but this renter has conditions: she must be given free rein to strip the wallpaper in the living room and kitchen and paint the walls any color she pleases. The audacity! I can't believe that someone would dare propose such drastic changes to a house they expect to occupy temporarily.

Missy must have let slip some hint about my present financial desperation, and I guess this potential renter thought she had me over a barrel. This roused my self-righteous indignation. I was inclined to say not only *no*, but *heck no.*

I restrained this impulse and told Missy I'd consider it. I really am trying. What's more important—saving the wallpaper that my mom and I picked out and put up together when I was ten years old? Or keeping my lifelong home?

I envisioned the wallpaper in the living room, and vividly recalled how I used to trace its designs with my fingers. For the first time in a long time, I thought about the old olive green paper that was there before. Mom and I tried to scrape it off, but it was cemented on so securely that we risked tearing off chunks of sheetrock, so we had to put up the new cream paper with the purple-flowered vines on top of it.

Did you know that peeling away misconceptions is like stripping old wallpaper one layer at a time? One doesn't even realize how many coverups there have been and how the room has slowly become more confining over time until she begins scraping away and finds more layers underneath.

There is a fundamental flaw with this sort of undertaking, though—namely, that the determination to get to the bottom of something, once ignited, is not easily extinguished. It tends to catch on other elements in the room—the carpet, trim, furniture, and fixtures. If one is not careful, she may find herself scrutinizing the room's size, purpose, place in the house, and perhaps the very concept of a home. She may even question the jurisdiction in which it resides and the illusion that her life ever satisfied her at all.

FRIDAY, APRIL 29

(Phoenix, AZ)

It's nearly impossible to work out which threads of Jeremiah's stories are real and which are lies. I'm compelled to stamp *false* on everything he's ever told me, but it's not that simple.

Is Jeremiah brilliant, or is he sick? Or worse—is he both?

He's a chess player and a mathematician at heart. I am inclined to attribute to him a degree of cunning that leaves little room for error. He seems to know that the best lies are wrapped around truths, and he uses this to manipulate his followers' sympathies.

Yet, even with my emotional x-ray machine (Empathy) turned on full blast, I have detected a high degree of authenticity in him all along. Perhaps Jeremiah believes so passionately, so madly, in everything that he does, that he has passed beyond all comprehension of right and wrong, means and ends. Meanwhile, I have passed beyond all comprehension of where he ends and I begin.

When one reaches the mythical proportions that Jeremiah Promise has in my mind, it's impossible to tease apart all the threads of truth from fiction. My memories of him are tinged with loyal trust the way that old photos are marred by lens flares and color bands.

Speaking of loyalty—Jeremiah had mine from the start. I was so busy trying to prove my worth to him that I never stopped to consider whether *he* was loyal to *me*.

He has a contract with Jude, but not with me. He pays Jude, but he doesn't pay me. No contract, no money, no means of independence, no real power. He has willfully kept me stumbling in the dark, dependent upon his every whim.

This pervasive fear I've felt of being left behind, cast off, and forgotten cannot be wholly unfounded. There were many times Jeremiah could easily have assuaged my anxiety with just a pinch of reassurance, but he chose to withhold it. Or rather, he would bomb me with excessive praise on rare occasions and brush me off the rest of the time. This never felt right, but I assumed it was my fault and strove dutifully to please him.

Are these really the actions of a loyal and caring teacher, guide, or friend? What is he, then? Friend or foe? Innocent or guilty? Is he sincere or deceptive, careless or self-protective, earnest or disinterested, foolish or wise? He is all these things at once, inseparable, and non-linear. I can neither love him nor hate him absolutely because, even now, I can see his humanity peeping through. Curse these complexities.

SUNDAY, MAY 1

(Phoenix, AZ)

Wholesome Healing Ministries, a registered religious institution, has the legal right to accept and use donations as it sees fit—tax-free. Jeremiah Promise is not required to provide any records of the ministry's financial dealings to the IRS. It's true. I looked it up.

In fact, the IRS is remarkably apathetic about the fiscal goings-on of all 501(c)(3) exempted organizations. Unless someone shoves indisputable proof under its nose that the ministry's donation money is being used for non-religious purposes (loosely defined), the government remains staunchly indifferent to such things.

I found one notable exception. Four years ago, amidst a suspicious surge in registered tax-exempt organizations, the Senate Finance Committee launched a massive investigation into six of the nation's most prominent and wealthy televangelists. Bartholomew Lambrecht was not among those named in the articles I read. Apparently, there exist in this country at least half a dozen more prominent, wealthy, and dubious faith healers than he.

The investigators lacked the authority to compel their subjects to disclose financial records or impose a penalty for non-compliance. The inquiry dragged on for years, ran mostly in circles, and was officially closed last year with inconclusive results. The ministries in question were neither condemned nor cleared, and the rest of us are left to wonder how celebrity preachers pay for Malibu mansions and private jets.

Even as I write this, a desperate part of me wants to rush to Jeremiah's defense. *He's nothing like them. He may keep some of the money, but it isn't necessarily earmarked for selfish purposes. He must be skimming it for a good reason.*

I'm eager for every modicum of relief that comes from reframing my impressions and softening the words I use to describe Jeremiah's actions. I don't like this about me. I find my readiness to excuse Jeremiah appalling. He doesn't deserve a feather-light euphemism. The word is *embezzling*, not skimming.

So that's it then. Jeremiah Promise is an embezzler. That's what it's called, even if what he's doing is not technically punishable by law. Ask me if I care what's right and what's wrong in the eyes of the law when the lawmakers look the other way in such matters. Legal or not, what he's doing is unethical and immoral—and worst of all, it's a misrepresentation. A lie.

Jeremiah was right. Betrayals are like mice. Where there's one, there are always a dozen more. He has gone to the trouble to cover up his questionable practices, which makes me wonder what else he's hiding.

SATURDAY, MAY 7

(Phoenix, AZ)

"And another thing!" she exclaimed, stabbing the sky with her index finger. This is what I would look like if I spoke my mind freely every time the pressure of my thoughts overwhelmed me. But I keep my declarations mostly buttoned-up, as if constricting them with a tight enough collar might force

either insight or resolution.

Impressions and hypotheses spin nonstop in my head. With each revolution, I try to identify the troublesome spurs that pluck at my conscience. I've given names to a multitude of Jeremiah's faults—deceit, disloyalty, dissoluteness—but there are other, finer points to be made that cannot be reduced to single words. I have discovered some today that I don't even want to acknowledge. I'm embarrassed by my unwitting complicity in certain evils. Ignoring them doesn't make them go away, however, so I might as well admit what's troubling me today.

Jeremiah's secret relationship with Carmen does more than violate his ethics or cause me personal offense. It also reveals something distinctly vexing about the way he treats women (particularly the ones he is closest to). He seems to have a system: he chooses a mark, makes her feel extra special, then abruptly discards her in favor of something newer and shinier. If he cannot rid himself of certain marks—one of the hazards of taking on employees and devotees—then he makes them stand by and watch while he shows everyone else more respect, consideration, and charm.

Carmen and I may have more in common than I ever wanted to admit. We both got in too deep with Jeremiah, and it's been bad for both of us. Carmen and I don't have to get along, don't have to be friends, don't even have to discuss any of this—but I should not resent her for falling into his trap. The same thing happened to me.

Now, with the pregnancy rumor, I can't believe Jeremiah dared to tell me that he pleaded with God to make things right. As if, naturally, I should agree that the top priority here was to cover his own tracks. Where's the remorse? Where's the repentance? Where's the concern for human life? Jeremiah is only interested in protecting his reputation—which leans heavily upon the *appearance* rather than the practice of integ-

rity. This, I can neither respect nor condone.

I am tempted to use Jeremiah's arrogance against him. Wasn't it he who put me in charge of human relations? I speak to the masses so that he doesn't have to—it wouldn't be difficult for me to slip a few subversive words in each of their ears. Had I the authority to speak out against him, I could ruin him with aspersions alone. Character is everything in this business—even if it's only skin deep.

It would be so much easier if this all turned out to be a bad dream. Perhaps tomorrow, I'll wake up and find that Jeremiah is a good man with a master plan that's laced with covert twists and turns. Perhaps the wisdom of his machinations will blow us all away in the end.

This is a sweet dream, but not a probable one. Such flights of fancy only raise my hopes to dash them from a greater height. No more of this nonsense. There are no magical revelations nor gushes of clarity coming for us now. They have gone the way of those enchanting looks, smiles, and talks that Jeremiah and I used to share—ripe with promise but left on the vine to rot.

SUNDAY, MAY 15

(South Lake, TX)

I tune out Jeremiah's sermons all the time now and allow my attention to wander quite a bit during the Crusades. I am not entirely deaf to his antics, however; today, these words brought my attention back with a snap: "Behold sister Yolanda's perfect faith! Praise Jesus, hallelujah!"

Uh-oh. What did sister Yolanda do?

Jeremiah called the woman up to the stage and announced that she had just donated her last five dollars in the world to Wholesome Healing Ministries.

Hallelujah!

I was horrified. After the show, I tracked the woman down and tried to reason with her. I told her she should not have surrendered the very last of her money to this sham of a ministry. Whatever her situation, I could guarantee her that the money would do more good in her hands than it could possibly do in Jeremiah's. I even tried to press upon her my last twenty dollars to make up for the five she had given, but she wouldn't take my money. Yolanda Jones just smiled serenely and said that Jeremiah had prophesied greater riches in her near future. Bless me for trying, but God would provide. There was nothing I could do or say to change her mind.

Wednesday, May 18

(Houston, TX)

Jude has a gift for appearing out of thin air when I need a reason to get out of my own head.

I found him in the hotel lobby when I returned from a frustrating afternoon walk. I had just been to the dry cleaner to pick up my Crusade dress, but it wasn't ready, and the attendant was rude about it. I had tried calling Missy to check in with her and chat, but she didn't answer the phone. I got gum on my shoe—not just on it, but *inside* the split in the sole. And just as I was crossing the street to return to the hotel, a car turned left on red and almost ran me over.

It was a relief to see a familiar figure standing at the front desk as soon as I stepped into the hotel lobby. Jude's back was to me, but I recognized his steely glimmer. The desk clerk had just handed him something. When I reached his side, I found him scowling at a thick, hand-addressed envelope. The instant he noticed me, the letter disappeared into his pocket.

"Checking mail, good idea," I remarked. "Anything good?"

Jude glanced at me curtly and walked away.

I don't think he intended to give offense. Careful observation has led me to conclude that Jude usually means well, even if his manners are rough and abrupt at times. Here's the thing: I'm human, and sometimes I take things personally even when I shouldn't. Little did Jude know, his rebuff was my second-to-last straw of the day.

By the time I stepped into the elevator at four o'clock this afternoon, my patience was totally spent, and I was ready to retreat into myself and stay there until morning. Unfortunately, the day wasn't quite done. The elevator doors opened, and Jeremiah stepped in. He was heading upstairs (to Carmen's room, I presume). No hello, how are you, what's new, nothing like that. Instead, he glanced down at my shoes and asked, "Are you ever going to upgrade those old things?"

He'd barely breathed a word about my appearance before, and now he thought he could offhandedly shame me? I whirled around and snapped that my shoes were none of his business, and by the way, I wasn't the swindler here. Maybe if he wasn't so selfish, I could afford to buy new shoes.

Sigh. I meant to say all this out loud, I really did. My heart pounded, my whole body shook, and in the end all I could do was turn to Jeremiah with a glare and say, "Never."

Friday, May 20

(Houston, TX)

My faith in Jeremiah first emerged from the vapors of the universe as a delicate and ephemeral thing. It was an eager baby bird that couldn't survive without my nurturing and care. Over time, it grew into an independent beast capable of savagely possessing me and preventing its own demise.

This beast no longer answers to me. I cannot expel it like pus from a flesh wound. It has become an integral part of me—it saturates me to the bone, envelops me like a magnetic field. Part of me desperately wants to escape it. I ought to be able to leave Jeremiah and never look back. But he and I persist in some binary orbit from which I cannot break free. Each time I reach the apogee of my disregard for and disgust with him, some indefatigable force pulls me back in again.

Which force?

Hope.

Indefatigable hope.

I bend and twist and hack away at the invisible fist that grips me by the collar. It won't let go. Stop prevailing, you silly, stupid thing! You have outlived your usefulness. I suppose Maya Angelou was right about humans requiring hope to survive. Hope may keep me alive, but it also keeps me weak. I cannot seem to latch onto a resolution. I flounder in ambivalence. Should I confront Jeremiah about the money? Should I wait patiently for the matter to resolve itself? I can endure almost anything if I do it with conviction, but these thorns of uncertainty tear at my conscience and bleed my fortitude. I pray for external guidance, but none manifests. So, I look inward for guidance, but there's too much! A cacophony of voices speak to me, and I can't discern what "feels" right because all my feelings clash.

SUNDAY, MAY 22

(Houston, TX)

Another dream about Jeremiah. He was leading the way through a network of rope bridges high up in a forest canopy. I followed behind him and half-listened to his litany of excuses for taking the long way to our destination.

We came to a fork in the path. Jeremiah told me that he wanted to visit a friend in a hut to the left, but he had to do it alone. He took a handkerchief out of his pocket and bound my wrist to the rope guide. It was for my own good, he told me—he didn't want me wandering off.

I awoke from this dream with one clear thought: ambivalence is itself a sign. It is more than a sign. It is a tool. When one finds herself bound, instinct compels her to wriggle back and forth, stretch and loosen the restraints until, in time, she wrenches herself free.

SATURDAY, MAY 28

(College Park, GA)

I always seem to be passing Jude in hotel lobbies, hallways, bars, or dining rooms. I have finally discovered the reason for his omnipresence: he is surveilling. Jude situates himself in some strategic spot and pretends to read, but he absorbs everything around him. Few things escape his

notice. When I sneaked up on him this evening, it was purely by accident. He was reading one of those mysterious letters that he's been collecting from hotel front desks the world over. My curiosity inadvertently bumped me into stealth mode. A soon as Jude noticed me beside him, he stiffened with annoyance, crumpled up the paper, and stuffed it in his pocket. Something tells me those letters may never see the light of day again.

"Love letters?" I teased.

"Of course not," Jude snapped. "It's just my brother."

"You have a brother?" I asked.

"No—my other brother," he said. This confusing coverup did nothing to discourage my love letter hypothesis.

"You must be fastidious about updating your mailing address," I observed. That's no small feat, considering how often we change cities. Jude didn't respond—in other words: *I'm done with this conversation.* I decided to stick around anyway. Better to brave Jude's tacit annoyance than return to my room and risk being waterboarded by troubling thoughts.

I attempted to draw Jude into a critique of the porpoise-shaped tile pattern in the hotel foyer, but small-talk plinked ineffectually off his armor. He seemed to be paying attention to something else. His eyes darkened and changed shape. I sensed the subtle drop in atmospheric pressure and fell silent.

For several minutes, Jude's attention indirectly followed one man's every move around the room. I watched Jude observe the man, trying to discern the connection between them. After the interloper left, Jude explained that he was not a guest at the hotel, but he probably had business with someone that was. Not a pleasant kind of business. This guy was ex-military, ex-police, or both. He was carrying, but he wasn't a cop—probably a bounty hunter. I gazed at Jude incredulously. How could he discern all that just from a few discrete glances?

"It's my job to discern things," said Jude.

When I paused to critically evaluate what I had seen, Jude's assessment made sense. The uneven fit of the man's jacket (leather on an eighty-degree day), the furtive manner of his movements, the deliberate path he took through the hotel, and his prompt departure.

"He was anxious," I told Jude.

Jude raised his eyebrows. "How do you know that?"

"I could just . . . feel it," I shrugged. When that man came near, I felt the vibratory intensity of a jackhammer pass behind my chair. It made my muscles clench—but I didn't think much of it because things like that happen all the time.

I expected Jude to scoff at me, but he did not. His eyes narrowed as he mulled over my observation for a minute, and then with a nod, he filed it neatly away in some private corner of his mine. I'll admit, a strange little thrill scurried up my spine when I realized that Jude and I had just used our powers of observation to collaborate. That was fun! It was fascinating to glimpse the world through his eyes.

Friday, June 3

(College Park, GA)

Madison Square Garden is the topic of the hour. Jeremiah booked it for October, and he looks forward to "joining the ranks of the greats that have preached there before" him. It'll be our biggest venue of the year—not only because the stadium seats twenty thousand, but because Jeremiah plans to broadcast live to other auditoriums, or "satellites," around the globe.

It's becoming more apparent every day that the Jeremiah Promise train is leaving without me. I've never felt farther from him than I do now. I always assumed I'd be there to celebrate our successes together, but this does not feel like a victory.

SATURDAY, JUNE 4

(College Park, GA)

I almost resolved to burst into his room yesterday evening and tell him everything—and I mean everything. What a relief it would have been to unburden my mind.

Then I thought about his likely response. His probable look of surprise. His indignation. His stunned reserve. That dismissive wave of the hand and those sweeping phrases of denial. "Look, you can't prove any of this. I don't have time for this kind of drama. And by the way—*I never loved you.*"

Then it would just be me sobbing pathetically while being led away by some unsympathetic stranger. I couldn't bear the indignity of that. Jeremiah doesn't deserve the chance to make me feel even smaller than I already do. I wish my heart didn't still ache for him. I wish my loyalty would break, and my longing for him would snuff out like an abandoned campfire. I used to play a little game of Devil's advocate with myself: what would I be willing to do for Jeremiah Promise? How far would I go? What would I give up? There was a morbid thrill to dreaming up daring hypotheticals, knowing each time that the final choice would always be the same: anything for Jeremiah Promise.

When I look at him now, I see a man whose suits are expensive, but whose values are cheap. I pity this man. I want to put my hand on his shoulder and speak earnestly with him, friend to friend. But he is beyond reach and reason now.

MONDAY, JUNE 6TH

(College Park, GA)

It's all long walks and circling thoughts, but zero resolution. I keep hoping for the answers to miraculously come, but they don't. The powers that be have turned their backs on me. *This one's on you,* they say.

I walked far today, but my steps were more compulsive than they were exploratory. I hoped to induce exhaustion so that I might finally sleep, but there were too many boogeymen waiting for me at every turn. The pale visage of a plain and solemn face rose up in a plate-glass storefront beside a smiling, cherry-lipped mannequin. I forced myself to stop and look, really look, at the contrast between the two and etch their differences deep into my memory banks.

In this light, it was obvious that no man in his right mind would choose the bleak specter on the left over the perky peach on the right. The former ought to have known better from the start. Her indignation and outrage were unwarranted, her broken heart superfluous. And yet, of all the reasons for her to agonize, it was Jeremiah's "romance" with Carmen that disturbed her most. Can you believe that? So petty, so unworthy.

I resolved (once again) to steel my heart and drive out silly preoccupations once and for all. A moment later, I passed a gift shop that featured a rack of novelty license plates. The first name that caught my eye was *Jeremiah.* I hurried on by, turned the corner, and was immediately accosted by an elaborate display of fancy chess sets in an adjacent

shop window. See? Every time I make up my mind to disown Jeremiah Promise and be done with him, reminders of him chase me down like vengeful wasps. I used to think these sorts of signs were magical. Now they look like cheap and demented tricks.

I have never hated loving someone before. I've never sought to destroy feelings that persisted without my permission. My instinct was to walk farther and faster, put miles between myself and the object of my twisted affection—as many as Earth would allow. Yet no matter where I go, or how far, I cannot seem to escape the trouble that lives in my own heart.

I caught sight of a different face in a different pane of glass. This one was smaller and harder. It fit inside the exclamation dot at the end of a big, bright advertisement for a storewide sale. Everything up to 50% Off! Including my self-respect. I scowled at the face, and she glared fiercely back at me.

I walked on and thought about the profound futility of imposing my will on the world. I honestly thought that if I set out to fix humanity with the noblest of intentions, all the forces of the universe would rush to my aid. I did not imagine that anything insidious or exploitative would hitch a ride on fate's master plan—or that fate might not have a master plan. Or that the future is a wilderness where evil proliferates like poisonous moss, and I lack the power to stop it.

As the volume turns up on life's perceived injustices, I am overwhelmed by the urge to shake awake the people that slumber all around me. I want to demand answers to these questions: Why aren't you concerned about the hazards that creep closer every moment? Can't you sense the danger? Doesn't it terrify you? Then I remembered that not so long ago, that woman in the glass also struggled to wake from her comfortable slumber. No one fixes anyone, no one saves anyone, and no one wakens anyone before she is ready to stir.

By this time, I was miles from the hotel. A stomach rumble warned me to plan my next move carefully. If I wanted sustenance, I would have to turn back. I had foolishly allowed my means to dwindle to such a degree that I couldn't afford to stop for food along the way.

Just as I crossed the street and pointed my feet in the direction from which I'd come, I looked up and glimpsed one more face. It hovered, life-sized, in the void of a vacant storefront. This one was the least changed of all the apparitions I saw today. There were more lines on her face, and she seemed to have forgotten how to grin, but her eyes were still wide and traced with rose-colored rims.

This face was the most tragic of all. This was the one that could not assimilate the grim, rough, and unjust realities of the world. Try as she might, this one could achieve only flickers of transformation. Where could she go from here? She couldn't go back to ignorance. She couldn't continue forward into deeper complicity. She was hopelessly, desperately stuck outside her element, and she was miserable.

Enough phantasms for one day. I trained my eyes on the sidewalk and did not raise them again. By the time I returned to the hotel, I had reached a resolve: there's only one place in the world for all these reflections and me—the only place we ever fit, and that's home. Home may be a bit worse for wear and sullied by unfulfilled dreams, but it's the place that has withstood every storm so far and will undoubtedly stand up to more.

On cue, a rush of sensations propelled me further into my resolve. I could smell the cedar of my bedroom closet. I could feel the faucet knobs in my hands and taste the iron in the tap water. I anticipated the simple pleasures of summer heat and winter's bite. Yes, it's time to go home. This time, for good.

Tuesday, June 7

(College Park, GA)

Mom used to say that every time one speaks the truth, she gains an ounce of power. I wonder if power can also be lost to silence? If so, then it's no wonder I have lost nearly everything by now. May these final words reclaim just enough of my strength to get me home again.

Dearest Jeremiah,

You were, and always will be, my miracle.

You inspired me, and others like me, to become a better, stronger, happier, more resilient version of myself. It's an immutable fact that you changed my life, and for this, I will forever be grateful.

I must confess that my feelings for you have evolved into something more complicated and enduring than gratitude. I wanted to tell you many times, but I knew deep down that you did not return my affection. I hoped that this unwanted part of me would eventually turn and walk away, but instead, it clung to me tighter and dug in its claws.

My situation, as it stands, has become very painful. It has come to my attention that you have engaged in more than one unethical practice during your tenure as head of Wholesome Healing Ministries. In addition to your affair with Carmen, I know about the extreme under-reporting of Crusade donations, Hrithik Mukherjee's multiple bank accounts, and the wrongful deaths of several congregants that you supposedly "healed."

I agonize daily over both my feelings for you and the hard reality that even if some version of "us" (you and me) was possible in this life, it would turn me into things that I don't want to become: a secret, a liability, and an accomplice.

Admittedly, I have no hard evidence of any laws that you've broken or crimes you've committed. I only have my conscience and my heart, which tell me that my suspicions

are all true, and though I love you, I cannot condone what you do. It's essential to me that you personally exemplify the standards of conduct that you preach. It was your strong moral character that mesmerized me from the first, and now I'd rather lose you altogether than stand by and watch as my respect for you sinks lower with each step you take up the ladder to fame.

Despite everything, I still see a lot of good in you. I understand that even the best intentions can go astray, and I sympathize. People don't often talk about what happens when fame's ladder is presented to you—how it changes you. The first few steps are simple, innocent, safe. But as you climb higher, the distance grows between you and your roots. You start to lose sight of where you came from and what first inspired you. You lose sight of the things that make you who you are, and then you forget altogether. You become somebody else, a person with different motivations and values. You learn about frailty and corruption, and you begin to forget what's good about the world. Perhaps you wonder if it's even worth saving.

This much I can see, but unfortunately, I don't know what to do about it. I've tried warning you, but you won't listen. I've tried to help you, but you shun my efforts. I cannot endure this Sisyphean cycle of hope and disillusionment forever, nor can I, in good conscience, remain. I must go.

I wish you the very best.
T.B.

Saturday, June 11

(Miami, FL)

I asked Jude, "Have you ever had one of those instant connections with someone that hits you like a meteor hurdling out of the wild blue sky? You know the chances of it finding you—a single speck out of billions—are truly astronomical, so you never expect it to happen. When it does, it comes on so suddenly and flattens you so fast that there's no time to step out of the way. You're struck. And you're changed.

"Now there is a stranger in your life that's not strange. He comes with a tailored set of rules, most of which defy the laws of physics. It takes an impossibly short time to read each other's thoughts. You have a million bits and pieces in common with each other, and you don't even have to change a thing. You wait for the deja vu to be explained. For your fascination to dim. For things to go back to normal, but they never do. The feelings never tarnish. The way he looks at you takes your breath away—not just the first time or the second, but every time.

"Then one day, you take a look at yourself and realize that you became someone else while you were chasing this one. You spent your whole life believing that you were a strong, independent woman with a good head on her shoulders and a strong moral compass that would never, ever go astray. One day, you learned the truth: somewhere inside us all lurks a version of ourselves that would do anything, give anything, become anything, for *true* love."

"I am acquainted with troubles of the heart, yes," said Jude. A strange and foreign impression bumped against me like a black cat in the night. There it was, at last—a raw and genuine emotion from Jude. It was as if he'd drawn back the cover from the top of his well and permitted me a brief glance inside. What I saw there was sadness, and my throat clenched painfully. Before I could ask him anything further, Jude pointed out that I still hadn't answered his question: *why* was I leaving.

"I can't go on like this any longer," I said.

Jude paused to consider my response. Then he said, "I underestimated you."

He recalled the time he condemned me for my blind faith and admitted that his initial judgment of me was harsh. He didn't think I had it in me to give all this up on principle, and he respected my decision. "Character is determined by the choices a person makes when the price of doing the right thing is more than the price of doing anything else," he said.

Well, it was nice to know that Jude finally approved of me. Too bad we had to have this talk at the eleventh hour.

He said that he had seen in me a genuine desire to help people. Now, more than ever, I was in a unique position to do some good. If I wished to leave, he wouldn't stop me. But I ought to know what exactly I'd be giving up if I left.

I interrupted with the argument that by aiding and abetting Jeremiah's immoral endeavors, I canceled out every positive thing that I had ever done. Jude disagreed. I was missing the big picture. As the only person in the ministry (and perhaps in the world) that has intimate knowledge of Jeremiah's indiscretions but is not contractually bound to silence, I am more dangerous to him than he realizes. Jeremiah made the same mistake that Jude did. He underestimated me. He failed to see me as a threat. A lot of power now rests at my fingertips, but that power is not worth much unless I pick it up and put it into service— like a hammer.

Jude said one more thing before we parted ways, and his words continue to ring in my ears, try as I might to dampen them.

He told me that there were three kinds of people in the world—wolves, sheep, and sheepdogs. It was the sheep's nature to graze innocently in the field and the wolf's nature to prey upon the sheep. Were it not for the conflicting natures of the sheepdog—whose sharp fangs made it formidable, but whose altruistic heart compelled it to protect the innocent—all the sheep would soon be slaughtered by the wolves.

What does he expect me to do with this!? My mind is already made up. I'm leaving—it's the right thing for me. Once my connection with Jeremiah Promise is finally broken, the ragged ends are healed, and my mind is clear, I can try again. Somehow, someway, someday, when I am stronger, I will contend with him. Our story isn't over, but for sanity's sake, this chapter must end.

SUNDAY, JUNE 12

(Miami, FL)

I remember the first hour that I sat by myself after receiving the news that my cancer was gone. It was not a celebratory time like you'd imagine it to be. I didn't cheer or cry or make a list of people to invite to the party. I was still and quiet, an empty vessel that needed to be refilled with new hopes, dreams, and expectations.

One of the first decisions I made was to live each day of my life without regret, so I tried to exist in constant truth. Believe me, I tried. I spoke my mind and refused to comply with anything that didn't suit me. My fall back into old people-pleasing habits and needless self-restraint was so gradual that I didn't know it was happening. It always seemed like the right thing to do at the time—to stay quiet, look away, let it slide. Ruffle no feathers, stir up no dust.

Now, look at me. I've shied away from the impetus to act or speak up too many times, and my conscience cannot abide. It has amassed a tally of razor-sharp loose ends, each one designed to usher me toward death, one small slice at a time.

No more. Today, I dig in my heels and say *enough*.

"When the day of Pentecost had come, they were all together in one place. And suddenly a sound came from heaven like the rush of a mighty wind, and it filled all the house where they were sitting. And there appeared to them tongues as of fire, distributed and resting on each one of them. . ."

My bags were packed. The letter addressed to Jeremiah was stuck in my waistband. I meant to sneak it in with the reports that I hand over to Jeremiah every evening after the Crusade. By the time he found it there, I would be gone.

I ascended the stage of my final Crusade as if I was walking the plank. How grave an occasion this would be! How fateful and calamitous! As I walked, I thought tragic thoughts about my current predicament— about how hard I've worked to get nowhere. About my loss of peace, love, and money. About all the hard work I've done to justify my darling Jeremiah's failings and protect him from everyone's scrutiny—including my own. I had spent a year of my life running full speed in the wrong direction, and I had earned the right to feel sorry for myself.

I let the tears flow down my face. I chuckled bitterly over the poetic justice of my decision to leave Jeremiah after suffering through all that fear of losing him. Leaving him quietly was a small gesture, I realized. It would be a tiny tap of the hammer whose full impact may only be noticed later, if ever. Jeremiah would not miss me after I'm gone. I might never know what, if anything, I meant to him.

When I reached my seat on stage, I pulled myself together and prepared to face the crowd with stoic courage. I would pretend to be a part of all this one more time. I would endure *one more* cursed show and then be done with this business forever. Would anyone notice my spirit's silent protest against the injustice of Jeremiah's practice? Probably not.

In retrospect, my act was madness. Why did I bother to attend one more Crusade? If my intent was to startle Jeremiah with my absence, I might have been better off slipping away in the night.

It was never really about obligation, honor, duty, or even a last chance for redemption. No, clever presentiment. It was about buying time. Something big loomed on the horizon, and I must have sensed it the way that birds do when they fall silent just before the storm. I had asked for guidance, begged for signs, and the powers that be weren't about to let me leave just before they gave me my answer.

It didn't come until the end of Jeremiah's sermon. His pregnant pause caught my attention. It was time to unleash the donation brigade. What was he waiting for? He requested the congregation's full silence and concentration. Then he turned toward the left side of the stage and began to clap for some unseen entity.

"Let's welcome to the stage God's Chosen US Presidential Nominee, Bartholomew Lambrecht!" he shouted. Out from behind the curtain stepped the infamous man. The tip of his shadow brushed me as he passed by. I leaped from my chair as if touched by hot coal.

BL raised his arms high as he made his way to center stage. "Praise Jesus, hallelujah!" He roared and clapped Jeremiah on the shoulder. "May the good Lord richly reward my friend for his hefty campaign contributions! With his help, and *His* help, and the help of all you good people out there, our victory at the polls next year will ensure that we spread the Gospel of Jesus Christ to every sinner in America!" Cheers and *amens* erupted from the audience.

I glared at the two men on stage. I couldn't believe that this mythic figure I had been taught to loath and fear was standing right in front of me—standing beside Jeremiah Promise. It didn't make any sense. Then suddenly, something clicked, and I lunged.

What did I mean to do at that moment? What did I intend to say? We shall never know because Jude intercepted me and hustled me off-stage before I even got close.

"Don't do anything stupid," he hissed in my ear. I struggled, but it was pointless. After the blind passion of my impulse passed, even I could see that Jude was right. Thank goodness he stopped me. I might have squandered my chance to do something truly meaningful in this life.

My tectonic plates have shifted. Not by much—maybe by a few quarters of an inch. Yet these are the sorts of small deviations that grow in magnitude as they make their way to the surface. To say that I'm angry with Jeremiah is an understatement. I'm mad at myself for thinking that my silly little ball-peen measures to persuade, inspire, or coerce him to change would actually accomplish anything. His deviance is far worse than I imagined. The time has come to reach for something mightier— a sledgehammer.

I'm done playing the victim and allowing myself to be dragged along by the whims of Jeremiah Promise. I am not a victim. No. I am someone with fire on my mind.

Do you hear that resounding click, click, click? Those are flicks of the spark wheel.

I have reached my limit of forgiveness. I will not tolerate Jeremiah's "indiscretions" anymore—not when his twisted ambitions lead him to unleash a villain on millions of innocent people. I see now that my aim must extend beyond the *intention* to do good in this world. Good is not enough if I don't actively seek to combat evil.

My head throbs. It's that peculiar sort of deep brain pain that no pill can assuage. I don't know exactly why the feeling comes on this way, but I know now what it is. It's the pulsing vein of volition.

I've torn up the letter that I wrote to Jeremiah and fed it to the flames. I'm staying. My business here is not done. I am the source of Jeremiah's power, you see. I gave him all my faith and love, everything I had. Now I will take it all back.

Tuesday, June 14

(Miami, FL)

Curiously, I slept.

I dreamed that I was the conductor of a speeding train. The train ran so hot and fast that it caught fire, and I had to slam on the brakes and call for emergency assistance. There were only two passengers on the train, and both jumped off and ran into the woods to gather buckets of water from a nearby stream. We tried to contain the flames, but they spread quickly to the trees and underbrush.

After months of tossing and turning on the shifting tides of a troubled conscience, I'd given up hope for the big moment when my qualms would clear, and I would sleep soundly through the night. Perhaps the ability to rest was never about waiting for peace to arrive, but in discovering a way to carve out a few moments of stillness amid the ceaseless turmoil of life.

Today, the question resumes: If I can't go on like this and I can't leave, what can I do?

I mulled it over all day, and when I found Jude in the hotel lobby this evening, I made a beeline to talk to him. He received me dryly without looking up from his copy of *The Prince*.

"You're still here," he remarked. I told him about the goodbye letter I wrote to JP and about tearing it up. I said I was ready to stay and fight. So, now what?

"Now what, *what?*" asked Jude.

"What's the plan?" I asked.

"Plan?" He shook his head and turned the page of his book. No answer was coming. Wait—what? All the talk, all the soul-searching, all the sound and fury, and no plan? He had to be kidding me.

With an air of annoyance, Jude closed his book and put it down. Did I have a plan? No. Then why did I expect him to have one? Read Sun Tzu, he said—the opportunity of defeating one's opponent is provided by the opponent himself. If I must have a plan, it's this: do nothing. Watch and wait.

Friday, June 17

(Orlando, FL)

I have been fantasizing about crushing JP under my heel. At least once per day, my mind ventures down some fantastical path of plausible ruin. How can I expose his corruption in a bold and conspicuous way? How can I attain the sweetest revenge?

Apparently, I am prone to obsess about all things involving JP, whether positive or negative. This seems to be the effect that he inspires in most people and the secret of his success. But as long as outrageous personal feelings color my plans for JP, I make little progress. Like Einstein said, we can't solve problems using the same kind of thinking we used to create them.

This is where anger comes in handy. It quiets the mind by whittling down my focus to a laser point. *It's not just about you anymore,* anger warns. *Justice for all is the objective now, whether it comes in the form of deafening thunder or a quick, quiet snipe.*

I feel like I have all the critical pieces of the puzzle already, but I lack the mundane in-between parts that hold the whole picture together. I *know* that JP is stealing ministry donations in secret, and I'm certain that he's using them to finance BL's presidential campaign. How do I prove it? How do I get him in trouble for it?

Al Capone was sent to prison for tax evasion, and Bartholomew Lambrecht was brought up on charges of fraud. These weren't the most glamorous of indictments, but they were effective. I did a little related research today.

For a person to be charged with mail fraud, there would have to be proof that he purposely misrepresented himself or his business to solicit money via US mail. Wire fraud is similar, except it involves the phone, radio, or television.

For a person to be charged with tax evasion, there would have to be proof that he knowingly reported false information to the IRS. This would have to go on for years before a pattern of willful evasion could be established. I don't even know if JP files taxes. With the ministry's tax-exempt status, he likely has quite a bit of leeway. Any money deemed a "donation" is presumed to be at the ministry's disposal and utilized at its sole discretion, no questions asked.

What can be proven? That is the question.

WEDNESDAY, JUNE 22

(Orlando, FL)

If I didn't know better, I'd think that my enmity for JP was the cause of his recent streak of misfortunes.

We're in Orlando this week for no reason at all because our Crusade venue fell through at the last minute. That's a first for Wholesome Healing Ministries. A couple of days ago, a popular gossip rag published an interview with JP's father's wife regarding his affair with JP's mother. Apparently, the story JP told me about his parents was true, and it's now making its way into the public eye. He chewed Carmen out in front of everyone for letting that information reach the press—although, honestly, I don't see how Carmen could have prevented that.

On top of all this, JP somehow broke his right index finger and now has to wear a brace. I'm not sure if that was a consequence of his usual clumsiness, or something more sinister.

SATURDAY, JUNE 25

(Orlando, FL)

Just like that—poof!—Carmen is gone.

Her husband found out about the affair and flew all the way here to confront JP face-to-face. Jude intervened before the situation came to blows. A heated conversation was had behind closed doors, and then

Carmen's husband stormed out. Carmen left that same night.

It's strange the way that certain problems have a way of working themselves out.

SATURDAY, JULY 2

(Washington DC)

Tomorrow, JP will share the stage with the illustrious Reverend Joseph Mendez. I got to know the reverend pretty well over dinner yesterday evening. The man charmed me creditably; he expressed a boundless fascination with my interests and hobbies. He wanted to know my point of view on everything. At least a dozen times, he pulled me away from the general topic of conversation at the table to share a relevant anecdote or joke. He complimented my quick wit and comprehension. He flattered me.

The reverend's open and friendly manner imposed upon me a profound sense of intimacy. Was I flattered that the famous man singled me out in this way?

No.

Well, to be honest—no and yes.

I was surprised, embarrassed, and pleased that so handsome and distinguished a man should single me out. But I soon sobered to the reality that the man's fast friendship made no sense, and his extravagant praise did not ring true. I possess little beauty or influence, and I tend to become awkward and shy in the presence of impressive men. An hour of chit chat isn't enough to reveal the redeeming aspects of my character. The reverend couldn't have meant all that he said about me. His flattery was insincere. I merely reflected his praise back at him.

I sneaked several comparative glances at JP and Reverend Joseph throughout the evening. Does charisma come naturally to men like these, or are their techniques learned? Sometimes Reverend Joseph's expressions and mannerisms reminded me so much of JP that I wondered if they had attended the same charm school.

By the end of the evening, one thing was clear: the magical connection I used to think I had with JP could be recreated. Almost any charismatic man could use the same formula to stir similar feelings in me. Any man could make me blush by leaning in and gazing intently. It wasn't hard to make me feel special. Such manipulations were predictable and reproducible, and I bought into them because I *wanted to.*

How disheartening.

When I saw Reverend Joseph today, he was not particularly friendly toward me. In fact, he barely seemed to recognize me. This inconsistency confirmed my suspicion. I am mortified to realize that this hot-and-cold treatment was JP's game, too. His just took longer to play out.

My understanding of the man I thought I knew continues to roll back. History rewrites itself without the filtered hues and attributes that I gifted him. The truth hurts. Let it hurt.

SUNDAY, JULY 3

(Washington DC)

JP stayed after the Crusade today. That's unusual. I soon discovered the reason: an attractive young woman separated from the crowd and sidled up to him. I recognized her from another Crusade in another city. Jeremiah greeted her with that broad, eager smile that I once thought he reserved just for me. The whole scene unfolded in a predictable

sequence. JP laughed and feigned timidity as he inched closer to her. Eventually, he found some innocent reason to touch her on the shoulder. She grinned, giggled, blushed.

I remember clearly what it was like to be her. How I cherished every meeting of the eyes and every accidental brush of the fingers. It was strange to watch this process from the outside and see it for what it really was. The young woman didn't realize that she was already tangled in the faith healer's net. She thought she was in control and seducing JP with her coy head tilts and arched back. She held his attention with a series of minor questions and complaints. Her forearm hurt in this one spot. Would he mind taking a look? No, not there, *there*. Come to think of it, her wrist hurt a little, too. And her hip was stiff. Was that normal? I resisted the impulse to think unkind thoughts about this young woman. She was no sillier than I had been.

JP knew that I was watching them. He suspended me in his periphery but refused to acknowledge me until I turned to leave. Then he called after me to ask if I'd spoken to the reporter that was here earlier.

What reporter?

The vexed eyes of the young lady shifted from me to him. She disliked this interruption and was anxious to reclaim the faith healer's full attention.

I shrugged and told JP that if there was an unwelcome reporter, Jude would know about it. Ask him. Then I turned around and tore through the grasping threads of Jeremiah Promise's net like tissue paper.

Tuesday, July 5

(Washington DC)

No matter how much anger, clarity, and conviction I summon, I keep losing stamina like water through a sieve. The sheer volume of suffering that surrounds me weekly is more than I can process. It's all so frustrating and disheartening! Nearly a month has passed since I decided to stay and fight, and it seems to be all I can do to keep my head above water, much less devise a plan to take JP down.

I did not mean to unload the details of my battle with Empathy on Jude this evening. It just so happened that one insightful remark led to another, and before I knew it, a personal admission was the next logical step.

I described to Jude the ambient energy field that surrounds most people. I can't always see it, but I can feel it—especially when I pass near them. A walk down a city sidewalk can be a barrage of impressions—joy, sorrow, frustration, anger. A highway drive can suddenly plunge me into a smog of road rage. I can't seem to regulate how or when others' feelings affect me, and this phenomenon only intensifies with each passing day.

I didn't expect Jude to find this topic interesting. He struck me as someone who assigned little value to soft skills. But he heard me out and asked a few follow-up questions: how do I explain this sensitivity? Am I especially attuned to micro expressions, mirror neurons, or electromagnetic fields? Have others corroborated my experience?

I nodded to a nearby table and described the emotional climate of the group seated there. Jude listened to my assessment with interest. He

explained that reading emotions was an aspect of psychological profiling. He was open to the idea that there were multiple ways to accomplish this—assuming the empirical evidence was there.

As for my problem with Empathic exhaustion—I should learn to compartmentalize, Jude advised. That's easy for him to say! When one is predisposed to stoicism, it's a short trip to compartmentalization.

I rushed to explain that I've made all kinds of attempts over the years to suppress, ignore, dismiss, and deny my feelings. There were five whole years in my early twenties when I literally could not cry. I found that suppressing and ignoring emotions only served to deaden all my senses. That was no way to live.

To help people, I need to empathize with their pain. This allows me to understand them and invest in the solution to their suffering. When they feel better, I feel better. Unfortunately, when they feel worse, I feel worse. Sometimes the cost of Empathy is more than I want to pay. Sometimes, survival requires me to give away pieces of myself.

"How much suffering have you solved?" Jude asked. Did he really expect me to quantify something like that? When I didn't answer, he began reciting tenets of the Marine Corps.

"Every Marine is, first and foremost, a rifleman," he said. Recruits do not pass basic training unless they excel in marksmanship. Why? Because no matter what they later become, they are soldiers who must always be prepared to fight.

Jude's second pearl of wisdom was to "have a kill plan for everyone in the room." I chuckled, though I knew he wasn't joking. It seemed a bit extreme in this context. We were not at war. Or were we? Wasn't I the one that used words like *battle* and *survive* to describe my circumstance?

I get what Jude was trying to say, and I agree that it's dangerous to remain in a position that I am not fit for. My present situation doesn't care that I'm sensitive. It's a greedy beast that will eat me alive if I don't take steps to protect myself. Like it or not, I'm in the midst of a fight, and to survive like a soldier, I must think like a soldier—weapons, armor, and all.

SUNDAY, JULY 10

(Washington DC)

I assumed that I would be able to cast faith aside at this juncture and forge ahead without it. Ironically, faith found its way into all my conversations today. I ended up saying a lot of things about it that I didn't know were in me, and most of them I said to Abigail Mobley.

Abigail Mobley, what a tragic one. Last decade she lost her mother to an aneurysm. Last year she lost her husband in a boating accident. Last month she gave birth to a stillborn baby boy. She hadn't come for healing; she had come for answers. Why was God punishing her? What had she done to deserve all this?

I hear variations of these questions every week. People want to know *why,* and they are usually satisfied with the answer that God has a plan. Abigail's problem was that she didn't know if she believed in God anymore. How could she? All her life, she'd been told that God was good, God never gave a person more than she can handle—but this time He *had.* Her burden was unbearable.

A look of alarm appeared on her face then. She feared that Satan was speaking to her, corrupting her in her frail state. Terrible ideas had been coming to her. She often dreamed up wagers about what she would do to get her loved ones back. There was no limit to her depravity.

One quick glance inward toward my own shaken faith, and I felt strangely relieved. I wanted to say, "Don't worry, Abigail. That's *not* Satan speaking—that's grief." Grief may drive us to the edge of desperation, but it cannot throw us over. Thinking wicked thoughts is different than doing evil deeds. As long as she knew the difference, God was still with her.

Her life wasn't fair. She didn't deserve so much pain. Still, it was up to Abigail to find the meaning in it. If she wanted to believe that God was punishing her, I couldn't convince her otherwise. I could only suggest that sometimes we have to lose everything to find ourselves. To discover our purpose. Perhaps her purpose was to learn to turn utter darkness into light—something one can only master by doing. No one wants hard lessons thrust upon them, but those who survive their trials have the rare chance to help show others the way.

Some kind of faith is essential to this process, of course. Our world is rife with chasms and pitfalls. Without bridges of belief to span the gaps, we would eventually reach impasses in every direction. Faith is the way forward—whether it be in stone, mortar, science, or God. Faith in someone is optimal, but faith in oneself is essential.

Monday, July 11

(Washington DC)

Perhaps faith is a form of armor.

Every time my faith in JP was shaken, my defenses weakened and open me up to attack. I fell prey to illness, fatigue, sprains, strains, headaches, and insomnia, and allowed social interactions to drain me to the quick.

Yet it never seemed to matter that JP wasn't the bastion of moral

purity that I thought he was. It was enough that I believed in him. The intensity of my conviction gave me strength.

I need to invest my faith in something new, and yesterday evening I stumbled upon just the thing. Walking down 11ᵗʰ Avenue, I glanced over and saw the glint of a 1911 Wheat Penny in the grass. That's it! Such a simple solution. I've been over-thinking things—the answer was right under my nose. My lucky penny is working wonders from the safety of my pocket. I already feel more energetic and optimistic.

WEDNESDAY, JULY 13

(Washington DC)

I can do NOTHING to impress Jude. I ran into him in the elevator and excitedly told him about my success with the lucky penny. He shook his head and interrupted, "Bad idea."

That's it. The elevator doors opened, and he stepped off.

Why I continue to seek Jude's approval on so many matters, I don't know! He's not the expert, and we don't have to agree. Unfortunately, Jude's ominous remark left me feeling uneasy. I don't like the ease with which he planted a seed of doubt in my mind, or the rate at which it has begun to grow.

FRIDAY, JULY 22

(Philadelphia, PA)

It occurred to me that the secrets to protecting oneself while defeating one's enemy might lie in the game of chess. Perhaps I ought to learn

the rules. I asked Jude if he knew how to play. Could he teach me? Jude chuckled and asked what the point would be. Chess is a game. If I wanted to learn strategy, I should study something useful, something with a direct application—such as risk management. This was the scientific method that he used to assess basic security threats. Personal security was at the heart of the matter, was it not?

Jude walked me through the process. Step one: identify the assets. What are they? At first, I thought he was asking for tangible assets, so I mentioned my house. Wrong answer. We were not drawing up a financial balance sheet. An asset could be anything that needed protection, including intangibles. In this case, my valuables were things like energy, health, empathy, compassion, and faith.

The next step in risk management was to identify threats. What and *who* endangered my assets? The people, I supposed—their insatiable needs. I'm an emotional sponge that has no choice about what it absorbs. Jude asked me if there was anyone else, and I tentatively conceded that JP might still be a suspect. I have done all I can to abolish my feelings for him, but something may still linger—

"What about you?" Jude interrupted. Me? A threat to myself? Nonsense. Jude pressed upon me one of his dark and pointed looks, but he let the matter slide and carried on.

Step three: identify vulnerabilities. I complained that this one was tricky because abstract problems called for abstract solutions. I couldn't just put shiny, new padlocks on all the doors and windows and call it a day. Jude argued that people tend to focus too much on locks. The best locks in the world cannot stop the most determined intruders. Security is about layers. The more vulnerabilities one considers, and the more types of protection one uses to compensate for them, the more secure a thing is. Take a safe deposit box at a bank, for example. Sure, it is guard-

ed by lock and key, but it is also enclosed within a vault, housed in a facility monitored by cameras and motion sensors, regulated by locked doors, patrolled by security personnel, and perhaps even fenced in and lit up by floodlights. None of these layers is impervious on its own, but they take considerably longer to infiltrate when they are stacked on top of one another.

I tried again to name my vulnerabilities. Eyes? Ears? Skin? These were the means by which the outside world got in. Heart? Gut? These were the epicenters of compassion and empathy…

Jude nodded slightly and advised me not to give answers as if they were questions. It was his job to describe the process, not to dictate my interpretation of it.

On to step four: risk analysis. What do I stand to lose if I remain vulnerable to threats? What are my most significant weaknesses? The risks must be assessed before it is possible to determine how to negate them.

"My heart is my weakness," I said.

"I doubt that," said Jude.

He spread open the front of his flannel and pulled up his T-shirt to reveal a black ballistic vest underneath. "However, if you want to protect your heart from mortal wounds," he said, "This is one way to do it."

I was confused again. After all this theorizing, it was suddenly okay to present a concrete solution to an abstract problem? If so, then why did he declare my lucky penny a "bad idea?"

Jude explained that the efficacy of all things was mostly in our minds; however, the bullet-proof vest had the added advantage of real-world testing and certification. Its function was verifiable and reproducible. Its protective powers could be believed *and* proven. The lucky penny's purpose was based entirely on superstition invented and perpetuated

by me alone. If I could create its power, I could just as easily destroy it.

He made me a baffling offer: if I wanted a ballistic vest, he would help me acquire one. But he warned that this was only one layer of personal protection, and I should continue to search for more.

Monday, July 25

(Philadelphia, PA)

Skin.

Skin is my most essential boundary. Its fundamental purpose is to hold my native matter in and block external forces out.

I've been called "thin-skinned" plenty of times in my life. It seemed to be an immutable fact of life about which little could be done, so I learned to laugh it off. Yes, that's right, my skin is thin. Careful what you say—I might bleed on you!

The consequences of my empathic condition are not really faults of my physical skin, though. My body's rind is not that much different than anyone else's. The real issue is, like Jude said, *mostly in my mind.* It's my figurative boundaries that are thinner than most. This is the reason I absorb the feelings of others willy-nilly. I lack the mental skin to filter them out.

I've decided to take Jude up on his offer. I need a model of imperviousness to build my defenses around. Being strapped into a ballistic vest shall instruct me daily to create a mental barrier in its image—both strong and flexible.

Friday, August 5

(Woodstock, VT)

Rest.

Nutrition.

Hydration.

Meditation.

Visualization.

Vigilance.

Living in the present moment.

Limitation.

Prioritization.

Preparation.

Washing away the residue of negative influence.

Walking in nature.

Grounding.

Good friends.

Positive experiences.

Creative expression.

Solitude.

Stillness.

Saying *no.*

Monday, August 22

(Detroit, MI)

Jude's safe deposit box metaphor is foremost in my mind every day. I'm building my new ideology around it. So far, I've identified many of the layers he mentioned (box, vault, building, fence) as various types of boundaries. Boundaries I'm getting the hang of. The Crusades offer countless opportunities to assess my mental and emotional weaknesses and test methods of fortification. I'm learning to discern my radius of acute Empathy and shuffle outside of it when things become too intense. I dodge overly-personal topics with strangers and limit the length of time I spend with any one person. I'm making rest into a daily ritual. When my defenses falter, I draw inspiration from my ballistic vest.

I'm now ready to level up and examine other aspects of Jude's metaphor.

Floodlights—what are they, in and of themselves? What do they do? Lights shine into the darkness and reveal the unseen. They are agents of discovery. At present, my knowledge is limited, and my circle of illumination is small. To broaden my vision and comprehension, I must commit to learning all that I can about myself and the world.

Motion sensors and security alarms—these are the early warning systems that are triggered by special sensors. They represent "other" senses, like intuition, anticipation, and all the little ticks and twinges that alert my body to trouble. Best to pay attention to these and learn to interpret their signals.

Security cameras—vigilance and memory. These show the world as it is and hold it accountable for its actions. They remind me to be aware, both of myself and everything outside of me. I must cast off the filters of emotion and expectation to see things as they really are. Once I see them, it will be possible to accept them; and once I accept them, I will finally break free of illusion.

Thursday, September 1

(Indianapolis, IN)

I have passion: powerful and compelling emotions.

I have conviction: a fixed and firm belief.

I have determination: a resolute sense of purpose.

What about self-discipline: the planned and controlled training of oneself for the sake of improvement? Do I have that?

The distinction between determination and self-discipline came to me as I gazed out my hotel room window early this morning. I saw Jude heading out for his six o'clock run just as I've seen him do every day this week, rain or shine.

Are there any routines that I practice with strict regularity? I'm astonished to find that nothing comes to mind. There are things I do because passion moves me to do them, like drawing and walking in nature, and there are things that I work at tirelessly because conviction and determination drive me to pursue them. But there isn't really anything that I do because self-discipline dictates that I must, come high tide or low. When passion wanes and convictions waver, I end up adrift without an anchor.

I resolve to add the dimension of discipline to my life. It won't be easy, I'm sure. There are factors to consider: how does one reconcile her rigid regimen with twinges of contrary intuition? Feelings mat-

ter. Sometimes they provoke a sudden change of plans, and sometimes that's for the best. Perhaps it's a matter of learning to distinguish between good pain and bad pain, fear of danger and fear of discomfort, essential pursuits, busywork, and distractions. I don't yet know the formula for all this, but I am determined to figure it out.

SATURDAY, SEPTEMBER 3

(Indianapolis, IN)

It's official. My home is in foreclosure. What to do? I might perhaps dash home and try to halt the proceedings, but I lack the impetus. My past life is dissolving by the minute, and I am strangely unmoved.

SUNDAY, SEPTEMBER 11

(Columbus, OH)

I dreamed of a slate-gray farmhouse in a cornflower-blue field. A coarse old oak tree with thick, sprawling limbs grew in front of the house. Its branches sprouted teacups instead of leaves, and little birds roosted in each one of them.

As I drew near, I saw Freddie waiting for me on the front porch. He was tipped back in a chair with his feet up, and when he saw me, he grinned and waved. Boy, was I glad to see him.

I'm not yet done with grief. Perhaps I never will be. Loss of life is only one of many casualties to be mourned. Among the others are loss of ideas, identity, faith, hope, and home.

Jude warned me to be wary of hidden adversaries. Now I know what he meant. Un-befriended grief is an insidious energy thief that hides inside of me. How shall I manage it, then? How shall I prevent it from consuming me? The answer seems simple, but it will not be easy: accept it, honor it, bring it into the light, and in time, grief will assume its proper place and proportion in my high council.

WEDNESDAY, SEPTEMBER 14

(Columbus, OH)

The starker my resolve becomes, the more forcefully and frequently I must repeat my iron-clad reasons for going up against JP. It feels as if I'm battling a shadow in some deep, untouchable reach—one that cannot be defeated by ordinary means. If it could be, then the last of this turmoil would have been extinguished long ago.

What debate remains to be won? All my arguments have been polished to a high shine, and all are profoundly right. Something else must be at work here, some errant suspicion or misplaced fear. What are you? You can't hide indefinitely, so show yourself!

With that, the word comes to mind: *self-doubt.*

Ah, yes, self-doubt—the inexorable, indefatigable, unconquerable quality that cannot be ignored or strong-armed into submission. Coddling only encourages it. Contention and superficiality only aggravate it.

What do you want from me, self-doubt? How can I appease you? Let's stop spinning in spiral debates and earnestly embrace the complexity of all things. Come, step out of the shadows. Take a seat at my table and tell me what you think.

Self-doubt warns me that countless trials lie ahead, and they will test everything I know. Do I really want to proceed any further down so treacherous a path? Am I sure? Because self-doubt makes no exceptions for friends. It will scrape and tear at everything inferior until only the bare bones of conviction remain. Only then will I know which beliefs are built to last.

Fine, I say. Let's get on with it. Something big is close at hand, and I cannot afford to flinch when the critical moment arrives.

Monday, September 19

(Columbus, OH)

Jude made a bizarre observation today: he said that JP looked to me for leadership cues. Preposterous! JP hardly looked at me for any reason, least of all for guidance.

Now that I've had time to think it through, I see some truth in Jude's claim. There were a few occasions in the beginning when JP sought my advice, and I fancied myself a trusted subordinate. His manner of humbling himself always struck me as odd, though. There was a bitter and exaggerated flavor to it. My senses were not calibrated to his subtleties then, but when I examine them now under my magnifying glass, I see his barbs of contempt. Those overdrawn hesitations, superfluous gushes of praise, and perplexing half-smiles of his were hints of resentment, all.

I assumed from the start that he wanted an equal partner in the ministry, so I strove to make myself invaluable to him. I wracked my brain for ideas and inspiration, but I never meant to compete. Did he think I was trying to outdo him? He teased me with talk of trust and responsibility, but he never intended to empower me. To JP, I was merely a life-giving organ—which he resented but couldn't afford to cut free.

He probably knew that I could see his leadership failings. They were evident even before Freddie's murder (yes, I said murder) and his affair with Carmen. I saw his weakness when he began banishing ushers without cause, bickering at staff meetings, and preaching fire and brimstone after claiming he never would again. He knew that I saw, and he hated me for it, so he heaped on me all the human-relations "dirty work" he didn't want to do. This was his mistake.

Jeremiah Promise may be the fearsome face of Wholesome Healing Ministries, but the body is a composite of everybody else—Jude, the crew, ushers, volunteers, congregants, and me. Without us, he has no dominion; without him, we simply have no head.

SUNDAY, SEPTEMBER 25

(Buffalo, NY)

I didn't even think; I just stepped up to the mic and started talking. I don't remember exactly what I said; I only remember being incensed that JP was over an hour late. This time he had gone too far. His blatant disrespect was unacceptable, and I was poised to do something about it. I strode up to the podium and spoke to six thousand folks about a few things that had been on my mind lately. The good parts, of course—about love, courage, self-sacrifice, and such. I received my fair share of *hallelujahs* and *amens*.

When JP finally arrived, he was livid. He didn't chew me out like I thought he would. I sensed fear beneath his rage, but he couldn't bear to show it, so he demanded that I leave the stage and not come back. Fine. Gladly.

Jude and I exchanged looks as I passed him on the way out. At no point did he lift a finger to intervene. Interesting.

Thursday, September 29

(New York, NY)

Is it better for a leader to be feared or loved?

I know what Jude would say: he'd quote Machiavelli, the brilliant political philosopher, and contend that it was better by far to be feared. I would argue that few brutal leaders in recent history have managed to hold onto power for long, and Jude would point out that *no* leader can hold the reigns indefinitely. All positions of power are temporary, and even the most loved leaders are hated by some.

Sure, love is ever the human ideal. Yet noble sentiments tend to go out the window when it comes down to critical moments of self-sacrifice and self-preservation. Fear is almost always more potent than love. If the two were pitted against each other, it could never be a fair fight.

Pie in the sky, then: under what conditions *could* gentle love prevail in a world dominated by fear? I'll admit, I couldn't think of an honest way. Love does not triumph because it doesn't compete. It grows in the absence of more pernicious things. For love to reign supreme, fear would have to be assassinated in its sleep.

Tuesday, October 4

(New York, NY)

It is the eve of transformation. Tomorrow we alter history.

The clock has stopped. Energy crackles and sparks around my head like lightning. As I write these words, I sense the gathering of storm clouds and the ascension of immense potential. From this, I draw the strength to push fiction to a distant horizon. No more conjectures bred of uncertainty and dread. No more waiting to see what tomorrow brings. I am tired of gazing into the unknown, wondering what saints and monsters lurk under cover of darkness. The time has come to manifest my will. From now on, my word is the law. I decide what tomorrow brings.

Tomorrow will begin tonight as mobs descend upon the city. Some will have come for us, and some will have come for the other protest. The world doesn't know it yet, but we will soon prove that revolts against the status quo are all tributaries of the common good.

JP and I will be together at dawn, sitting face-to-face in his hotel suite while Jude guards the door. Jeremiah will not acknowledge me. He will lean forward with his elbows on his knees and steep in the glory of his fame. I will study the top of his head as if I'd never seen it before and realize that his metamorphosis is complete. He has become a stranger to me, but one whose black curls, angular face, and luminous eyes stir painful recollections of someone I used to adore. A part of me will still wish I was wrong about Jeremiah Promise. I will allow myself only one more minute to contemplate the power of "if only" before I put it away for good.

If only I had never met him.

If only I had never loved him.

If only things had played out differently. To think, how much evil I might have readily condoned, how much wrongdoing I might have overlooked, *if only* he had loved me back.

But perhaps everything played out precisely as it was supposed to. I was destined to fall in love and destined to suffer for it. Does love really change anything or anyone? Sure. One's love changes oneself. Changing oneself is the only hope we have of changing the world.

Voices in the hallway outside will alert us to the approaching twist of fate. Moments later, Jude will escort two FBI agents into the room. They will handcuff JP and flank him to the left and right. With one long, fiery backward glance, the Man Himself will walk out of my life for good.

"How did this happen?" He will wonder as he walks the gauntlet of reporters and shocked onlookers. At the trial, the damning evidence will be revealed: a stack of interest statements from half a dozen bank accounts belonging to private citizen Hrithik Mukherjee, a.k.a. Jeremiah Promise—all dutifully reported to the IRS by their respective financial institutions, but not by the Man Himself. This sort of discrepancy was just suspicious enough to raise a few bureaucratic eyebrows and trigger a few red flags. Perhaps a few phone calls had been placed to nudge things along, but for the most part, the ball of fate rolled here on its own.

At this point, Jude and I will be alone in the fancy hotel suite. He will ask me if I'm ready. I will say, "Absolutely not." He will tell me that the car is here, and it's time to go. Forward march.

We will glide through the halls, the elevator, the hotel lobby, and the waiting crowd outside. Reporters will shout questions about the infamous faith healer that had come out in handcuffs, not five minutes prior. *No comment!* Jude will plow ahead and part the seas for us every step of the way. Rage, righteousness, and single-minded focus will compel us onward.

We will crawl through crowded streets, move barricades aside, traverse dim underground passageways, and listen to our own footfalls echo on hard, polished surfaces. Time will lay still like a landscape without a beginning or an end. There will be no rushing nor anxiety because this will be the moment that everything else in my life has been leading up to. This will be NOW.

Tam will dress me in Jeremiah Promise's suit and pin up my hair to make it look darker and shorter. Jude will pull up the video feed on his tablet and show me the inside of the arena. It will be hazy and twilit and packed from bottom to top with humming, swaying, praying disciples. Opiate grins will play at their lips. In their half-hypnotized state, their minds will be open, ready, waiting for the message.

With each stride toward the stage, I will envision my heels plunging deep roots into the earth and gripping its core with resounding resolve. Before I ascend the risers, I will look back at Jude. He will nod to me. This will seal our tacit agreement to stick together come hell or high water. Up the steps, I will go.

From behind the curtain, I will emerge a peculiar and misshapen visage of Jeremiah Promise. I will raise my hands, and the crowd will roar. Then I will tell them a story.

Once upon a time, there lived a handsome prince that spoke of all the good he meant to do in the world, but who failed to honor his word...

I will talk to the people about nobility.

Integrity.

Compassion.

Empathy.

Faith.

Love, and the beauty and wonder of all things.

I will talk about pain.

Illusion.

Fear.

Regret.

Treachery.

I will talk about the wolves that disguise themselves as sheep and the sheep that disguise themselves as wolves. Then I will unpin my hair and let it down so they can see I am not Jeremiah Promise—no! I am the mirror-bearer, come to show the people the truth about themselves.

In vivid prose, I will call forth the stories of others' personal strife that had inspired me to overcome my own. "We are a congregation of sufferers, forged in the fires of sacrifice and baptized in the holy waters of patient endurance," I will say. "Fire strengthens, and water purifies the soul. Together, they clean and close the wounds of humanity. The new flesh that forms over them is made of love, empathy, and compassion. Sufferers have the power to understand and help each other far better than the unscathed and unproven."

I will describe the common threads that connect us all: the search, the hope, the hunger for things greater than oneself. Our pilgrimages may sometimes lead us astray, but at least they bring us together. We converge—not because we are sick, but because we are strong.

"The Bible claims the meek shall inherit the earth," I will say. "It's time to stop confusing 'meek' with 'weak.' Jeremiah Promise made that mistake! He was a charlatan who sought to pad his pockets and his secret agendas with our miracle money. He abused his power; he prospered while we languished. Enough! We don't have to take that. Together we are more powerful than any one man. United, we can break mountains and part seas. It's time to shake things up. Rise up, fight back!"

The congregation will writhe and wring their hands with the agony of awakening. Then there will be a deafening shriek of exultation as the dam begins to break. Bodies will rush, gush, and crash down from their seats in the stands. Jude will pull me from the path of destruction before I'm swept underfoot.

The people will fight their way outside and overrun the streets. They will converge with the protestors already out there marching against financial inequality and corporate corruption. Barricades will be broken. Conflict will erupt. People will fight to the death. All roads will lead to anarchy, and from it, freedom will be born into a brave, new world.

. . . How cathartic would that be? How triumphant? If only the matter was that simple. I fear nothing will ever be simple again.

Perhaps people *could* rule themselves, in theory. A wise community *could* create a doctrine of the common good and choose to adhere to it rather than submit to the yoke of corrupt leadership. But . . .

It is 12:01 a.m. on October 5, and it occurs to me that all my calculations are based on error. Have I never asked the question before now—why? Why are Jeremiah's disciples and others like them subject to his corruption? Is it because they are too sick or too poor to resist? Is it because our society allows them no voice to speak out when they have a grievance to share?

Shh. Listen. Hear that? Silence. That is the sound of complacency. Who is speaking out against Jeremiah Promise and others like him?

Not his true believers. Those are people that will give up their last five dollars to someone like Jeremiah Promise. They will go to their graves believing that the miracle didn't work because of their trifling sins. They don't want to self-rule, to make choices, or to be free. They just want to continue their adequate slumber. Even if some of Jeremiah's disciples turn away from him in disgust tomorrow, the next day, they will seek a new ruler. If this is true belief, then I am not True Believer. I relinquish the name and rank. Who am I now? I cannot take back my given name because I am not her, either. I am neither.

It would be a miracle if the FBI came to arrest Jeremiah Promise tomorrow. No phone calls have been made. No financial investigation has been opened. Not yet. But never mind that, we will not be compelled onward by rage and righteousness, anyway. We will only go 'round and 'round like cogs in a wheel guided by some unseen hand. Memories are short, hopes and dreams are easily fleeced, and history will find a way to repeat itself until finally, the bough breaks.

My consolation is that Jeremiah Promise has weaknesses—not the least of which are pride and arrogance. He has made mistakes, and he will make more. Like many rising despots that have come before him, Jeremiah Promise will induce his own downfall. His disciples will need a new leader. Until then, I wait.

Acknowledgments

When I made up my mind to write this book (no more putting it off, no more excuses), everyone in the world seemed to have something to say about it. Whether they were strangers, acquaintances, friends from way back, the lady at the park, the guy at the gym, or that social media "friend" I never met in real life, something about this endeavor compelled many different people to reach out and connect with me. Whether they knew me well or not, most offered overwhelming support and encouragement, and for this, I've felt truly honored and grateful. Thank you, thank you, thank you.

Let me not gloss over the small handful of people that were not so supportive, though. To the ones that doubted and discouraged me: cheers to you. I couldn't have done this without you.

I'd like to give special thanks to Small Ham and Owly, who took the journey with me and shared (sometimes exceeded) my enthusiasm for the minutia of plot and character development. Without your kind refrains, "I need this book!" and "I can't wait to read it!" . . . this story might still be more dream than reality.

Thanks also to Military Mike for inspiring a character, allowing me to pick your non-linear brain, and demonstrating infinite patience while I blew too many self-imposed deadlines to count.

Finally, thanks to Mom and Sister for always being there, supporting me, and believing in me no matter what.

About the Author

M. Funk has always had a fondness for creative expansion, whether it came in the form of multiple college degrees, several small businesses, or a heap of artistic pursuits. What's a girl to do with an infinite supply of curiosity and an insatiable passion for learning, she wondered? There seemed to be no satisfying career for so nomadic a student as she. But wait! There was! She could be a writer. She could use her observations and experience to write stories—realistic stories—intertwined tales about interwoven lives—and gradually build a universe of her own. That's precisely what she's set out to do.

When she's not suspended in the ether of careful observation, M. Funk lives in Minneapolis, MN, and pays regular visits to the captivating raptors that inhabit the pond nearby.

To learn more about M. Funk's writing universe or delve into the personal details alluded to above, please visit MFunkWrites.com.